Advance Pra[ise for]
Stevan Allred's A Simplified
Map of the Real World

"In *A Simplified Map of the Real World*, Stevan Allred creates one of the unforgettable locales of modern fiction—Renata, Oregon, a small town that takes us to the largest places in the heart. The people of Renata struggle with broken dams and families, with dangerous curves in roads and marriages, and with dreams that are both reckless and brave. These are stories as beautiful and honest as the landscape Allred loves. Gorgeously written, *A Simplified Map of the Real World* will make you wonder why you haven't been reading Stevan Allred all your life."

—Scott Sparling, author of *Wire to Wire*

"Death and high jinks, love and rage—the ordinary doings of a small town are not so simple. Stevan Allred has clear vision and he's a loving and joyful teller of tales. In his hands, these voices are angry, foolish, wise, heartbroken, and true."

—Joanna Rose, author of *Little Miss Strange*

"Much like being ambushed by a sneaker wave, I simply surrendered to the futile and claustrophobic circumstances Stevan Allred forces the community of Renata to endure in this linked collection. As human beings we all know there are two sides—or multiple ones—to every story, and as readers, it's pure indulgence to experience Allred's deft ability to shift between various points of view to give us a 360-degree perspective of the intertwining lives of his characters as they meet head-on their spectrum of woes, each more heartbreaking than the last."

—Polly Dugan, author of *So Much a Part of You*

"I don't know how he works his magic—probably naked at the typewriter or some other trick to get so much humanity and humility on the page—but Stevan has built a world full of beautiful and messy people living beautiful and messy lives. These stories are great on their own, and even stronger together. You'll feel like you know these people and this place better than you know your own people and place. You should be ashamed of yourself for not having read this book yet!"
—Yuvi Zalkow, author of *A Brilliant Novel in the Works*

"Stevan Allred's *A Simplified Map of the Real World* is on my short list of truly hard core Oregon literature. Whether you laugh or feel sad or want to shout "amen" at Allred's political swipes, you will be engaged by this wildly enjoyable collection."
—Matt Love, author of *Of Walking in the Rain*

"The Northwest town of Renata, the families, the connections between all these characters, their idiosyncrasies and quirks, their tribulations and moments of light, Stevan Allred makes it all very real. He intrigues from the first words and won't let us put down each story until we know exactly how it's to turn out."
—Jon Bell, author of *On Mount Hood*

See more reviews and praise at forestavenuepress.com

A Simplified Map of the Real World

From my ticky little mind to yours —

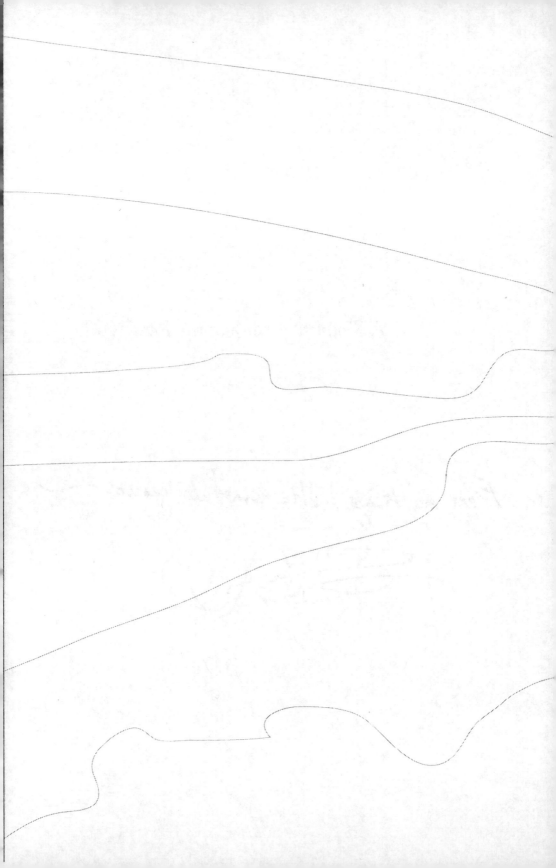

A Simplified Map of the Real World

RENATA

The Renata Stories

Stevan Allred

illustrated by Laurie Paus

FOREST AVENUE PRESS
Portland, Oregon

ISBN 978-0-9882657-2-1

Library of Congress Control Number: 2013937353

First edition 2013
Printed in the United States of America
by Forest Avenue Press
Portland, Oregon

Cover design: Gigi Little
Maps of Renata: Stevan Allred and Gigi Little
Illustrations: Laurie Paus
Interior design: Laura Stanfill
Copy editor: Annie Denning Hille

The author is grateful to the editors of the following literary journals, in which these stories first appeared, sometimes in slightly different form: "On Formal Occasions, Hummingbirds" in *Beloit Fiction Journal* (Spring 2004), in the UK by *The Text* (July 2006), and online at *Phantasmacore* (June 2011); "His Ticky Little Mind" in *Mississippi Review* (October 2005); "Conflations of a Hard-Headed Yankee" in *The Iconoclast* (December 2005); "A Simplified Map of the Real World" online at *Carve Magazine* (July 2006); "In the Ditch" in *Inkwell* (September 2006); "Trish the Freaking Dish" in *Rosebud*, under the title "Cleavage" (May 2007); "Sink Like a Steamroller, Fly Like a Brick," in *Real* (October 2007); "The Painted Man" online at *Bewildering Stories* (March 2008); "The Idjit's Guide to Intuitive Mastery of Newtonian Physics," "To Walk Where She Pleases," and "Trish the Freaking Dish" in the UK by *The Text* (August 2011).

Forest Avenue Press
6327 SW Capitol Highway, Suite C
PMB 218
Portland, OR 97239
forestavenuepress.com

For my father,
James Allred,
one of the world's thirty-five
great readers

Ry Allred

... in the high
ignorance of love ...
abstractions are just abstract
until they have an ache in them.

– Stephen Dunn

Contents

A Simplified Map of the Real World

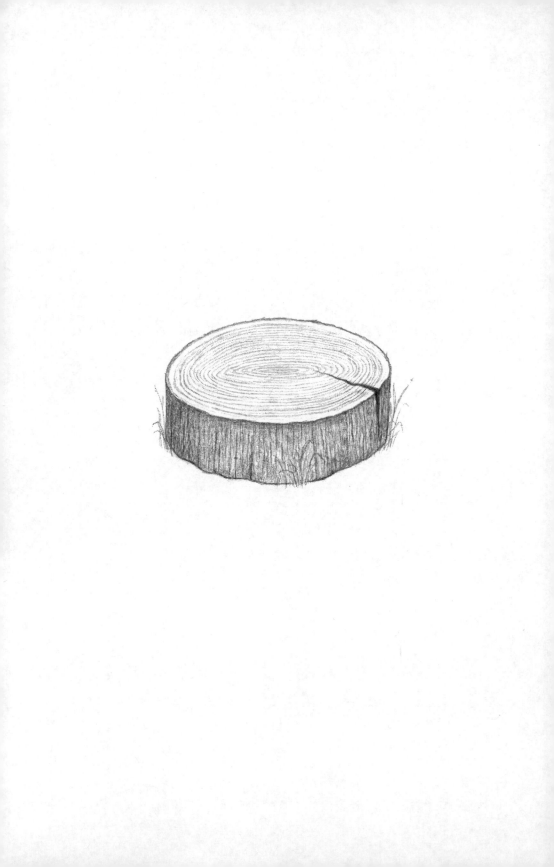

His Ticky Little Mind

THIS ALL BEGINS WHEN I come home from visiting Mother in the rest home last week and taking her down to the Norse Hall for the monthly dinner. Good eats at the Norse Hall, and Mother may not be able to remember what year it is, but she'll sit there and tell you how that secret pinch of nutmeg made her creamed carrots the envy of all the ladies down at the grange, and that's about all the female companionship I can handle these days.

It was Saturday evening and almost dark. That long busy drive from the city was behind me and I was eight miles past the last red light when I made the turn onto Gossard Road. I've lived on Gossard Road my whole life, and my whole life whenever I turn onto Gossard Road, the world has been made whole again, a place small enough that I can keep track of everything that matters and big enough to hold everything I need.

That first quarter mile the road rises and makes the tree line beyond sink, so you feel the heavens opening up big as God above you. The evening star was bright, and it had risen in its customary spot in the southern sky, which at this time of year puts it almost directly above the bungalow, which is the house

I was born in, the house I now live across the road from. It was my parents who sold the bungalow and the farm that goes with it to Volpe.

Something wasn't right. Underneath the evening star should have been the silhouette of an oak tree standing plumb and true, the only tree on that particular stretch of Gossard Road tall enough and near enough not to disappear below the top of the rise. I come up to the top of the rise and pull over in the wide spot where I like to sit for a minute and see the whole valley stretched out before me, with my little piece of paradise smack dab in the middle, the heart of the heartland, and the best forty acres in the whole damn section.

It must be in the nature of things that paradise wouldn't be paradise without there was a snake running loose in the middle of it, because all that's left of that oak tree is the butchery of a stump left to stand there tall, dark, and ugly.

The headlights of my truck picked up the big white ovals where Volpe cut off the lower branches. There was no lights on at Volpe's house except for the TV, which he's got the biggest damn TV in the whole damn county. The oak tree was laid out in rounds where he sliced it up after he dropped it. Volpe worked on a logging crew when he was fresh out of high school, so the man knows how to drop a tree. He had to take the fence down at the far end of his yard to keep it from getting smashed when he dropped it.

The sky was just this side of full dark, and those fresh cut rounds lay there white as a sliced cucumber, and sliced up the way it was, there was nothing left to do but split those rounds into firewood. Enough firewood to keep Volpe warm for five or six winters easy. When I was a boy I spent whole summers in that tree, me and my brothers and sisters and our cousins who lived on Gossard Road. We built a pirate ship high up in her branches and sailed off to the new world. We hung a swing from her thickest branch and we swung ourselves dizzy. We laid in the dirt beneath her and looked up at puzzle pieces of blue sky through her branches, and we made a game out of putting those pieces together.

Now everything that tree ever was would go up Volpe's chimney and be gone forever. Everything except the stump. He left that stump standing twelve feet high to provoke me. I know how his ticky little mind works. We been neighbors for thirty-four years, and we went to all the same schools before that, and I got plenty of history with Volpe. That stump sat in the view from my front porch to his like the upraised middle finger of Volpe's hand.

I know a dick when I see one.

I DIDN'T EVEN GO in my house after I parked my truck. Walked straight over to Volpe's and knocked on his door.

"Evening, Arnie," he said. On the TV was one of those fishing shows where some guy takes you out to a river and pretends he ain't bragging about all the fish he's caught. Volpe's wife never would've let him buy a TV that big, but Volpe and me, neither one of us could keep a wife past the time our kids grew up and moved out of the house. I never thought my marriage to Viv would fail the test of time. They left us less than a year apart, and Volpe told me right after Viv left, he thought his wife caught the leaving disease from my wife. Like his wife didn't leave first, and like that artificial inseminator fellow she ran off with had nothing to do with it.

There was a dish of ice cream half eaten on the coffee table in front of Volpe's recliner, and the word "mute" in blue letters across the bottom of his big TV. I stepped back from his front door and pointed at his butchery.

I said, "What'd you do that for?"

"And what a fine evening it is," Volpe said, "thanks for bringing it up."

Volpe stepped past me and I got a whiff of whatever fancy

cologne it is he puts on now that he's divorced. He stood out in the yard, looking up at the evening sky.

"Have you seen the evening star?" he said. He was sideways to me. The man's got no more chin than a hen does, and a long stick of a neck, and with his big beak of a nose cantilevered out over the bottom half of his face, he looks like he's part weasel.

"Going to be hot in August without the shade of that tree," I said.

"I got air conditioning," Volpe said. "I'll be all right."

"That so?" I said.

A pair of bats was working the sky over our heads, all swoop and flutter, quiet as the grave, doing their level best to keep the flying insect population down to a dull roar. Volpe's face was white and bloodless in the porch light. I stepped down and stood so I could talk straight into that chinless face of his. "Why on earth would you cut down your shade tree?" I said. I knew for a fact that my grandparents had situated their house to take full advantage of the shade of that oak.

Volpe's mouth pulled up into that tight curve he's been smirking with since he was five years old. "Have you seen my new satellite dish?" he said. "I been meaning to ask you over to watch one of my five hundred channels."

He walked out into his yard further and pointed up at the roof. "You mount it so it faces the southern sky," he said. The satellite dish was a round white circle against the darkening sky. It had that baked-on enamel look of a household appliance, but there was something sausage-like about the bulbous gray hunk of electronics that pointed at its center.

"Wasn't getting the kind of reception I needed," Volpe said. One of the bats flew low over his head and Volpe swatted at it. He pointed at the oak tree laid out like a dead relative down the length of his yard. "Did you see all that rot running through those rounds?"

"You couldn't put that dish on the back corner of the house?" I said.

Volpe tightened up his smirk and put crinkles at the corners of his eyes, just in case I didn't already know that he was laughing at me. He stuck his hands into the back pockets of his jeans. His arms are so long the man can practically tie his shoes without bending over, so his elbows stuck way out, and that left his gut wide open and just begging for me to sucker punch him.

"Well now, I suppose I might have," he said, "but right here is where the signal is strongest."

Course it ain't me that's got a history of throwing the sucker punch, it's Volpe.

"You want a dish of ice cream, Arnie?" he said. "Rocky Road, it's your favorite."

I said no.

It was going to take a whole lot more than ice cream to patch this up.

COME SUNDAY MORNING, I got up early, fixed myself a pot of coffee, and sat out on the porch. There was a chill in the air and I was glad for the bourbon whiskey I sweetened my coffee with. I had my binoculars in case any interesting birds came by, and I was set to spend my one day off right there in the heart of the heartland.

The bungalow was a whole lot more noticeable without the oak tree between us, the way it occupied the morning sun that tree used to occupy. That stump was stupid and butt ugly both. Butt ugly because it stood there like a big old stick stuck straight into my eye, and stupid because it was a whole lot more work for Volpe to cut down that high than it would've been to take her closer to the ground. He had the extra difficulty of handling a thirty-six inch chainsaw while he was up a ladder, and he had to move the ladder at least twice to get the job done.

Volpe came in from mucking around out back of his house

with his John Deere tractor, which he owns the biggest damn tractor in the whole damn county. If you want your hay field plowed up for putting in Christmas trees, and you want the job done quicker than you could do it yourself on the kind of tractor most folks around here own, Volpe's the man you call. I had a clear shot of his living room window, and Volpe come in and turned that TV on, and even at two hundred yards, the picture on that TV was so damn big I didn't hardly need my binoculars to see that all he was watching was some stupid gardening show.

We used to set up a card table and play cards in that living room back when he and I was married men with families. A regular routine we had, with our wives taking turns on the roast beef and the kids running around in the yard after dinner. My Viv used to make potatoes au gratin that would make a dead man drool, and Mary Sauerberg Volpe's pies were grand champions at the county fair so many times she had to quit entering and give somebody else a chance. Good eats for sure, and for a good solid twenty years if it wasn't the Gossards over to the Volpes' on a Saturday night, it was the Volpes over to the Gossards'.

Viv and Mary Sauerberg were friends in a way that Volpe and me never were. Our wives did all kinds of things together, from joining the Skip-A-Week Quilt Club to running the church socials to going to A-robics together. There was twelve years of age between them, with Mary Sauerberg seven years younger than Volpe and me, but that didn't stop the two of them from getting along like a house afire.

But Volpe and me are a different story. Volpe's been a bully his whole life, the only difference being he's gone from using the size of his fists and the mean look in his eyes to using the size of his wallet and the size of his farm operation to back everybody else down. Back in grade school, one time I hit a softball down the third base line right between Volpe's legs for a stand-up double, and Volpe tried to convince everybody it was a foul ball. He come running over to where I stood on second base and got right in my face.

"Foul ball," he yelled, "it was on the line."

"Was not," I said. "Hit the ground in fair territory."

"Was too," he said. Back and forth like that, was not, was too, the way kids do. His eyes all screwed up tight and he kept punching the ball at me, trying to knock me off second base. Everybody gathered around us and taking sides, and Volpe getting madder and madder at me when I won't back down, and then the bell rings for the end of recess, and everybody starts back to the classroom. Soon as I step off second base Volpe tags me with the ball and says, "You're out."

"That so?" I said. He figured he'd beat me, his mouth all smirky and he's holding the ball up like he'd just won a MVP trophy. I nodded like I was agreeing with him, and then I nailed him with what I says next.

"Well," I says, "I guess if I'm out at second 'cause you tagged me, then that must've been a fair ball that got me here."

That was the first time he hauled his fist back and punched me in the nose. I let him do it, and then I walked right in to the classroom with all that blood dripping down my face. Got me the good citizen of the month award because I didn't hit him back. Hah.

Volpe's a good bit slicker than that now, or he'd never of got himself as fine a wife as Mary Sauerberg. Viv and me both was friends with her, because Mary Sauerberg was always good company. I knew her older sister when I was in school, and while Ruth Sauerberg didn't have Mary's looks, they were both women who were raised to be friendly and kind to everyone, and that included a lump of coal like me. Mary Sauerberg would get me to talking about whatever cabinets I happened to be building at the time, or she'd ask me if I'd seen the osprey that was hanging around Jimmy Ahlquist's pond, and I would find that I had more to say to her than I did to most people. She had a way of leaning in when you talked that showed you just how fascinating your subject was, and maybe she'd widen those big green eyes of hers, or raise up an eyebrow to show you how she had a question. You could answer that question if you were paying close enough attention to keep talking about whatever it was that brought that eyebrow of hers up. And when you did answer it, she smiled real pretty to let you know.

Of course that left Viv and Volpe to talk between themselves, and what Viv and Volpe mostly talked about was our kids and how they all got along. At least that's what I heard when I was within earshot. Volpe's the kind of guy who thinks that who a person turns out to be is all in the breeding. He had them prize Herefords after all, and he was always bragging on what good stock they were, and how many ribbons his kids won down to the county fair. The years his kids went on and won ribbons at the State Fair he was damn near impossible to be around, and since the only beef any of us ate came from his herd, he had plenty of occasions to remind us all what a smart cattleman he was.

Viv never seemed to mind all his bragging, though. I asked her about it once, after the Volpes had been to our house for Saturday night dinner, and Volpe had gone on and on about his Reserve Champion Hereford cow at the State Fair and all the careful breeding he'd done to get the bloodlines that made her what she was, and then on and on about how his son Michael Jr. was going into the Marines, the toughest branch of the service, where he was sure to become an officer. "Don't you see how he talks about his cattle," I said, "and how that's so when he talks about his kids you'll understand they're such fine children because he picked out the finest heifer in the county to breed himself to?"

With Viv you know you've crossed the line when her lower lip gets all bunched up, and she shakes her head back and forth like she's saying no to an ant, but the movement is so small you have to know her a few years before you see it.

"Arnold," she said, "it's bad enough you think women are no better than cattle, but you have to be some kind of idiot to think it's not going to hurt me when you call my best friend the finest heifer in the county." She pulled herself up so that all of her five foot two frame was plumb and true. She said, "You wish you'd married her instead of me, don't you."

No use explaining that I called Mary Sauerberg a heifer because that's how Volpe talks. Too late to put the shackles on when the milk cow's already bolted for the barn door. And no use saying that the thought that I would have rather had Mary Sauerberg for a wife never even crossed my mind, but I said it anyway.

"Talk is cheap, Arnold Gossard," says Viv, "and I see how you look at her."

It took building Viv a special cabinet to hold her sewing machine so it fit into a corner of the dining room to patch that up.

The summer before Mary Sauerberg left, her and Viv went on a tear to lose the weight they put on having all those babies. Viv especially, she being the stouter of the two. The Volpes' two boys were already gone by then, and we were down to Roger, the youngest of our three. The five of us'd sit down to Saturday night dinner, and Roger would bolt his like a stray dog and then run off to be with his friends. It was the summer before he went off to college, the first summer the Volpes had after Ray, their second born, moved out and left them a married couple on their own again.

There was a night over to the Volpes' when I ended up doing the dishes with Mary Sauerberg, and when we got done, Viv and Volpe had gone off for a walk. They walked up to the top of the rise where the wide spot in the road is, and if you look away from where our own farms are you can see the next valley spread out like a patchwork quilt. We could see them silhouetted against the evening sky looking out at the rest of the world, and then as they walked back toward us, the sound of their voices came to us on the wind, but not what they were saying. And as Mary Sauerberg and I sat on the porch we were quiet, the way friends can be sometimes, until Mary Sauerberg said something that sounds different now when I think about it than it did when I heard it first.

She said, "It's a good thing to have friends when the people you love move away."

There'd been a lot of moving away, what with our kids growing up, and that's what I thought she meant. But Mary Sauerberg herself would leave Volpe in less than a year's time, and that had to be already on her mind. So she wasn't thinking of the four of us being empty nesters together, she was thinking about Volpe still having Viv and me close by after she left.

It was Viv who told me why Mary Sauerberg left. Volpe was too proud a man to talk about it until the hurt wore off, and his hurt didn't really wear off until Viv left me. There's nothing like watching another man suffer the way you have to help you forget your own sorrow. In the year that went by between when Mary Sauerberg left and when Viv left, we still had Volpe over for the occasional dinner on a Saturday night, but Volpe took to spending most of his Saturday evenings down at the The Cazadero, where they had that video poker. He sold off his Herefords and had a pile of cash to play with, and I think he had his eye on one of the waitresses there for awhile. Least ways that was the gossip that Viv carried back to me from the women down at Curves, where she went for her A-robic workout.

I come home one night after delivering a set of kitchen cabinets over to Viola, and I pulled over in the wide spot at the top of the rise. There was just the barest sliver of a moon that night, and way off at the other end of Gossard Road was the remnants of a burn pile that Jimmy Ahlquist had lit in the morning. The smoke gave the night air a campfire feel, like Volpe and me and everybody else on Gossard Road was pioneers who got here last year and was still setting up our homesteads. I felt peaceful with that smell in the air, and I set there a while in my truck with the windows open. Our house was dark, and I was wondering when Viv was going to get back from running her errands.

After a time I started the truck back up and drove on down to home. I'll be goddamned if Volpe's front door didn't open just before I got to his place, and who should come out of it but Viv. She saw my truck and she saw me slow down, but she just waved her hand at me like I was to go on by. She was looking down at the ground like she had to be careful where she walked, and she was in her high-heeled shoes, but she was on Volpe's nice smooth concrete walkway from his front porch to the road, and she'd walked there ten thousand times at least.

I drove on down to our place and parked the truck next to the pole barn. There were a lot of reasons why Viv might be down to Volpe's for a minute, but the thing was I'd called her twice while I was out, and I had the feeling she'd been down there for hours. It don't take hours to bring Volpe a lasagna the way she'd done from time to time, and walking over to his house in high-heeled shoes didn't make no sense at all.

Viv was up in our bedroom when I come in. I had to look in half the rooms in the house to find her because she hadn't answered me when I called her name. She had the closet doors open all the way, and she was just standing there, staring at all our clothes hanging on the bar.

"I'm going to reorganize all this," she said. "I'm going to throw out all my clothes that don't fit." She'd been to the beauty salon and got her hair fixed up, and she was wearing a new dress that showed off her waist she'd got back with all them hours she spent down to Curves.

"You're all gussied up," I said. "Where you been?"

"You know where I've been," she said. "I've been down to Volpe's." She said this with her hand on her hip, and her mouth all squinched up the way she did when she thought the question I'd asked was stupid.

"What you got to wear lipstick to go down there for?" I said.

"I'll wear lipstick any time I please," she said. She reached into the closet and pulled a dress out, one of her house dresses that had no more shape to it than a sausage did, and she threw the dress down on the bed. It was only then that she looked at me.

"What is it, Arn?" she said. "What is that look on your face?"

I had no answer for that, seeing as how I could not see what look I had on my face. All I knew was that Volpe was not a married man any more, and that my wife didn't look like my wife any more, and that the two of them had spent the afternoon together doing I didn't know what. Everything changed when Mary Sauerberg left.

Viv said, "You think I've done something wrong?"

It was hard to tell. What I knew was that she and Mary Sauerberg had secrets between them and that Viv must've known Mary was leaving. She hadn't seen fit to tell me what was coming until it was already here and gone, and now she was keeping company with Volpe and not telling me until I caught her at it.

"I don't know what you've done," I said. "That's what troubles me."

Viv was looking me right in the eyes with the same hard look she used on that real estate fellow who came knocking on our door asking if we wanted to sell. It was a barbed wire fence of a look that backed a slick city fellow with a dark suit and a silk tie right off our front porch and into his car. But I had done nothing wrong, and I stood there and took that look from Viv, and I sent it right back at her. They say good fences make good neighbors, but there we were in our own bedroom and each of us with a fence in our eyes to keep the other one out.

Viv turned finally, and started in pulling clothes out of her side of the closet and piling them up on the bed.

"What's for dinner?" I said.

She kicked her high-heeled shoes off and they landed on the floor of the closet with a clunk and a clunk.

"Whatever you find in the fridge," she said. "I had dinner with Michael."

Dinner? With Michael? Not even Mary Sauerberg ever called Mike Volpe by that name, and neither one of us'd ever had dinner with Volpe without the other one there. Viv could've blown me over as easy as you blow out a match after she said that.

I come home a week later to find Viv's side of the closet empty and her car gone. She left me a letter in an envelope with my name spelled all the way out like I was some stranger. The letter said she was filing for a divorce. I would not be able to take her for granted any longer, she wrote.

I couldn't tell if she left me because I was jealous and she felt guilty, or if it was because I was jealous and she hadn't done a thing, but it was one or the other. If taking a person for granted was reason enough to get a divorce, there wouldn't be a married couple left in the whole damn county.

THAT WAS LAST FALL. Volpe come over a week or two after Viv left to tell me he knew how I felt, and then he offered to mow my lawn for me like I was some kind of invalid or something.

I haven't said ten words to Volpe between then and now. The crows were lined up on the telephone wires in front of his house making quite a racket about how the tree they were used to roosting in was gone. He'd finished his breakfast, which was oatmeal by the color of it. He got up from his chair and turned the TV off, and a few minutes later Volpe rolled out of his driveway on his big John Deere. Going off to plow up somebody's forty acres for Christmas trees.

I poured a judicious amount of bourbon whiskey into my coffee and finished it off, and then I got up and moseyed on over to the bungalow. The closer I got the taller and uglier that butt ugly stump got. His lawn was covered with wood chips all around where he'd sliced up the oak tree into rounds. The rotten spot running through the rounds that Volpe'd mentioned the night before was no bigger than my fist, nowhere near big enough to pose any real hazard to his house. He could've had that tree milled into some fine boards for cabinetry instead of wasting it all on firewood.

I sat on one of the rounds and started in counting the rings on the next one. Two hundred and seventy-eight years that tree had stood before Volpe cut her down. It couldn't have hurt me any worse if that tree'd been a wedding oak that my ancestors planted. You cut down something that's stood the test of time as long as that tree has and you're messing with something that you haven't got any right to mess with.

There wasn't but one thing to do to make the world whole again. I headed out to Volpe's barn and found his chainsaw in his tool shed off the back side. It was a big woolly bugger of a Stihl, and he'd had the saw a long time, but it was clean and the chain was sharp. I hauled the saw back to the oak tree and fired her up.

I ain't no logger but I have dropped a few trees in my time, same as anybody around here. You have to cut a wedge out of the side where you want the tree to fall and then backcut to the tip of the wedge from the opposite side. To do it just right you leave a half a finger's worth of wood between the two cuts, and you pull your chainsaw out and then you can push the whole tree over with your hand.

That tree was four feet thick at the base, and it was more work than I like to do on a Sunday, working that thirty-six inch bar back and forth, chips flying off the chain like a rooster tail and the rip of that chainsaw loud in my ears. I had to go back to Volpe's barn and borrow a couple of splitting wedges to keep the trunk of that stump from clamping down on the bar. The whole job took me a good forty minutes. Oak's pretty hard wood even when the chain's as sharp as Volpe kept his.

I had my choice of which way to let her fall, and I chose to let her fall across Volpe's walkway. I figured a man that would leave a big dick of a stump like that to stand in my view was a man you couldn't trust to keep a proper distance from your wife. It only made sense that I would block the way into his house with it. That way he'd have to go around it to get to his front door, and maybe going around it would make him think about what a stupid thing he'd done. I dropped that twelve foot tall stump neat as you please right across his walkway.

Thing of it was, even though I'd done such a bang-up job of dropping the stump right where I wanted it, I felt like I'd just shot a horse with a broken leg. There are times when a man has to finish something that somebody else started the best way he can, but that ain't a time to take a lot of pride in what you've done.

Running that saw put some serious sweat on my forehead. I hauled Volpe's saw back to his tool shed, and then I walked right into his house through the back door and got myself a tall drink of water, with ice out of Volpe's fancy fridge where you get the ice right out of the door. I can remember Mother right here in this kitchen complaining about having to defrost her freezer all the time. She'd have given up her left titty for a frost-free behemoth like this one.

I went into the living room to see how the view was between our two houses now that I'd dropped that stump. There was my porch with my chair on it, and I could just make out the coffee cup I'd left on the arm of the chair. I might want to plant a shrub of some kind at the corner of my porch to screen the view a bit. Wouldn't want Volpe to catch me sitting there with the binoculars aimed at his place.

The remote control for Volpe's big TV was sitting right there on his coffee table, right next to a satellite TV guide the size of a newspaper. I've looked at the big TVs in the stores but it always seemed like you'd need a room the size of a church for a TV that big to make sense. But here it was, and here I was, and it seemed like going back over to my place was open to an interpretation of cowardice that I surely wanted to avoid, so I sat down in Volpe's recliner and turned the TV on.

My God the picture was big at this range. People were maybe halfway to lifesize, even bigger than lifesize when they had a close-up. The sound came from behind me and beside me and in front of me, and when I found a movie that had a car chase in it I felt like I was on a roller coaster. Too much for me, but then I ran across a show where a guy was talking about saw blades and how to fine tune a chop saw, and that was real interesting. The guy had some good points to make about the ball bearing in the pivot, but he was all wrong about using the thinnest blade you can find. You want a thick blade, or else the blade will follow the grain of the wood and you won't get a straight cut.

I started feeling a might peckish after a bit, so I got up and checked Volpe's freezer. Sure enough he had some Rocky Road in there, so I scooped myself out a big bowl of it and sat back down in front of the TV. Man that ice cream tasted sweet. I kept flipping channels around until I found a movie with that weightlifter fellow in it, and his wife thought he was just a computer salesman but really he was a secret agent and he knew all about her stepping out on him, and stupid as it was, I settled in to watching it.

I sat there long enough to determine that a TV that big was a nice thing, but not a nice enough thing that I need to have one. And surely not a nice enough thing that it was worth cutting down a three-hundred-year-old oak tree to make it work right. I sat there until I heard the sound of a big diesel engine coming up Gossard Road on the other side of the rise. My neighbor was coming home.

I stood up and walked out on the front porch. There was that stump lying right where I dropped her, and I looked up to the top of the rise. Here comes Volpe on his big John Deere.

I climbed up on that log and stood plumb and true. Some things in life are worth a good punch in the nose.

In the Ditch

WHAT A DISAPPOINTMENT RAY'S turned out to be. You raise two boys the same way, you feed them, make sure they get their shots and their dental check-ups, you teach them both how to chop wood and say please and thank you, you show them how to throw a perfect spiral pass. One of them grows up straight and true, brings home nice girls with good bones and good manners to meet his parents, goes to college and then, when the shit hits the fan, he answers his country's call to duty.

The other one can make fifty free throws in a row but he won't go out for the basketball team. He dyes his hair strange colors and plays a mouse in some stupid local theater thing. He sleeps till noon and flunks out of college. You run into him in the city when you're out on a hot date and you've promised her the best steak she's ever eaten. There's your kid, sitting absolutely still on a box on a street corner in a suit. This might be okay, except every inch of him—his face, his hands, his clothes from the top of his fedora to the bottom of his shoes—is painted silver. His chin rests on his hand and his elbow rests on his knee. He's so still he looks like some goddamn statue, and he has a cigar box painted silver on the sidewalk next to him and there's three ones and a few quarters in it.

You say his name, but he doesn't look up. You say it again, "Ray, it's your dad," but he refuses to look up. He is dead to you, a silver ghost, a deserter. He won't raise so much as an eyebrow to let you know that he's heard you. There doesn't seem to be much point in introducing your date to a statue.

You want to slap him, but you're afraid if you do he'll just fall off the box. There he'll be on his side, on the sidewalk with his silver legs still bent at the knee, his silver chin still resting in his silver hand, the creases in his silver suit wrinkled just the same, like a goddamn cartoon, and what do you say to your hot date then, huh? Tell me that.

YOU CALL HIM UP the next day and ask him what the hell he thinks he's doing.

"Performance art," he says.

"Oh really," you say. "When did you take this up?"

"A year ago," he says.

"If that's performance art," you say, "shouldn't you actually perform somehow? Play a musical instrument, do tricks with coins, pretend you're stuck inside a glass room that isn't really there?"

"I'm not a mime, Dad," he says, "and it's not easy sitting still like that. It takes tremendous focus."

"And how much do you make for this tremendous act of focus?" you say. "Three bucks an hour? Four?"

"I don't do it for the money, Dad." He spits the word "Dad" out like it's a stink bug that flew into his mouth. "But if you must know, I average eighteen dollars an hour."

He's lying, you know he's lying, he's always played fast and loose with the truth. No way does he make eighteen dollars an hour for painting himself silver and sitting on a box. He's never had a lick of sense about money. His mother coddled him because he was her baby, the last child she would ever have. He was always a mystery to you. How could two boys from the same breeding lines wind up so different?

YOU SPEND YOUR LIFE with someone, you sleep with her, eat with her, you bathe together and take family vacations together, you stand by her side at her father's funeral and you hold her trembling hand in yours, and you think you know her.

And then your wife comes to you and says she has something to tell you. She sits you down at the kitchen table and tells you she's in love with someone new. She has her lipstick on just so, and her hair is brushed back from her face and held there with a tortoise shell comb, and she has on the diamond earrings you gave her for your twenty-fifth wedding anniversary, half a caret each. There isn't going to be a thirtieth. The way she talks to you is as calm and composed as if she were announcing that the vacuum cleaner was in need of repair. You want to take her face between your two hands and bite down on her nose. You want to hear cartilage crunch between your teeth. You want to spit her nose out on the floor and stomp on it with both your boots while her face bleeds and bleeds and bleeds.

When you ask her who this new man is, and she tells you it's Andy Buchli—a man you have known for five years, a man whose hand you have shaken within the friendly confines of the vendor-vendee relationship, a man you have invited onto your property in his capacity as an artificial insemination technician for your herd of prize winning Hereford cows—you are stunned like a steer in the slaughterhouse.

"Are you pregnant, Mary? Is that it?" you say. "Are you going to have his child?"

"I don't want another child," she tells you. "Besides, he's had a vasectomy."

You get up and leave. You tell your wife to pack her things and to be gone before you get back. The only thing you know for sure is that the world has gone completely cockeyed when your wife leaves you for a guy who's been clipped. You get into your truck and you start driving. You don't know where you're going at first, but it isn't long before you drive by Rickabaugh's place with his herd of Black Angus, and you know then you're looking for Andy Buchli. That skinny little fuck of a man who spends his days with his skinny little arm stuck up one cow's twat after another. Randy Andy, you think, and that makes you laugh a quick snort of a laugh, even though you're about as far from being amused as you are from ever being able to forgive your wife. Randy Andy, what a disappointment he's turned out to be.

You owe him a good thumping. For weeks you drive the back roads looking for him in his All West Breeders truck, which is painted a conveniently bright shade of green. You cruise all the way out The Hogback to Kurmaskie's herd of Red Brangus. You drive past Sam Weller's place with his herd of Charolais and his brand new silo. You drive Wildcat Mountain Road all the way to the end where Bill Rossing has those shaggy Scottish Highland cattle that look like yaks. You want to come across Randy Andy in his bright green truck on a deserted country road where you can force him into the ditch and then drag him out by his ears and stomp his guts. You will kick his balls so hard they'll go sailing up his throat and lodge at the top of his gorge where they will slowly, slowly choke him to death. You will take his skinny little fuck of a body over your knee and break his back like a matchstick.

Your sex drive went south for the winter after you found out about Randy Andy and your wife, but it comes back late the following summer, right after the divorce papers show up in your mailbox. Your hot date is Belinda Parry, and she is the first woman you've dated since the divorce. She has the kind of sturdy thighs you look for in a woman and she owns her own insurance agency. You've gone out with her three times, and when she asks you in for a nightcap on the third date, you think your chances are pretty good.

You've already told each other the stories of your respective divorces. She has wavy hair that she dyes auburn. You know this because you've just seen the hair dye box in her bathroom. You're sitting on her couch, both of you sideways with one knee drawn up. You are mirroring her gestures because you read somewhere that this is a good way to build rapport, and today's women want rapport. She has long fingers with the nails painted a deep shade of red, and you can't stop thinking about how much you want those fingers to stroke you. She has a fifteen-year-old daughter who spends the weekends with her father. You ask her what she thinks of your son painted silver all over.

"He's very creative," she says. Creative is just another word for weird, but you don't say this out loud.

"Creative is good," you say, "but he's drifting. He's got about as much direction as a boat with a busted rudder." You are playing the caring parent because parenting is something you have in common. She has a redhead's fair skin and eyes the color of the ocean on a map. She has crow's feet and an easy smile but she is not an easy woman to get into bed. She is better than market grade, she is choice even, but she is ten years too old to be prime. You took her for a walk down by the river on your second date and you held hands. You watched the moon rise, a slender crescent of a moon, and she allowed you one soft lingering kiss.

"Some of us take longer to find ourselves," she says. "We can't all be gung-ho Marines."

Gung ho is what you have always been. Long before Mary ran off with Randy Andy, way back before you knocked her up, and the day her old man looked you straight in the eye and said, "I know I can count on you to do the right thing," back even before you bought the Gossard place and planted your first forty acres of Christmas trees, you were a young bull o' the woods. A choke setter, a rigging slinger, a timber faller, a pay-day partying scary skookum of a lumberjack who could drink till closing time, fight your way past the other drunken lumber-jacks in the parking lot, fuck some gin-jollied barroom Jane till dawn, and still put in a full day's work when the sun comes up.

You finish the pear brandy in the glass with the stem so delicate you could snap it in two like a matchstick with just your fingers. You set the glass on the coffee table and you take Belinda Parry's hands into yours. You count the buttons down the front of her dress and imagine unbuttoning them one by one. You gaze into the ocean of her eyes and murmur that her perfume makes you think of daphne because that's a line that worked with Mary all those years ago, and you lean in close. She closes her eyes and her face tilts up, her lips are parted to meet yours, you kiss her softly and your lips and her lips are getting to know each other like a cow nuzzling her newborn calf. You need this, and there's something fierce underneath your soft kissing that you want to bring out in the open, and the way she is kissing your upper lip with both of hers, with just the slightest bit of suction, you know she must be feeling something fierce as well. You slide your tongue forward between her lips and touch the tip of her tongue. She pulls her tongue back and breaks contact.

She says, "Slow down, tiger," and she gives you a soft push in the chest. "Let's take this one step at a time."

You have no idea what the next step is. You were sure that sticking your tongue in her mouth was absolutely the next step, but Belinda Parry's steps are not the steps you know.

She takes your hand and stands up. She leads you to the door, and she kisses you again, briefly.

"Go home, tiger," she says. You could beg, but you want something more than charity sex, and anyway you're pretty sure that Belinda Parry is not that kind of charitable. You could cajole, you could joke, you could offer the solace of a double mercy fuck, but then how could you ever come back a second time? You could go macho on her and demand that she give you what you want, but she's already told you one of the things she hates about her ex-husband is that he acts like he's entitled.

Instead you bring her hand to your lips and kiss it. She gives you a look that is full of promise for the next time. You offer her your most confident smile as you turn to leave.

You review the situation as you drive home. You thought the third date would be the charm. You wonder if seeing Ray was just a little bit too weird, and for a moment you'd like to slap your son silly. You'd like someone ten years younger than Belinda Parry to show you the steps, someone prime, but you haven't met anyone like that, so Belinda Parry will have to do for now.

You remind yourself that Belinda Parry is a single mom past forty. You decide to wait before you call her again because you are sure her desperation will blind her to yours.

SIX MONTHS AGO YOU had a prime herd of polled Herefords, the finest herd in the county. Your son, Michael Jr., went to the State Fair four years running and won the FFA Reserve Champion Brood Cow ribbon twice. He has taken your side in the divorce, unlike that mama's boy Ray, the deserter. One of the hardest things you have ever done is write the email to Michael Jr. telling him you are selling the herd. You don't want him coming home from the war to an empty corral but you have no choice. Every time you look at your cows you see Randy Andy shoving the syringe loaded with bull semen inside them all the way up past his elbow. You want to strip his long latex glove off his arm and strangle him.

You feel better after you sell the herd. Your honor is intact. You keep the gomer bull because he's young and you want to fatten him up, and Randy Andy has never touched your gomer. Months go by and you realize you've stopped thinking up new ways to kill his skinny ass.

You tell Belinda Parry about your cattle herd the night you exchange your divorce stories. It's the second date, and after you go for your walk by the river, you sit in your truck and talk for an hour and a half while the moon rises. You tell her all about Randy Andy, about the bottle of top shelf Kentucky bourbon you gave him at Christmas every year, about how much you liked talking bulls with him. Here was a man who knew his bull semen, a man who had worked both sides of the business—collection and delivery. A man who did his job and never complained. You tell her about Mary and her cunt of a lawyer, a woman with a big head of curly hair the color of galvanized steel and big round glasses, a woman who never smiled at you during the entire deposition. She asked you a string of questions that made you sound like someone who neglected his wife so he could run his farm business, someone emotionally distant who forgot birthdays but remembered the details of every cow he'd bred and the wholesale price of every Christmas tree harvest going back thirty years.

You know you're coming across like some pathetic whiner so you start talking about your Herefords. You start with the color, that rich deep red and how it sets off their curly-haired white faces. You tell her how after twenty years of carefully selecting the right bulls, you had calves with lower birth weight and faster gain to market. You tell her how you finished them with ninety days of grain and sold them to a broker who dealt with the best restaurants in the city. You tell her how your breeding program increased the marbling of your beef by 7.7 percent over the years. She likes hearing this, she tells you she likes your passion. You tell her when the truck left with your herd you sat in your living room staring at a blank TV until it got dark out. You tell her how the only animal you kept was the gomer.

"What's a gomer?" she asks.

You explain to her that a cow is only in heat for twelve hours every three weeks, and how you have to watch your herd for the signs if you want to control your breeding program. You tell her a gomer is a bull who's been clipped so that he still mounts but he can't impregnate, and when you see a cow letting the gomer mount, that's when you call All West Breeders, and they send out Randy Andy to do the deed.

"A bull with a vasectomy," Belinda Parry says. "I like that."

You think maybe Belinda Parry will ask if you've had a vasectomy, and you think that would be a good sign, but she doesn't. Instead she asks you this: "Did you keep the gomer for a pet?"

A pet is the furthest thing from your mind. Cattle are a business, a way to put food on the table. She takes your hand in hers and strokes her finger down the edge of your palm. It feels so good you ignore the stupidity of her question.

"I've fattened him up," you tell her. "I'm going to eat him."

She stops stroking your hand when you say this. It's only a minute or two later that she asks you to take her home.

A WEEK GOES BY with no phone call from Belinda Parry, but you remain strong. You have chosen your course of action and you will stick to it until it bears fruit. It's early Sunday morning and there's nothing to eat in your refrigerator, so you drive into town for groceries. There's a fog hanging low on the countryside and you drive with your headlights on. You ran into Ray yesterday when you went into the city because you can't get the kind of steak you're used to anywhere else. Ray was working inside some low-rent taco stand and he called your name out as you walked by. You don't like it when he calls you Mike, but you let it go.

"I heard from Michael," he tells you. "He says it's getting pretty scary over there. He says two of his men were killed by a roadside bomb."

You refuse the free taco that Ray offers you. You're sure that Michael Jr. would never use the word scary to describe the war. You can't help but notice the ring piercing the center of Ray's lower lip. You've never seen it before, and when you ask him when he got the goddamn thing, he tells you he's had it for a year. He tells you he always takes it out when he knows you're going to see each other.

"Because I knew it'd freak you out, Dad," he says. You want to rip the ring right off his face.

"But I'm glad you've seen it now," he says, "so we can stop pretending." A customer comes up to the taco stand before you can ask, "Pretending what?"

AT THE SHOP 'N' SAVE you get a basket and you cruise the grocery store aisles filling it up. You buy salad in a plastic bag and a cucumber for slicing. You buy sausage and eggs and bread for toast. You buy cream cheese and blue cheese and bunch onions for chopping. It's Sunday morning and the store is pretty empty, but you keep your eyes open because somewhere you've heard that the grocery store is a good place to meet women. You are looking for someone prime, a woman with long bones and the right shape, a woman who will know when to follow your lead. A woman too young to have crow's feet, because once a woman hits forty, she goes downhill fast. Instead you see a woman who is the right age but with a narrow, pinched face who is definitely no better than market grade. You see another woman with a pretty face who is shaped like a pear. You see Belinda Parry in a pair of tight jeans and a denim jacket. She's in line at the checkout counter, and you put on your most confident smile and you suck in your gut and walk right up to her.

"Hey stranger," you say, and the way she smiles back makes you glad you've cut out all that ice cream you used to eat. Her cart is three-quarters full. She has laundry detergent in a big box, a case of beer, light bulbs, a bag of carrots, and a gallon of apple juice. She has potato chips and chocolate chips. She has a pair of pantyhose labeled "Nude." She has bacon and eggs and a box of rice and beans.

"I'm going back to my place," you say, "to make one of my famous omelets. Care to join me?"

"I'd love to," she says, "but not this morning."

She looks past you at someone and gives a little wave. She has a shiny silver bracelet on her wrist that catches the light, something elegant and Navajo, the kind of thing you used to buy Mary for your anniversary. A man beelines his way to the two of you, a man with a carton of orange juice and a box of some feminine hygiene product that makes you want to turn and run.

The man holds up the box and says, "This what you're looking for?"

"That's it," Belinda Parry says. The man puts the juice and the feminine hygiene product into her cart and he looks at you. You are hoping that he will be introduced as her brother, her priest, her eunuch. He looks fifteen years younger than you and he wears a big belt buckle that lays flat across his flat belly. You suck your gut in even tighter and you smile your most confident smile at him.

"Ned Scheible," Belinda Parry says, "this is Mike Volpe. Mike's one of my best clients."

You don't like being introduced as her client but you cling to the lovely lilt in her voice when she said "best." You shake hands with Ned. You squeeze hard and Ned squeezes right back. Belinda Parry touches her bare skin where her collar is open above her breasts.

"Ned's a biologist with the Fish and Game department," she says. "He grew up around here, maybe you know him?"

"Fish and Wildlife," Ned says. He lets go of your hand, and you feel a sudden coolness on your palm. "Out here for a month working on a salmon habitat restoration project."

"Right," you say, "I read about that in the paper." You know the Scheibles, sort of, but not this Ned. The grin on his face makes you want to stomp his guts.

The conveyor belt at the checkout stand starts to move, and Belinda Parry grabs the package of pantyhose labeled "Nude" and puts them on the belt.

"Nice meeting you, Mike," Ned says. You have to stand aside so he can join Belinda Parry in line.

"See you around, Mike," Belinda Parry says. "Call me up sometime, okay?"

Sure thing, you tell her. You head off for the beer cooler even though beer is the one thing you have plenty of at home. It's a walk-in cooler, and you can waste enough time in there to be sure they'll be gone before you come back out.

THE FOG IS THICK and pure when you drive home. It gets whiter as you drive up Handel Road to the ridge where you live. This is good, you think, you will erase the past the same way the fog erases the world around you. You will start your life over this very morning. You are going to have to go on a serious diet and start working out if you ever hope to land a woman above market grade. You are going to call the mobile slaughterer tomorrow and have the gomer butchered so that you won't have to drive all the way into the city for a decent steak. You will eat nothing but steak and salad, and you will do sit-ups until your belly is so flat you will never have to suck in your gut again.

You drive fast because you know every dip, every twist and turn of this road. The fog is your best friend saying you can do better than that slut Belinda Parry. Erase the past, the fog says, and take control of your new life. What humiliates you will fall away, and what you need will be revealed to you. You deserve better than a wife who cheats on you and a worthless son who pretends to love you.

You see your sons the way they are in the pictures on your mantle. Michael Jr. is in his dress uniform. His hat is a white as pure as the fog and the brim is shiny and black. He looks directly into the camera without the hint of a smile. His eyes are the eyes of a man who does his duty. A man who knows something about honor and how to defend it. He has your strong nose and narrow cheekbones and your earlobes, which are not attached all the way around to your face.

Ray's picture has him smiling raffishly out of the frame. His hair is slicked back and he has a diamond earring in one ear. It's his head shot, he's told you, the one he uses to advertise himself for acting jobs. His cheekbones are wide, like Mary's, and his eyes are shifty and hazel like Mary's, and his earlobes are all part of his face, like Mary's. That raffish smile is Mary's too, and you are going to stop calling it raffish because that word is Mary's word, and you are done with all things that are Mary's. Including Ray, because—you see it so clearly now, how could you have pretended otherwise all these years?—Ray is not your son. This explains so much. You don't know whose son he is, but you know goddamn well that a woman who can run away with Randy Andy could have done you wrong twenty years before.

Ahead of you, in the fog, you see taillights. You come up on them quickly because whoever is driving is slowed down by the fog. You come up on them and you see they are the taillights of a bright green truck. This is your lucky day. This is the last piece of unfinished business you need to erase. You have the whole world in your sights and you are ready to pull the trigger.

You floor it, and you slide over into the oncoming lane. Won't this be fun, you think. You can't wait to see the look in Randy Andy's eyes when you pull up alongside of him. You are gaining on him quickly, you are almost even with him, and he has his arm out the window, waving you on by. But you will not go on by. You will herd him into the ditch like the frightened little sheep that he is. And then you will give him the ass whipping he so richly deserves.

Ahead of you, in the fog, someone switches on their headlights. They are coming straight at you, and they are close, way too close. You glance over at the bright green truck next to you, and you see that it is not the All West Breeders truck. Horns are blaring in front of you and beside you. You wrench the steering wheel to the left and boom, just like that, you are driving in the ditch. The other cars pass each other without crashing. Gravel is spitting under your tires. You hit a mailbox and flatten it. The ass end of your truck fishtails when you hit the brakes. Tall grass is ticking against the window next to you. You come to a stop in a place where the fog is especially thick.

You know this spot. You're next to the Hildebrandts' field, the one Jimmy Ahlquist leases for Christmas trees. You open your door and get out, pushing through the tall grass. The paint on your truck is grass stained down the side. The bumper is dinged hard where you hit the mailbox. Your left wheels are buried deep in soft mud. You cannot get the truck out going frontwards or backwards. You cuss your truck for not being truck enough to get out of this ditch, you cuss your ex-wife for being the lying, cheating cunt she is, and you cuss Randy Andy for not being here when you need him most.

You get rid of the other two drivers when they come back to see if you're all right. You don't need anybody's help. You will walk home and get your tractor, and you will come back to pull your truck out. You are totally alone, on a back road, in the ditch. Far away, on the other side of Hildebrandts' Christmas tree field, you hear the soft clank of a bell, the kind of bell that goat herders put around the neck of the lead goat.

"Hello," you call out. You listen for a reply. Nothing but fog fills your ears.

What Good a Divorce Is

IN THE BEGINNING IT was all about the dresser. One minute
Viv was driving along, thinking about what a dud her ex-husband turned out to be, and the next she was pulled up next to
the trailer at the Goodwill donation site, loading up a dresser
that didn't exactly belong to her.

When she hit fifty she began to wonder when her real life
was going to start, the life she'd imagined when she was a
young woman, the life where her nails were painted to match
her lipstick, and she was beautiful, at least in the eyes of her
husband. A life without all the compromises she'd made to
stay married to Arnie. The last year she was married she lost
forty-two pounds, and she'd kept pretty near all of it off ever
since. Forty-two pounds was a lot of days where she had nothing but salad for lunch and dinner both, and it was a lot of
hours on the stationary bike at the gym, and it was no dessert at all, ever. She wanted Arnie to notice, that was all. She
wanted him to at least mute the flippin' TV when she came out
of the bathroom on a Saturday night with her hair all done up
and her lips painted red with a lipstick called Rita's First Kiss
and a negligee from Victoria's Secret. Who the hell else was she

supposed to feel sexy with if it wasn't her husband?

After she lost all that weight she started dropping hints about a cruise, or maybe a trip to Maui like the one the neighbors took. She pictured long walks on the beach at sunset, holding hands and kissing each other like they were teenagers again. "They had such a good time," she told Arnie, "Mary told me all about it. The water's so warm you just walk out into the waves and go swimming anytime you want."

"That so?" Arnie said. He stared out the window with a pair of bird watching binoculars in his hands. If she stood there long enough he would crack his knuckles, she'd seen him do it ten thousand times.

It was infuriating. As if those two words and cracking his knuckles were enough to hold up his end of the conversation.

AFTER SHE LEFT ARNIE she developed a kind of radar for old furniture. There was a lot of old furniture out there in the country that dealers in the city would pay decent money for, if a person knew what they wanted and how to fix it up for them. She hit all the garage sales and the church rummage sales, and after a while the word was out, and people started calling her when they had something to get rid of. But taking things from the Goodwill was never a part of it until she saw her cousin Jeff's old dresser sitting there.

She didn't know what it was at first, only that she'd seen something across the highway that made her turn around and drive back for a closer look. It was nothing special as a dresser, just a four drawer in a plain box, the kind of cheap but sturdy thing factories churned out after World War II for all those soldiers who were starting families. It was still painted the same medium gray, but what Viv cared about were the decals. They were cowboy decals, one on each drawer, really nice ones with colors like an old movie poster. The bottom drawer was a cowboy on a bucking bronco, and the next one up was a cowboy twirling a lasso over his head, and then a saguaro cactus in front of a big sunset with a cowboy sitting on a horse looking at it. The one on the top drawer was her favorite, a cowboy with a branding iron he'd just pulled out of the fire. The business end of the branding iron was red hot, a circle with a V in the middle. Circle-V brand, V for Viv, and that dresser was meant for her.

She was a tomboy growing up, and she used to go over to Jeff's house all dressed up like a cowboy, and there weren't enough hours in the day for her to play cowboys with Jeff. If it was rainy out, they turned his bedroom into the Circle-V ranch. Jeff had a bedspread with cowboys and Indians all over it, and wallpaper with six shooters and spurs and cowboy hats. The bedspread was where their cattle roamed, and in front of the dresser was the corral. The ranch house was the closet, and they would close the door and lay on top of each other and make snoring noises, their six shooters clanking in the dark.

Her aunt and uncle had given the dresser away to some friends more than forty years before. She tried to hunt it down once, but the friends had long since moved. But here it was, like it had dropped through a wrinkle in time and landed right in front of her. It was in pretty good shape, too. There were some big scratches down one side, and the corners were beaten up, but it was nothing she couldn't make right with some sandpaper. The main thing was the decals were in almost perfect shape. Fifty years old and no kid had ever drawn a mustache or devil horns on those cowboys. There were a couple of chips in them, a nick here and there, but that just added to their character. Maybe she was being nostalgic, or sentimental, but when she saw that dresser again, she just had to have it.

There was a big sign on the side of the Goodwill trailer that said stealing from the site was a felony crime. But this wasn't stealing, not really. After she lost all that weight she gave a whole closet full of clothes to the Goodwill. And she knew for a fact that some of the things that went to Goodwill ended up in antique stores and shops that specialized in vintage clothing. She'd given the Goodwill a little clutch purse that belonged to her aunt, and a couple of months later she ran across the very same purse in a shop on Antique Row with a fifty dollar price tag on it. So the Goodwill owed her something, and here was a piece of her childhood that nobody would care about the way she did. Not taking it would be an even bigger crime, a crime against her own good fortune. She wouldn't sell this piece, she would keep it, so nobody could say she did it for the money. She did it for love.

It only took her thirty seconds to load the dresser into the back of her little truck.

THE SECOND PIECE OF furniture was a different matter, as was the third, and the fourth, and a few more after that, and the bottle of nail polish that found its way into her purse at the Hi School Pharmacy. The second piece was a half round table with a drawer, perfect for a telephone or a place to put pictures in stand-up frames. She'd seen one just like it in a shop for ninety-nine dollars. The one at the Goodwill donation site had a cigarette burn on it, but she stripped the finish off, sanded it, and put a dark stain on the mahogany so the burn barely showed. She was getting by on a measly little alimony check and the eight dollars an hour she made working part time at the video store. She got fifty in cash for the table, not so much given how many hours she spent fixing it up, but it was the fifty dollars she needed to buy that teddy at Victoria's Secret, the creamy one with a hint of peach and all that frilly lace. When she wore it she could at least imagine she was sexy, even if she had jeans and a work shirt on over it.

The thing of it was, Goodwill had gone corporate. She read all about it in the newspaper, how they hired some hotshot executive and paid him half a million a year, and how he turned the Goodwill business around to where they were selling forty million dollars worth of stuff every year. They were opening a new store every six months, and she couldn't see how carting off a piece of furniture every now and then hurt anyone. If that table had been in one of their stores it would have had a ten dollar price tag on it, and she would've paid it. All she was doing was cutting out the middleman. It's not like the Goodwill even knew about that table.

She did feel a little bit bad about Daryl. Daryl was at the Goodwill trailer from nine to five every day, with his bag of miniature chocolate bars and his look of perpetual amazement, as if he could never quite catch up to what was going on around him. He always smiled when she dropped off the clothes that didn't fit her any more, and he always said, "Would you like a receipt, ma'am?" If she said yes he licked the end of his pencil and marked a careful X next to the word "clothes," and just as carefully tore the receipt off a pad. He had a round face that reminded her of Arnie, except Daryl's ears didn't have those ugly tufts of hair growing out of them.

She was pulling out of the Goodwill donation site one evening with a dining room table in the back of her truck when the sheriff came screaming up in his car, red and blue lights flashing, cutting off her escape. He stepped out of the car like he meant business, one hand on the gun in his holster and the other shining a big flashlight into her eyes. Viv was so terrified her knees barely held her up when the sheriff told her to step out of the truck.

She didn't even bother to try and explain herself. "I'll put it back," she said, "I'll never do it again, just please, let me go." She had her arm in front of her face to keep the light from blinding her. The sheriff lowered his flashlight and told her to turn around and put her hands on top of the truck. The pat down he gave her was quick and impersonal, like Arnie's idea of foreplay. He handcuffed her and put her in the back of his squad car.

"I was right across the highway," the sheriff told her. "I saw the whole thing." The smirk on his face when he said this made her want to slap him. He took her to the county lock-up, where she spent the night in jail for the first time in her life, curled on a cement ledge, knees to belly, her shirt pulled up over her mouth and nose in a vain attempt to filter out the smells of the holding cell. There was the reek of stale vomit, of unwashed bodies, and a chemical, almost metallic stink that clung to the impossibly skinny woman who paced the floor all night long. For weeks those smells settled in her lungs like an itch she couldn't reach, and whenever a whiff of it caught the back of her throat she gagged, and felt angry, and mistreated.

SHE SAW ARNIE COMING out of the liquor store a few weeks after she got arrested. He was crossing the street in front of her with a bag tucked into one arm. She had an itch to stomp on her gas pedal and make him into a hood ornament, but instead she pulled up along side of him and rolled her window down.

"Viv," he said. The bag he carried was big enough for a half gallon of bourbon, and it gave her some satisfaction, be he only bought bourbon by the fifth when they were married. He must have a lot of sorrow to drown if he couldn't look her in the eye with the bulge of that half gallon of bourbon in his bag.

"Having a party?" she said. He stared off down the street before he answered. His truck was a block away, in front of the cafe where he'd taken to eating his meals since their divorce. He hadn't shaved in a couple of days.

"Naw," he said, "no party. Just stocking up."

"That so?" She waited for his gaze to swing back around and meet hers but it didn't. "Just you and Old Grand-Dad, huh?"

There was enough of an edge in her voice that he finally looked at her. "How have you been?" he said. Two o'clock on a Friday afternoon and his eyes were rummy and rimmed with red.

"I saw your picture in the paper," he said. "It kind of surprised me."

"That so?" He heard it this time, because he shot her a look like he'd just sat down hard enough on a good-sized splinter to cut through the fog he was walking around in.

"You had your picture in the paper next to a child molester and a dope addict," he said. "People are talking."

Viv put her truck in neutral and jammed her foot down on the emergency brake just to hear the screech it made.

"People are talking?" she said. "Big whoop-tee-damn-do. I don't give a good goddamn if people are talking about me. Stealing a piece of furniture from the Goodwill is pretty small potatoes compared to those other two."

"It's big enough potatoes to be an embarrassment every time somebody stops me on the street and asks me what the hell is wrong with you," Arnie said. "You're a damn criminal, Viv."

He started walking to his truck, hustling right along, eager, no doubt, to get away from her so she wouldn't embarrass him any more. Well, she wasn't going to let him get away that easy. She got out of her truck, just left it there in the middle of the street with the motor running. This wasn't going to take that long. She stomped down the street in the spike-heeled boots she'd found at Goodwill and stood right in his way, and wouldn't let him go around her.

"You want to know what's criminal, Arnie? Criminal is when your wife loses forty pounds and you still don't pay any attention to her. Criminal is not taking me to the Norse Lodge Christmas dance so I can show off how good I look in a size six dress. Criminal is you take our vacation money and spend it on a new drift boat without even bothering to ask first."

There must have been something truly fascinating on the pavement between Arnie's shoes, because that's what he was studying as if his life depended on it. Viv was talking loud enough that people coming out of the cafe half a block away stopped and stared, but she didn't care.

"Let me tell you something, Arnie Gossard. If you had taken me to that dance we would still be married, and I would not have my picture in the paper for stealing furniture from the Goodwill trailer, and you would not be buying bourbon by the half gallon so you could go home and drink alone. So don't be telling me how embarrassed you are by my picture in the paper, because this is all your fault."

"That so?" The nerve of that man, trying to shut her up one more time with those two words.

"Yes," she said, "that's so." She took the bourbon right out of his hands, just snatched it so quick he never knew what hit him, tore the bag off, and she threw it down on the ground.

As it happens, Old Grand-Dad in half gallons comes in a plastic bottle, so all it did was bounce.

"What the hell has got into you?" Arnie yelled. He bent down to pick up his bourbon, but Viv was quicker. She jumped on his bottle of Old Grandad with both spikes. If he hadn't pulled his hands back she would have stabbed both his wrists. The bottle split open and bourbon poured out all over the street.

"You owe me for that," Arnie said. His voice wobbled, and there were tears in his rummy eyes, and Viv knew she'd got him good.

"That so?" she said. "So sue me."

What good was a divorce if you couldn't make a man cry? Her work there done, she strode off down the street, her spikes smacking the pavement with each step. She got back in her truck and drove away, but she was too worked up to run the errands she had planned. She headed out of town, thinking a drive up the river might be a good way to celebrate what she'd just done.

The highway took her right by where the Goodwill donation site sat on the edge of town, and there was Daryl. Even though the sheriff had warned her to stay away, she turned her truck around. Screw the sheriff, she hadn't even been convicted yet, and she was tired of men telling her what to do.

But before she pulled into the Goodwill donation site she took a slight detour and pulled into the Qwik Mart. She ran in and bought the biggest chocolate bar they had, a bar of chocolate big enough to make anyone sick if they ate the whole thing at once. She drove over to the Goodwill trailer, and before she got out of her truck she fingered the top buttons of her work shirt. She had the teddy from Victoria's Secret on underneath, and she unbuttoned her top two buttons, so just the lacy top edge would show. When she got out she held the chocolate bar in front of her chest with both hands.

Daryl came over to her, his face as round and innocent as ever. "Do you have a donation, ma'am?" he said.

"Yes I do," Viv said, and she moved the chocolate bar side to side a little. "It's a special donation, just for you."

It took Daryl a minute, but his eyes got wide and a little goofy, the level of his perpetual amazement rising up a notch. He smiled at Viv the way only a man who appreciates what he sees can smile.

"For me?" he said.

"Yes," Viv said. She handed him the chocolate bar. "All for you."

Her hands free, she ran her finger up the edge of her shirt, along the skin she'd exposed for Daryl. She had never flirted with a man like that in her life. Flirting was fun, even if it was with Daryl, who was staring down at the pad in his pocket as if he were trying to figure out if a chocolate bar was the kind of donation that required a receipt.

"No receipt necessary," Viv said. "This is just between you and me."

"Thanks," Daryl said. His eyes settled on her chest, on the lace across the tops of her breasts, and he blushed. Yes, she had him now, she'd cut through his fog. His eyes dropped, but he was smiling. He began to unwrap the chocolate bar as if it were a Christmas gift and he was going to save the paper to use again.

"Goodbye Daryl," she said, "see you next time." She got back in her truck and drove away. There was a flush in the skin of her chest, she could feel the heat there. She unbuttoned the third button on her work shirt. She felt the lacy edge of her teddy with her finger, and she thought she might drive over to the Hi School Pharmacy and check out some nail polish. They had something called Rockette Red, and it was about time she tried it out. She might even pay for it this time. Not that they'd miss it.

The Idjit's Guide to Intuitive Mastery of Newtonian Physics

JIMMY AND TODD BOUGHT the car cheap from Stubby Toobin. They thought they were looking for an old Willys Jeep, and that led them to Stubby, a tree-topper who was old enough to know what logging was before there were bulldozers and chainsaws. There were plenty of used-up, flat-topped loggers hanging around in the bars till closing time sent them home to their tin-patched shacks, old skookum sucker punchers minus a finger or two, who wouldn't let that stop them from throwing a punch if a brawl broke out. But everybody knew the story that made Stubby special. Stubby had once been a hundred feet up an old growth Doug fir he was rigging to be a spar tree for a clear cut. He had the high lead rigged to the main line block when a sharp tug from the donkey engine cracked the tree right through the rot hidden at the base, butt rot that Stubby should've known was there but had somehow missed. He was tied to the trunk with his flipline, so that as the tree fell twisting through the air, he had to keep jumping his feet around it to stay on top. He rode that tree clear to the ground, where it bounced four times, twisting each time with him underneath it or on top of it, flailing him around on his flipline like one of those paddle-balls kids play with, and each time he was underneath, it was his good fortune there was a swale where he landed so he was not crushed.

It was Stubby who talked Jimmy and Todd through the nit and the grit of what they wanted to do and how to survive it without breaking every bone in Todd's young body. What they came to, in Stubby's cabin, over a pot of coffee with bourbon bumps just to keep things interesting, was that Todd's chances would improve to well above those of a back alley crapshoot if he rode on top of the launch vehicle rather than in it, and to do that they would have to make some serious modifications. They needed something with an automatic transmission, not some old Willys Jeep with a manual, and Stubby had just the thing sitting in his yard along with all the other rusty hulks he'd accumulated over a lifetime of infatuation with what a man could do if he had the right machine and a brawny set of balls.

"Nineteen-sixty Plymouth Valiant with a PowerFlite transmission," Stubby said. "Ever seen one? You shift gears by pushing those buttons right there on the dashboard."

Todd and Jimmy, intuitive Newtonians and fledgling jump-happy jalopy drivers, knew right then that this was the car.

"Do you think," Todd said, "this would fly better if we put some weight in the trunk to balance out the weight of the engine?"

Nods all around. They were out to make their place in the history of crazy bone-crunch stunts. They called the car Duane, because they bought it the day Duane Allman died.

THEY SAT, THE THREE of them—Todd, Jimmy, and Mike Volpe—in aluminum lawn chairs in front of the single-wide that Todd rented on the edge of Adelaide Hamby's place. Volpe had showed up unannounced on a Sunday afternoon with a case of beer and what he called "a little proposition." Jimmy was there because he was always there that summer, the summer of 1972, when Jimmy and Todd both worked swing shift at the mill, and Todd was still on probation.

They were three beers in and had most of the details settled—the where and the when, the pills, half up front and half on delivery, the cliff, and how the loggers would site-prep it for the jump—when the true nature of Volpe's proposition came to light.

"Hey," he said, "I've just had this crazy idea. What do you say we charge people to watch?"

Jimmy and Todd both raised their beer bottles and drank, staring messages at each other, danger from Jimmy to Todd, opportunity from Todd to Jimmy.

"How much you thinking?" Todd asked.

"To see somebody jump a car off a cliff and land in a lake?" Volpe leaned in to the space between them. He put his hand out, palm up, as if the gesture alone were enough to make money appear. "I think we can get twenty bucks a head, and I bet I can round up fifty people."

Todd, the balls in the brains-and-balls combo that was Jimmy and Todd, said "Nice chunk of change." He took a swig off his beer. "What is that, Jimmy? A thousand bucks?"

Jimmy nodded, but he was watching Volpe, waiting for him to turn his head and give the blue-eyed stare he'd used to close the deal with Todd so many times before. Volpe was a couple years older than Todd, he was as slick as warm bacon grease, and he'd made a career out of taking advantage of Todd's weakness for any kind of a buzz.

"What do you want out of this?" Jimmy asked.

There it was, eyes the color of a workshirt for an honest day's work, and a smile that asked them to believe that they were all in this together. "We split it fifty-fifty," Volpe said, "half to you guys for putting on the show and half to me for finding all the money."

Todd's head bobbed back and forth, as if his brain were scales balancing two things of almost equal weight. They'd gone from nothing to five hundred bucks in a heartbeat, but Jimmy didn't like it. Jimmy didn't like much of anything about Volpe, but Volpe had the pills, and Todd wanted the pills, and his brother wanting the pills was Volpe's thumb on the scales.

Jimmy shook his head no. What a weasel Mike Volpe was. Always had been. He'd always been a little scared of Mike. Mike was a big guy and a bit of a bully, but he wasn't nearly as scared as he would be if Todd weren't there. And he had to say something before Todd blew it and accepted.

"We're not stupid," Jimmy said. "First off, there's three of us here, and second, we don't need you to sell tickets for us."

He was an idiot for not seeing it himself. Of course they could charge people to watch. They'd been so involved in getting the car ready to go, or he might've realized.

"I'm a reasonable guy," Volpe said. "I could go thirds on the money."

The two of them stood up, Jimmy and Todd, Todd's hands in loose fists, just in case. That was the good thing about Todd, he would back you up without bothering to wonder whether or not he thought you were right. Volpe sat in his chair and pulled a pair of sunglasses out of his shirt pocket. He put them on and stared up at the two brothers, and then he stood up, a head taller then either one of them.

"We'll think about it," Jimmy said.

Todd picked up the case of beer and handed it to Volpe. "I still want those pills," he said.

Volpe smirked the smirk that made people want to punch him. "No deal on the pills," he said, "until we cut a deal on the money." He took his beer and walked over to his car, a red El Camino he kept shiny because he figured women liked guys with shiny cars. "I brought you guys the spot. That's got to be worth something."

"I said we'd think about it," said Jimmy.

After Volpe pulled away Todd said, "Three hundred bucks and change apiece? Why didn't you say yes?"

Jimmy walked over to their jump car, Duane. The push-buttons were the key to the whole thing. Todd might be crazy enough to jump a car into a lake, but he wasn't looking to die doing it. They'd poured three hundred pounds of cement into the footwells behind the front seat to balance out the weight of the engine so Duane would fly level until he hit the water. The greater the mass, Todd liked to say, the bigger the splash. They'd cut the roof off the car with a welding torch, removed the windows and the windshield, covered the back seat area with a piece of one inch plywood mounted to the body, and screwed an aluminum lawn chair to the plywood deck. All that so Todd wouldn't get his body tangled up with the steering wheel when he hit the water. They'd rigged up a throttle cable and hooked two steel cables to the steering wheel. All Todd had to do was put the car in drive with a broomstick on the push-button, gun the throttle, and keep equal tension on the cables like a water skier behind a boat. The car would go balls out and straight ahead until it was airborne, and after that, Todd could sit back and enjoy the ride.

"He's a weasel," Jimmy said. "You can't trust him."

LARRABEE'S PERSONAL IDJIT METER had gone from twitchy all the way to flippy-floppy by the time the dog days of August rolled around. He knew something was up from the way idjits stared right through him with no more regard than they would give a cardboard cut-out. That they were working too hard on keeping their cool showed in the careful construction of their supreme nonchalance. A man with nothing to hide had eyes that saw a man with a badge and moved on to the next thing, but an idjit with a secret can't deprive himself of the pleasure of making a big show of his own fabricated innocence.

But Larrabee could take no action on the basis of how his idjit meter was acting up. He needed facts, the who-what-where-and-when of the criminal act, and facts were exactly what he did not have. This was the normal condition of the rural law enforcement officer, who sprang to action, in the vast majority of cases, pretty much after the fact. Most of what Larrabee did in the way of investigative law enforcement consisted of waiting for some idjit to fall into his lap, so he sat in his cruiser in the various patches of shade that were his roadside lairs, and he sipped his coffee, and he waited.

So it was that Larrabee happened to be under the shade of a three-hundred-year-old white oak when Mike Volpe came tearing down Gossard Road in his red El Camino. The Gossards had complained to him for weeks about Volpe doing this very thing, driving sixty miles an hour on a gravel road where children played and dogs sunned themselves, raising a rooster tail of dust that hung in the still August air like a murderer's whispered confession. He'd come over the rise so fast that he was just hitting his brakes when he passed the cruiser, dumb enough to have gotten caught but smart enough to pull right over the very second that Larrabee hit the siren. There would be no high-speed chase today, and there was a note of disappointment in the way the over-amped purr of the siren trailed away to nothing.

Larrabee pulled up behind Volpe's El Camino and got out, and he saw how Volpe was watching him in his side view mirror, so he made sure that Volpe saw him unsnap the safety strap on his holster. Eleven years as a deputy and he'd never fired his weapon in the line of duty, but he found it useful to bring to an idjit's early attention that he could fire it if he chose to do so.

"Afternoon, Deputy," Volpe said. He smiled up at Larrabee the insufferable smile of someone who relies on his father being the richest merchant in town and a known contributor to the political campaigns of Larrabee's boss, Sheriff Winnemore, in order to get himself out of a scrape.

"Afternoon, Volpe. Could I have your license and registration please?"

"Yes sir, Deputy Larrabee."

Larrabee gave him a look that said "Don't get smart with me boy," but Volpe wasn't buying it. Not yet anyway. His license and registration were current. Larrabee had him for the speeding, sixty in a twenty-five, and on a gravel road, no less, which was enough to write him up for reckless driving. A one-eighty fine and a mandatory trip to driving school—probably good enough to get this particular idjit to slow down for a while. But Larrabee's idjit meter right then was twittering between flippy and floppy, so on the strength of that, he decided to roust Volpe to see if anything interesting would shake out.

"I suppose you think I was going a little fast," Volpe said. His voice was crafty and composed, and wasn't he cute, the way he said "little" with a long "e" and held his thumb and finger close together to show how "leetle" a little fast was.

"Just a scoshe," Larrabee said. "Would you mind stepping out of the car, please?"

Volpe got out and leaned his back against the car, his hands jammed into the pockets of his jeans. He had a logger's broad suspenders on over a plaid flannel shirt with the sleeves cut off above his elbows. The crews hit the woods before dawn in the summer and worked until the forestry regs said the day was too hot to risk a spark coming off one of their saws, which was a damn shame, in Larrabee's considered opinion, because it gave them that many more hours in which to drink.

"Stand up straight, please."

Volpe stood up. There was beer on his breath, but Larrabee didn't see any empties, at least not in plain view.

"Cross your feet. Now bend over and touch your toes."

Volpe complied with an indolence that was meant to infuriate, but when he bent over, four red and white capsules fell out of his shirt pocket and onto the ground in front of his feet.

The toe of Larrabee's shoe covered them just ahead of Volpe's reaching fingers. Volpe looked up at Larrabee, and Larrabee let him see that he was resting his hand on the butt of his pistol.

"Volpe," Larrabee said, "Mike, old buddy. Be a good fellow and step down to the front of the car, and lean yourself over the hood with your arms spread wide."

He had the idjit right where he wanted him now, and Volpe knew it, he could tell by the way the smirk fell right off his face. It was laying there in the gravel, underneath the toe of Larrabee's shoe. When Volpe was leaned over the hood of his car Larrabee bent down and picked up the pills.

"Vitamins?" Larrabee said. "Antihistamines?" He held one of the capsules up between his thumb and finger. "I know they ain't Tylenol because Tylenol says Tylenol right on the pill." Volpe had his cheek pressed tight to the hood of his car, but his eyes were on that pill in Larrabee's hand like it was the key to his entire future.

"Nothing to say for yourself, Mikey? Well, no matter, the crime lab will tell us what kind of illicit possession to charge you with."

He walked around behind Volpe and got his handcuffs off his belt. "Put your hands behind your back." He cuffed him, tight enough to feel them, tight enough that they would leave a welt if Volpe struggled against them the least little bit. He grabbed him by the shoulders and pulled him off the hood of the car. He said, "Stand up and face me."

The capsules were in the palm of his hand where Volpe could see them. "Here's the deal, Mikey. I can haul you in on suspicion and hold you until we find out what's in those pills, or you can tell me what the ding-dong is going on here. You and your skookum buddies are up to something, and I want to know what it is."

Volpe's eyes went from the pills to Larrabee's face and back again. He could detect no sign of a bluff in the sheriff's face. His old man was going to roll over him like a steamroller squashing a bug if he got hit with a drug charge. Those assholes, Jimmy and Todd, this was their fault. If they'd had the brains to accept his little proposition he wouldn't have had those pills in his pocket just now. He was screwed, and there wasn't but one way out of this mess.

And that was how Larrabee got the who, and the what, and the where, and the when.

THE SPOT WAS A deep alpine lake on the edge of a clear cut well up one of the lesser tributaries to the Kalish. The lake was tucked into a cove between two ridges, and there was a basalt cliff maybe forty feet high at one end. Below the lake was a war zone of slash piles and stumps, the ground scarified down to bare dirt. The loggers had bulldozed a dirt road from their clearcut on up to the basalt. It was nothing but an ungraveled bare dirt track, but the last six hundred feet of it ran straight for the edge of the cliff.

Larrabee could see all of this through his binoculars. He'd driven twenty miles on gravel roads to get to the spot from the back side of the ridge above, so they wouldn't see him coming. He parked his car alongside the road and hiked up to the top of the ridge. A bunch of men were milling around below, some of them with beers in their hands. A few women too, girlfriends most likely. He picked out Todd Ahlquist, who was leaning against the side of their tricked up car next to Stubby Toobin. "Duane" was spray painted on the lid to the trunk in big black drippy letters.

Jimmy Ahlquist was working his way through the crowd with a clipboard, and people were handing him money. There was probably a law against that. There were laws against damn near everything these days, but actual criminals were rare in Renata, and dangerous sociopaths were even rarer. What you had a lot of was some very independent minded people who were used to doing pretty much what they damn well pleased. It was his job to decide who to let off with a warning and who to lock up. Some days he felt like Solomon himself, and other days he was just some dickhead of a deputy sheriff, making it up as he went along.

He had this jump business sized up as a public safety issue. If there was a crime here, it was a crime without a victim. Nobody had put a gun to Todd Ahlquist's head and told him he had to jump a car into a lake. No doubt the boy had caught the fever when he ran that John Deere tractor into the river the year before. He was probably still on probation for that damn fool stunt, so there was probably a violation in that too, but it wasn't the kind of violation that got Larrabee's hackles up. The truth was, the night he'd chased Todd Ahlquist through town had been as much fun as anything he'd done as a deputy sheriff.

No two ways about it, a balls-to-the-wall, flat-out high speed chase was the best part of the job. Larrabee's patrol car was a Ford Fairlane, a police cruiser with a 429 V-8 under the hood and a beefed-up suspension, she would do one-forty on a straightaway, and who the goddamn hell did those idjits think they were, trying to outrun him on a tractor? He'd caught sight of the John Deere just as it crossed the highway, rear tires as tall as the roof of his cruiser. The cruiser gulped the distance between them like a greedy dog, but before he caught all the way up, the tractor jumped the curb and ran full tilt boogie between two Doug firs on the bluff above the river. Larrabee skidded to a stop. He threw his door open and jumped out in time to see the top of what must have been one helluva splash, the frothy white flash of water flying straight up until gravity pulled it straight back down. By the time he got to the edge of the bluff, the tractor had sunk, but in the moonlight he could see the roiled water around a large glassy oval, and Todd swimming hard for the other side.

Damn what a ride. A fellow would have to be crazy to

think you could make a tractor fly, but it was the kind of crazy Larrabee admired for the sheer balls of it, to live your life like you were a lit stick of dynamite tossed high into the air, and never mind what comes when the fuse burns all the way down.

The only question now was, was Todd in danger of doing himself any harm? Larrabee was going to look like a real idjit if something bad happened to the boy, so why he was contemplating risking his career to see the boy make the jump into the lake he was only just now ready to admit to himself.

There was a little bit of idjit in everybody. Even him.

He watched Todd climb up into the seat they'd rigged up for jumping the car. So be it. There was no way he could get down there fast enough to stop him now. Everybody moved over to the edge of the cliff, lining up on both sides of where the car would leap off. Everybody except Jimmy, who hopped on a little dirt bike and raced on down to the lake. He had a big coil of rope draped over his shoulder. He must be the safety crew, ready to help out if Todd needed it after he hit the water.

The jump car started moving. It picked up speed fast. It looked like Todd was steering it with magic, his two hands out in front of him but several feet from the steering wheel. The car bounced along on the rough road, Todd leaned back like a bull rider, and now Larrabee caught the sun flashing off the cables that connected his hands to the steering wheel. Three hundred feet to go, and the car was doing maybe thirty. Then forty, with a hundred feet to go, and maybe forty-five as the tires left the cliff behind. A collective shout came from the crowd, which had been silent until then. The car sailed out over the lake, flying level and true with Todd yelling a rebel's yell into the alpine air. The car fell through the air for as long as it takes to fall into grace, and Larrabee, not ordinarily a religious man, offered up "The Lord is my shepherd, I shall not want," as much as he could remember of the Twenty-Third Psalm, and he held his breath and watched it fall. The car pancaked, sending a great sheet of water blasting straight up that hid Todd as if behind a curtain. Cheers from the crowd on the cliff. The curtain of water fell back to the surface of the lake, and there was Todd, flat on his butt with the lawn chair collapsed beneath him. The car sank fast, there being so little air trapped in it to keep it afloat. Todd stayed still until the water reached his chest, and then he slapped the lake with his arms and started swimming.

Jimmy threw the rope out to him, but Todd was making for the shore already. The cheering went on and on, and Larrabee was laughing and clapping his hands together. He didn't give a rip what the law said about what had just happened here. If a man couldn't raise his middle finger and shake it in the face of gravity every once in a while then there wasn't much point to being alive.

Down below the clearcut, he saw dust rising behind a red car, coming fast up the road to the cliff. A red El Camino, and why in the hell was that idjit Volpe showing up here now? Larrabee hurried down the back side of the ridge to where his car was parked. The last thing he wanted was for a fight to break out.

Todd came out of the water so chilled he should have been shaking like a wet dog, but he was so high on adrenalin he didn't feel the cold any more than he felt the ache he would feel later where his butt hit the plywood when the lawn chair collapsed. Jimmy was waiting for him with his arms open and the beatific smile of someone whose every intuition about the laws of Newtonian physics has just been confirmed in the risky crucible of crapshooting experience.

"We did it bro'," Jimmy yelled, and he wrapped his arms around Todd and lifted him clean off the ground, swinging him in a high arc before he set him back down again. They stood shoulder to shoulder and faced the people cheering at them from on top of the cliff, and they each of them raised a triumphant arm, which drew even more cheers. They were crackerjack wild men now, they were certified, the newest members of a club you could only join by doing something skillful and reckless and potentially fatal, like Stubby Toobin had done.

"Free pitchers at The Ripsaw," Todd said. "I won't have to pay for a beer for months."

They looked at each other then, sobered by the mention of time. Todd had gotten his draft notice the week before, and he didn't have months. In less than thirty days, he had to report for his physical. Jimmy leaned his forehead against Todd's forehead. He wasn't old enough to even set foot inside The Ripsaw, let alone have somebody buy him a beer there. Todd would likely be in Vietnam when he turned twenty-one, when they should be here, celebrating together, like they were now.

"When you get back," Jimmy said, "the pitchers are on me."

Todd had no room inside himself for this. "Shut up," he said, "don't even talk like that." He wanted to get high, he wanted to wipe out any trace of the future bearing down on him, he wanted his whole life to be exactly like it was right now.

"This is the best goddamn day of my life," Todd said. "Let's go get drunk."

There was some kind of commotion up on the cliff, the crowd splitting open, and a county sheriff's car arriving in the gap. The door opened, and they both saw who it was.

"Christ," Todd said, "What the hell is he doing here?"

"Larrabee," Jimmy said. "Let's go see what he wants."

Volpe got out of his car with a fat book in his hands, the kind of book that government regulators kept their regulations in. He was damn sure going to see to it that those Ahlquist boys were not the beneficiaries of the kind of deal Larrabee had cut with him. They were trash, those boys, they were the runts of the litter, and they didn't deserve any leniency because they would never amount to anything. He marched right up to Larrabee and said, "Where are they? I want those sons of bitches arrested." He flopped the book open on the hood of Larrabee's patrol car. "Look here," he said, and he jabbed his finger at some persnickety paragraph that said it was a class C misdemeanor to abandon a vehicle in the national forest.

Larrabee was willing to bet there was a phone call from Volpe's father to the head ranger behind that book being in his hands. "That's a funny position for you to take," he said, "given your own selective idea of which laws you would like to obey in your own personal life."

Jimmy and Todd rode up on the dirt bike from the lake. Everyone was crowded around the sheriff and Volpe, but they parted to let the Ahlquist boys through. Todd was dripping wet and grinning, and Jimmy had the look of someone who has just found a way to cheat St. Peter at cards and get away with it.

"Them," Volpe said. "I want you to arrest them."

Todd and Jimmy went wide-eyed and shrug-shouldered, the very picture of "Who us? We ain't done nothin' wrong." Volpe's fists were balled up, and he took a step toward them, but the whole crowd took a step forward, ready to stop him. He worked as hard as any man in the woods, and for that he was due some respect, but the bottom line was, his daddy was the richest merchant in town, and Volpe logging was Volpe slumming, and that book full of Forest Service regs was all the proof they needed that Volpe was never really one of them.

Larrabee held up his hands. The crowd fell silent.

"I can't arrest them," Larrabee said, "unless you sign a complaint."

"No problem," Volpe said. "Show me where to sign."

Jimmy Ahlquist said, "What the hell do you mean, sign a complaint?" He looked around at the men in the crowd, men who made their living dropping trees the way they knew how, men who hated regulation of any kind. "The national forest belongs to everybody," Jimmy said, "am I right?"

"Damn straight," Todd said. "We got as much right to drive a car off a cliff as anybody."

Volpe's weasel of a face put on a scowlish threat, but

there were nods of agreement from all around, except from Larrabee, who looked over at the book of regulations on the hood of his car and cussed the paperwork this was going to force him to do. The thing of it was, if he couldn't talk Volpe out of signing a complaint, he would have to act, or face a suspension if he didn't.

Stubby Toobin stepped through from the back of the crowd. He got right up in Volpe's face, and he looked up at Volpe, more than a foot taller than he was, and he winked at him. Then he punched him hard in the gut, doubling him up and bringing his face down within easy reach. Stubby looked over at Larrabee, who simply looked back at him. He didn't say yes, and he didn't say no, and that was all the permission Stubby needed. One more punch to Volpe's jaw dropped him clean. Volpe was face down, one hand underneath him and one hand palm down on the dirt. His right hand, most likely the hand he wrote with. Stubby stomped down on it with the heel of his boot, and everybody heard the bones crack.

Larrabee leaned over and felt for a pulse on Volpe's neck. Still a beating heart. The way he figured it, the absence of any fatal injuries made today a pretty successful day.

"Well," said Stubby, "I guess he's changed his mind about signing a complaint."

"Nope," Larrabee said, "nobody's got any complaints here, near as I can tell. I didn't see nothing, and nobody else saw nothing, and that's all she wrote. Everybody got that?"

Nods all around. It was as fine a summer's day as anyone could hope for. Below them the lake sparkled, the mountain air was soft and clean with the scent of the firs, and the sun shone bright on the roof of Larrabee's patrol car. They all four of them stared at the car, Larrabee, Stubby, Jimmy and Todd, and they all four of them, if they only knew it, were thinking the same thing.

Just how far would that car jump?

The Painted Man

GOD ONLY KNOWS HOW many times I've sat like this, elbow to knee and chin to fist, pondering the mystery of my father. Whenever he came upon me in this pose, he would mutter "Mama's little thinker" as he walked by, and sometimes drag his hand through my hair from front to back, likely as not catching a strand or two in his ring and pulling on it, hoping, I suppose, to startle me out of my reveries. Me the thinker, and Michael Jr. the doer, and both of us the fruit of his same loins, both of us beloved of our mother but only Michael the object of our father's affections. For Mumsy and me, he had only scorn and the fierce critique of his cattle breeder's gaze, those hard, staring, china-blue eyes that were constantly fixing upon us, measuring and calculating and finding fault. He was possessed of the idea that all the things that mattered about a cow, a wife, a son, or a melon were determined by breeding. Hard work was necessary to bring out the qualities that good breeding implied, but once the genetic throw of the dice has been made, no amount of hard work will cause a cow or a melon to raise above itself any farther than the limits set by one's hereditary destiny.

He was a logger, a farmer, a trader, a schemer, and a loud-mouthed, cocksure, bourbon-swilling barnyard bully of a man used to getting his own way. He could out-work, out-think, and out-fight damn near anybody he ever ran up against. He scared the bejesus out of me, and so far as I can tell, the only thing I ever did to provoke his constant ire was to be born different from him, different from Michael Jr., different from the foreordained predisposition of his genetic imprint.

We put him in the ground this morning. I don't know whether to bring flowers or wear dancing shoes when I visit his grave, for neither fits the state of mind his death leaves me in. You cannot grieve for a puzzle, nor celebrate the death of a cipher. You have to make some sense out of the man first.

The last time I saw him was the night of Michael Jr.'s welcome home dinner, a night that was already heavily freighted even without my father's subsequent demise. Two tours in Iraq, and my brother comes back from the second one a captain, and this was the first time the four of us would be at table together in some years. The dinner was a full-on catered showpiece, with prime rib and a decent claret to go with it, and waitrons in white shirts and black pants and vests, pouring champagne into tall flutes my father must have rented for the occasion. There were engraved invitations sent out and engraved place cards telling us all where to sit. I have some modest experience in the catering business, and the whole grand production had to've set my father back several thousand of his precious ducats.

It was not at all your typical potluck with the neighbors, and more than a little strange because Mumsy left him some three years before, and now he'd gone out and added on a master suite in the back and remodeled the kitchen, at some quite considerable expense, even though he was living out there all alone. It's not like he needed more space, or that he was the kind of cook who needed a professional grade six-burner range top with a stainless steel hood. No, this was my father pulling out all the stops to show everybody how he was the biggest, swingingest dick in the county and still a man to be reckoned with, never mind that his wife ran off with another man.

I could've sworn dinner was at five, but I've never been good at keeping track of time. One of my many flaws, as far as my father is concerned, and the sole reason I ended up at my father's house an hour and a half before the party started. He had, God save us, a golf tournament on the TV in his living room, a TV the size of a Mini Cooper, and we stood there watching it with bottles of beer in our hands and the sound off, which was a mistake because it meant we had to talk to each other.

"You working?" he said. This is what he always asked me, and what he meant by it was have I gone out and found myself a real job.

"I'm in a production of *The Outsiders* at the Children's Theater. I play Dally."

"Kids' show, huh?" All of my brother's sports trophies are lined up on the mantle, shiny statuettes in gleaming and inauthentic gold of boys swinging bats and throwing footballs. Somehow sports were never kids' games in my father's eyes, and theater is never a man's work. I could pick up one of those trophies and oh, sweet drama, bash my brains out, putting an end to this conversation right now.

"More like young adult," I said, with as much sangfroid as I could muster, but my father is possessed of a considerable talent for ignoring such nuances. A clatter of plates came from the kitchen. I could go in there and beg the caterers for a job. I could start right now.

"They made a film of it in the eighties," I said. "Tom Cruise was in it."

"Did he play Dally?"

"No. Matt Dillon played Dally in the movie."

"Oh. Him."

Someone missed a six-foot putt on the TV. My father took a

sip of his beer and stared out the window. The rain had stopped. His cattle were slogging their way across the pasture to the barn, hungry for their evening ration of hay. My father would provide. There was water standing in the pasture in great puddles. His new pond was off in the distance, a magnet for the local mallards.

"What's new with you, Mike?" A twitch runs through my father's jaw whenever I call him Mike. That little jolt gives me such pleasure. I started doing it when I dropped out of college after my junior year, and when I saw how much it tweaked him, I couldn't bring myself to stop.

"You see my new pickup?"

Trucks, tractors, TVs. Mike was all about his stuff. Which exact model with which exact features which would allow you to do exactly what with all your most excellent stuff. He was the kind of guy who rented a bulldozer for a week and built himself a new pond and called that fun. There wasn't an ounce of fantasy in him. He didn't go in much for art, didn't like me being in the school plays with all those people he called fruitcakes, and he just about disowned me when I majored in theater. Thank God the cattle started bellowing loud enough to drag him out to the barn before he could show me his new truck.

And then Michael Jr. showed up, and I went out to the driveway to meet the warrior returned. What Michael Jr. and I have in common—a childhood together spent roaming the woods around this house, our genes, thousands of hours throwing a football back and forth and shooting baskets in the driveway—is barely enough to counterbalance how different we truly are. Michael Jr. is a golden boy, a quarterback, an Eagle Scout, a Marine. He believes in God and country and red meat, a man so much like Mike in all ways, save arrogance, as to make my own provenance a little suspect. I am a performance artist, a burrito slinger, an actor, a barista, an atheist. I marched against this God-awful war. I've never asked myself why do they hate us so much, because I know why. We are a nation of arrogant assholes like my father, of men who think they have it all figured out so there's no need to even wonder why anybody else might think differently, or God forbid, be different.

There is no sign of the war in Michael's face. His face is lean and tanned—he has clearly been spending a lot of time in the sun—but he is as steady of gaze and as sure of grip as ever.

"I'm glad you're safe."

"It's good to be home. Where's Dad?"

"The barn, feeding his new herd."

He has his uniform, his dress blues, in a dry cleaner's bag slung over his shoulder. Of course, Mike would want him to be decked out in his full regalia. Of course, those shiny new captain's bars would be on full display, proof of the superior breeding that produced Captain Michael T. Volpe Jr., sired by Mike T. Volpe of Renata, Oregon, through his dam, his breeding partner, the lovely Mary Sauerberg Volpe, also of Renata.

"You want to toss the old football around?"

And so we fell back on our childhood. As soon as Michael comes back out of the house, as soon as he tosses me the football that he still keeps in the closet of his old room, as soon as I bend over that football ready to hike it into the open clamshell of Michael's hands, spread as they are in that intimate space between my splayed apart legs, as soon as Michael says, "Hup one, hup two," we are boys again, and there is no war between us. There is only me running down the length of the driveway, dodging mud puddles like they are defensive lineman, there is only Michael throwing me a perfect spiral pass, the ball slicing through the air like a rifled bullet, and the leathery sting in my hands as I make the catch.

And then it is my turn to throw, and Michael's to receive. I am nothing if I am not a chameleon, and because I am the family clown, the funny man, the goofball, I make my voice sound like a cheap radio, and I drop into the hyperbolic schtick of a sports announcer. Anything to give the troops a laugh. "Third and eighteen, the clock's running down, and the Melonheads are down by five. They need a touchdown to pull out what could be the greatest upset in the history of men playing with their balls."

A chuckle from Michael, and he hikes me the ball and takes off. "Volpe takes the snap, he steps back into the pocket. The Neanderthals are blitzing, but Volpe has Knothead and Cajones blocking for him, he's got plenty of time to find his receiver." Michael is a joy to watch, the way he leaps clear over the biggest mud puddle, the stutter of his steps when he fakes left, then right, then runs left down the county road, his knees high and his legs pounding.

"There's Volpe in the end zone but he's covered, he's got Steroids and Testosteroni all over him, the two toughest defensive backs in the league. Here's the throw, a perfect spiral, going long for the win, and this is it folks, the game is on the line. Steroids and Testosteroni are on him like stink on a jockstrap, and Volpe leaps up between the two defensive backs, and oh my God, how did he do it, he makes the catch for the touchdown. And that's the game folks, the Melonheads win it on the amazing forty-yard pass from Volpe to Volpe."

Michael throws me the ball and hustles back for the next play, a big grin on his face. We're fine as long as I keep up with the patter, the ball sailing through the air between us, connecting us in the only way we know how to connect. I won't ask him how it feels to lose two of his men to a roadside bomb, and he won't ask me what in God's name makes a performance a piece of art.

Just then a shiny silver car pulled into the driveway and parked right next to my father's brand new pickup truck. Out stepped a woman in a clingy red dress, a dress that stopped halfway down her thighs while her legs kept on going and going, the kind of legs a dress like that was made to show off.

Oh, the sweet drama of flesh brazenly bared, but all I can think when I see her is that she must be lost, for she was miles out in the country and looked nothing like the people my parents know. She was made up as theatrically as a New York runway model, and such a downtown sort of girl, with those candy apple red high heels—spikes of course—and silver hoop earrings the size of a dessert plate.

Michael, always Mr. Hustle, got to her first. "Can I help you, Miss?"

She put her hand out to him and said, "You must be the guest of honor. I'm Danielle, I'm a friend of your father's."

"Yes ma'am," Michael said, everybody was ma'am and sir after he went into the Marines, and by this time I was near enough to her to take in her long fingernails, done up to match her dress and her shiny little clutch purse. And gentlemen, we are talking serious cleavage here. The dress was long sleeved, with one of those cut-out fronts where there's a collar around the neck and then a big circle of white skin that's all about the tops of her breasts.

I put my hand out to her. "I'm Ray," I said, "and this is Michael." Her touch was brief but firm, very professional. She had too much nose and not enough cheekbone to be a cover girl, but she was good with makeup. She'd made her lips look bigger without going overboard, and her eye makeup was in shades of brown that brought out the color in her eyes. Fierce eyebrows, and dyed black hair cut to frame her face like a centurion's helmet. She was maybe half my father's age.

"Ray," she said, and oh my God her tongue is pierced, "yes, I've heard about you," she said. "You're The Painted Man." And right there she let her eyes soften, not a lot, but there was something there, an opening maybe, or some kind of recognition. She had seen me perform. Perhaps she had even dropped a ducat into my open cigar box.

"Is your father inside?" she said.

And the two of us, Michael the Marine captain who's stared down the barrels of guns in Iraq, and me the actor who's stared into the black hole of dozens of live audiences, we're both so dumbfounded by this particular woman showing up for this particular dinner party that all we can do is point at the barn. Danielle let us know how much she enjoyed the effect she had on us with a post-modern version of the Mona Lisa smile, one corner of her mouth turned up an extra twitch for ironic distance, and just the slightest raise of an eyebrow.

"He's in the barn?" she said, and the both of us nodded, dumb as puppies.

She said, "But the party's in the house, yes?"

"Right," I said, "he's feeding his cows. He'll be right in."

"I have a piece of luggage," she said. "Maybe one of you could help me?"

"Yes ma'am," Michael said. She opened the door of her car and Michael pulled out the overnight bag that was hanging on a hook in the back seat. Her heels clicked down the walkway to the front door, and Michael, her obedient servant, followed her.

I sat down, elbow to knee and chin to fist, on the front steps to ponder. So this was Mike's date. Mumsy and I didn't even know that he was seeing someone, not that Mike was one to keep us informed of who was on his dance card. There was still a trace of her perfume in the air. I couldn't name the scent, but I could tell it cost more than I made in a week working the burrito cart downtown.

It was the pierced tongue that really had me flummoxed. Mike had quite a wonderful little meltdown the time he saw me with my lip ring, and even though I've long since let the hole close up for reasons of my own, I know how much it tweaked him.

What a puzzle he was. And Danielle. She belonged with Mike the way cats belong on jet skis.

THE DRIVEWAY FILLED UP with pickup trucks, and Mike's guests gathered inside. Before we sat down to eat there was a cocktail moment, so very civilized, a time to stand around and chit-chat and sip champagne. Waitrons circulated with trays of hors d'oeuvres, salmon mousse topped with caviar, tea-smoked hard boiled eggs sliced thin and topped with a bourbon remoulade, and petite smoked oysters sitting on a horseradish florette. All of it beautiful, and all of it selected from the I've-got-it-so-let's-flaunt-it list.

Mike, ever the politician of his own life, steered Danielle around while he worked the room, showing off his trophy girlfriend and reminding everyone why they needed to pay attention to him. They put on quite a show, a pair of well turned out bees buzzing every flower in the flower patch, and you could tell from the way she looked at him with those big brown eyes of hers that they were going to make honey when the evening was over. Michael took up a position in the dining room and held it with the perfection of his posture and the blue precision of his dress uniform. His shoes were shiny and black, and the bubbles in his champagne glass seemed, when I walked up to him, to be rising in formation, obedient to the captain's wishes.

"What do you think of Mike's date?" I said.

Michael rubbed his temple with the tips of his fingers, a gesture he makes when he's trying to wrap his mind around a new idea, like the idea that there's actually something called performance art that allows me to make money by painting myself silver from head to toe and then holding a pose for an hour at a time on a downtown street corner.

"I didn't know Dad was seeing anybody," he said. "She seems nice enough."

"She'd be my date," I said, "if Mike hadn't seen her first."

Michael gave me his you're-such-a-melonhead eye roll. "She's way out of your league, Ray."

"What makes you think you know the first thing about my

league and who's in it? I suppose you think she'd go out with a Marine captain?"

"Stay away from her, Ray." There it was, that my-turn-to-take-names-and-kick-ass Marine captain's smile of his. We were at war again, and for all the wrong reasons, and now I had to sue for peace or face the consequences.

"I was kidding, Michael. I have no intention of asking her out."

What is most unbearable about Michael Jr. at a time like this is the way he nods his head, as if he knew all along that I would back down.

"Did you see the pierced tongue?" I said. "What on God's green earth is he doing? Next thing you know he'll be buying a Corvette and taking up snowboarding."

"Why do you hate him so much?" His gaze was as steady as ever, but he wasn't trying to back me down. He really wanted to know. If there was no sign of the war in his face, this was the moment when he was different from the brother I knew, and absolutely direct with me. A moment, sadly, for which I was unprepared. A moment I let slip by because I thought he wouldn't need to even ask that question if he'd been paying attention when we were growing up, and I would be damned before I would help him answer it now.

"Mumsy's going to die when she sees her," I said. "This is cruel. This dinner should've been family only."

Michael shook his head. "Dad's happier than I've seen him in years. It's his house, he can invite anybody he wants. And Mom," he said, and there it was again, that tight-lipped, hard-ass Marine smile of his, "she shouldn't have left Dad the way she did. You want cruel? That's what was cruel."

MUMSY CAME WITH HER best friend Viv, and they were the last to arrive, my darling mother coming back to the home she left because marriage to my father was a burden she could bear no longer. She came for Michael, whom she adores, which is one of the enduring mysteries of my life, how she could love both me and Michael, different as we are. How can one heart love both the raw and the cooked? The bent and the straight? The wayward and the driven? What does love mean if it is so promiscuous?

I went to her as soon as she came in and helped her off with her coat, the shoulders wet because the rain had started up again. She had on a pin-striped business suit, a little severe for a dinner party, but she'd softened it with a blouse that was all feminine frills down the center. She had her hair done up in one those carefully casual buns with a couple of artfully loosened strands, and there were droplets of rain caught in her hair that reflected the light from the room. Such a beauty she is, and ever will she be. I took Viv's coat too, both their coats laid over my arm, their faithful courtier, and I stood guard between my mother and the rest of the room.

"You up for this?" I said. "Any time you want to leave, you just say the word, and I'll fake a seizure so you can take me to the hospital."

Viv laughed and said, "I'll have the seizure, Ray, you're much too young and handsome."

"Mumsy," I said, "don't turn your head, but there's a woman in a red dress in the dining room, near the head of the table, you see her?"

My mother's eyes left mine and then came back. "Yes, did she come with you?" She had that are-you-finally-getting-serious-about-someone smile on her face.

"I'm not that desperate. She's Dad's date."

Viv turned her head and looked straight at Danielle then. My mother's smile tightened a twitch, from in-on-something-delicious to I've-just-had-something-sharp-and-pointy-shoved-up -my-ass.

"What is that on the front of her dress?" Viv said. "A boob target?"

"I just wanted you to be prepared," I said. "You know Dad. He's going to find a way to flaunt it."

Mumsy said, "He already has."

SIXTEEN OF US AT the table, with my father at the head and Michael in his dress blues seated at his right hand. Danielle was on his left. He'd invited the mayor of Renata and a county commissioner and their wives. I was banished to the foot of the table, flanked by Mumsy and Viv. Between my father and me, on either side of the table, lined as it was with the gleam of rented china and the shine of rented silver, sat the local Christmas tree mafia with their dumpy little wives. These are the farmers who raise the trees that Americans put in their living rooms every year with an angel on top and cheap tinsel hanging off the boughs. I grew up surrounded by their plantations, Christmas trees in silent rows as far as the eye can see, watching how the Mexicans shear them every year with their machetes to make them into these perfect little gumdrops that bear the same resemblance to a real tree as a Hostess Twinkie does to an actual cake.

Before we ate, Mike stood up at the head of the table and waited for everyone to quiet down. "I'd like to propose a toast," he said, and he starts in about Michael, using words like honor and duty and sacrifice, talking about freedom and tyrants and spreading democracy, and generally making it clear what a hero his first-born son really is. He'd changed into a preternaturally white oxford shirt when he came in from the barn, and there he was, with Michael in his dress blues on one side and Danielle in her bright red dress on the other, like they were the goddamned American flag waving proudly for all of us to salute.

"In the Marines," my father said, "the tradition at a time like this is to say hoo-haw," and the way he said hoo-haw was like a whole platoon stomping their combat boots boom-boom, "so I'd like for all of us to hoo-haw my son. You ready?"

Strange to hear all of this from my father, who never served in the military because, as I understand it, his lottery number never came up in the draft, but who spoke now as if he had been a Marine himself, and stranger still for me, because all this fuss over Michael was made all the brighter by my own invisibility, parked as I was at the far end of the table, the son over whom my father has never made any fuss whatsoever. So all of us enlisted as we were in my father's congratulatory platoon, hoo-hawed Michael, the warrior returned from battle, and we raised our glasses and clinked them with our table mates, and said not a word about the self-deluding foolishness, the dangerous naiveté, nor the horror of the enterprise in which he was engaged.

Mike maybe got a little teary after he sat down, and then the waitrons brought out the prime rib, the blanched and baked asparagus, and the wild mushroom risotto. Everybody fell to, and for a couple of minutes it was nothing but the sounds of serving and eating and people saying how good everything tastes. But this is a table full of farmers, and we have had rain for thirty-one straight days, and it doesn't take these farmers too long before they start in about the weather. Weather is their lives, and they're going on about how high the river is, and how wet the soil is, and whether or not things are going to get as bad as the flood of '96.

Jimmy Ahlquist, whose farm is at the other end of Gossard Road from my father's, was sitting midway up the table from us. He had, as always, that sweet smoky smell clinging to his clothes and his long gray ponytail, and when I was a teenager I figured out that the way he puts up with Mike is he gets stoned before he has to talk to him. "Mike," he said, "How's that new pond of yours holding up?"

"Six foot of water at the deep end," my father said. "It's right up to the top of the dike."

"You've been out again to check it then?" Jimmy said. "Your dike is holding?"

"I'm keeping an eye on it," my father said.

"What about that crack on the back side you showed me?" Jimmy said.

"Crack?" Joe Scheele said. "What crack? How big a crack?" Joe was sitting across from Jimmy, and he's one of those guys who talks way too loud and sprays spit when he does it. His farm is the next farm down the creek from Mike's, and the pond sat right on the edge of his property.

Mike took the time to fork a piece of prime rib into his mouth and chew it up before he answered. Danielle watched him, her dress full of the cleavage of a femme fatale and her face full of the innocence of an ingenue, waiting for him to speak as if every word that fell from his lips were purest poesy.

"It isn't any worse than it was the day you saw it."

"How big is that crack?" Joe said. My father doesn't like him much, but they have to work together because when it comes time to harvest the Christmas trees, all these guys share the work crews and the trucks and the balers.

"Don't worry about it," my father said. "I might lose a little slice off the back of the dike, but I got it under control."

"Sixteen inches in thirty-one days, got to be some kind of record." This from Kirk Kurmaskie, a man whose nose and ears grow larger with each passing year, lending his face a certain elephantine quality.

It is at this point that my patience with this banal talk of the weather is utterly depleted. "Don't you think," I say, "that global warming is the cause?"

Everyone save Mumsy and Viv turns to stare at me, as if my bowels had just uttered an enormous fart, or some steaming pile of filth had just spewed forth from my mouth. "The increase in Category 5 hurricanes," I say, "and the melting of the ice caps, don't you all think global warming has something to do with it all?" Jimmy Ahlquist and his wife Michelle are nodding their heads, yes they think global warming has something to do with this, and the mayor too, but I am at war with everyone else down that long table, and my father has fixed his china blue eyes on me as if I have just announced that meat is murder.

Mayor Weston says, "Most of the world's scientists would say you're right," but Dickie Stubbs runs right over him. "Those scientists," Dickie Stubbs says, "they just make stuff up to keep their research money coming. Bunch of parasites if you ask me." You'd expect more from a county commissioner, except that if you knew Dickie Stubbs you'd know he's an anti-reproductive choice, immigrant-hating, evolution-denying son-of-a-bitch from the flat-earth wing of the Grand Old Party.

"There's no such thing as global warming," my father says. "This is just a wet year. Hell, they had nineteen inches of rain in a thirty-day period here back in 1916."

I can always trust Mike to put me in my place. Or try to.

"What I don't understand," Kurmaskie says, "is if there's global warming, how come we've got more snow in the mountains than we've had in a decade?"

"So how big is that crack?" Joe Scheele says.

My father says, "Can you pass the asparagus down? Has everybody had enough of that prime rib?" He holds his wine glass up and one of the waitrons hustles over and fills it for him. "I'm on it, Joe," my father says. "I'm checking it twice a day."

"You should've waited till the spring to build that dike," Joe says. "You built that thing so late in the fall it's still all bare dirt."

"Joe," my father says, "you're just mad because my water rights are older than yours. That dike isn't going anywhere."

The waitrons bring out little dishes of sorbet then. "The palate cleanser," my father announces, as if he is some great gourmand. At least it puts an end to his bickering with Joe Scheele.

Viv leans in, her voice pitched for Mumsy and me, and she says, "Arnie thinks that pond is a big mistake. They built it right on the edge of the gully back there, right where the waterfall used to be. Remember how pretty that was?"

"Where is Arnie?" Mumsy says.

"Oh, you know," Viv says. She tilts her head toward Mike's end of the table. "They're not speaking again."

Arnie and Viv lived across the road from us all the years I was growing up. I used to play with their kids. Arnie's still there, it's Viv who moved out, and Arnie and my father have been pissing each other off and then making up again since before I was born. They only got along as well as they did when we were growing up because their wives made them.

After dinner there was coffee, which my father sweetened for those who wanted it with Kentucky bourbon, and a strawberry-rhubarb pie. The farmers and their wives got their coats and started saying their goodbyes. I found myself standing in a loose gaggle of people, next to Danielle, who had Kirk Kurmaskie all to herself while his wife glared at him from next to the front door. We were all a little tipsy, and Kurmaskie was still holding Danielle's hand, even though they'd stopped shaking hands a full minute before. Kurmaskie was telling her how his barn was built over a hundred years ago from trees they logged right on his farm, and how the big brass bell in the cupola had come around the Horn on a sailing ship with his great-grandfather.

Danielle kept smiling and nodding at him, and when he stopped for air, she said, "That is so fascinating, all that family history, but I think your wife is waiting for you." She pulled her hand away from his and pointed at Joyce Kurmaskie. Kurmaskie had to turn all the way around to see his wife, who jerked her head toward the front door so hard that he almost tripped trying to get to her.

Danielle turned to me and deployed the world's most ironic smile. "Your father has some interesting friends," she said. I couldn't tell if she included herself in that irony.

"So what," I asked her, "do you do?"

"This and that. I'm going to art school," she said. "I do some modeling on the side. Life modeling, like for the life drawing classes. A little foot modeling for local catalogs. I'm up for a Mountain Dew commercial right now. If I got that, I'd have national exposure."

Actress, model, whatever, she was a girl on the make. Why else would she waste her time with a farmer old enough to be her father? She did have nice ankles sticking out above the straps on her stilettos, but I couldn't imagine her face being the one they'd want next to a bottle of Mountain Dew.

"How'd you meet Mike?"

"Mutual friends," she said. "I know someone who grew up out here."

Mutual friends, but not friends she was going to name. "You know," I said, "I couldn't help but notice your pierced tongue. I had the distinct impression that Mike doesn't like piercings."

"Well," Danielle said, and she stepped in close enough to speak softly into my ear, "I haven't heard any complaints. I think he likes mine."

Her hand was on my shoulder, and I swear she raised her finger up and scraped her fingernail ever so lightly down my jawbone before she walked away. Such a tease, and I couldn't help thinking that she might liven things up if Mike managed to keep her. She went to my father, who was talking to Mumsy by the front door. Mumsy had her coat, and Viv was there with her. Danielle walked up to my father and slipped her arm through his, casually proprietary. She said how much she'd enjoyed meeting everyone here, and what a lovely dinner this was.

"It's so quiet in the country," she said. "I just love waking up out here." She offered Mumsy her doe-y brown eyes and the smile she was no doubt hoping would land her that Mountain Dew commercial. Mumsy, trouper that she is, took it without flinching.

"Nice to've met you too," she said, and they actually shook

hands, as if they were at a business meeting. As if Danielle were not going to be the last woman to leave.

Michael changed out of his uniform, and he and I helped the caterers cart all their stuff out to their van. We said goodbye to Mike and Danielle on the front porch. My father had a cigar going, something else that was new for him, and Danielle took it from him and wrapped her lips around the end and puffed on it. She tilted her head back and blew a smoke ring, and she handed the cigar back to my father. It was pouring down rain, and close enough to midnight that it was clear we were going to have rain for the thirty-second straight day.

We got in our cars and drove away, Michael back to the condo he was staying in with a Marine buddy, and me to my dinky studio apartment on the edge of The Pearl.

THE CALL FROM MUMSY came the next afternoon, after a night when I slept poorly. Several times as I lay on the cusp of sleep, on the very tipping point between wakefulness and sweet oblivion, I was visited by dark bovine creatures. On two legs and then sometimes on four they ambled through a pasture on the dark side of twilight, walking away from me and then sometimes walking directly toward me, and always when I saw them I was filled with trepidation, and startled out of sleep.

Mumsy told me to sit down. Her voice had a squashed sound to it, the sound of holding in tears.

"There's been an accident," she said. "It's your father." She took a deep breath and let it out slowly. She said, "He's dead."

I hadn't bothered to sit down, but now I did. It was a Sunday afternoon, and I was still in my bathrobe, the Sunday *New York Times* spread out on the kitchen table, open to an article about the death of the American musical that left me wondering if I'd been born twenty years too late.

"What happened?"

"Arnie found him. He must've gone out to check the pond.

The dike gave way." She was breathing hard into the phone now, a whole string of hard breaths like she was trying to empty her lungs and couldn't. The words "he's dead" were a big brass bell ringing over and over inside my head, a loud sound that made no sense.

"He was buried," she said, her voice swamped but not yet drowned, "alive," she said. She let a sound out then, not a word, but a sound pitched high and edged sharp, like a bird coming home to a nest full of broken shells, her eggs robbed. Then she was quiet, even her breathing quiet, and I sat there waiting to feel something—grief, elation, overwhelming sobs, anything—but nothing came.

"When?" I said.

"Probably this morning," Mumsy said. "Arnie went over there because the cattle were making a lot of noise, like they hadn't been fed. Your father's truck was in the driveway, and Arnie thought that was strange, your father home and the cattle hungry."

He had his cigar in his mouth and his arm around Danielle's waist when he waved goodbye. Last night, he was alive last night. "Mom," I said, "this is awful."

She was crying now, but I was too numb to force even a stage tear. There was something lumpy turning over underneath my sternum, something small and inchoate, something too easy to push away. It wasn't how I wanted to feel. An absurd thought, given that it is the nature of emotions that they come upon us without consultation as to which of them we might choose. I was tossed aside, unable to find my bearings, a lumbering beast trying to find my way home.

"Mom?" I asked. "Are you still in love with him?"

She made a sound then, part hiccup and part sob, the inarticulate speech of her heart. I was envious. The instrument of her body was fully engaged, her emotions sharp and reactive, while mine were muffled and lethargic.

"Stop it," she said. She was crying hard, her voice choked

off and twisted around itself. "How can you ask me that now?" she said. "You can't ask me that now," she said, and then her voice turned raspy and mean, a voice I had never heard from her before. "We have a funeral to plan, damn it, and I need you to help me. Pull yourself together."

"I'm sorry," I said. But I was not sorry. Sorry would have been something, and I was a big empty vacuum, a void where my heart should have been, and there was nothing whatsoever inside me that needed pulling together. She knew this, Mumsy always knew, I could never fool her. "Pull yourself together" was merely a figure of speech, and what she meant by it was that I should fall apart, which was utterly beyond me.

"Does Michael know?"

"No."

"Do you want me to call him?"

"No. I'll call him."

"What do you want me to do?"

She blew her nose, long and hard, away from the phone.

"Come over here," she said. "He'd want a big fuss made over this. I owe him that much."

She was right, of course. We had obligations that could not be ignored. My father, dead, was not yet done telling us what to do.

THE NEXT DAY, WHILE Michael and Mumsy dealt with the funeral arrangements, I was at the house with a list of things to get. His blue suit. A white shirt and a tie. His address book. His wallet. I was to check in with Arnie Gossard about feeding the cattle, and about how much feed was left in the barn. Michael thought we should secure the house, maybe change the locks, look for valuables to remove. He told me to pick up Dad's mail so we could keep up with the bills.

I opened the drawer in his night stand, thinking I might find his wallet or his address book there. There was a copy of *The*

Pulse inside. That was odd. *The Pulse* was a weekly alternative newspaper aimed at twenty-somethings who couldn't be bothered to read the daily paper. They covered the local news, sort of, but everything was an enormous joke to them, except for which new band was the most cutting edge.

I set the paper aside. There were condoms in the drawer, and a bottle of lube. Not that this was news, given what we'd all seen of Danielle at the dinner party, but I gathered them up and took them to the kitchen. There was still garbage from the other night in there, and it was starting to stink. I pulled the wastebasket out from under the sink, and dropped the condoms and the lube in there. Even dead, my father was flaunting things. We all had to know what a stud he was.

I took the garbage out to the can on the back porch and headed back to the bedroom. Maybe his wallet was in his pants pocket. It was strange standing in that room that was not a part of the house I grew up in. It made the old part of the house into a dowdy little stepsister. The carpet was plush, the walls were a stylish dove gray, he had a plasma screen mounted on the wall so he could watch it from the bed or while he rode his stationary bike.

I went over to the nightstand. There was *The Pulse*. I'd already read this one, it was a month old, but I thumbed through it anyway, trying to find whatever it was that had made my father pick it up. The cover story was about some cop who had an affair on company time, and wrote all these X-rated emails to the woman he was bonking, also on company time, all of it reported with *The Pulse's* typical relish in all things salacious. No big whoop, and not at all the kind of thing my father would go in for. There was no way on God's green earth he was into any of the music, or the bar scene for twenty-somethings. Unless maybe Danielle was the one who brought *The Pulse* into his life. And then I thought of the personals, and I flipped to the back, to "Women Seeking Men."

A regular private eye I was, putting the pieces together. I

was sure I'd find an ad circled, maybe several, and that one of those ads would lead back to Danielle. Mystery solved. Mutual friends my ass.

But there was nothing circled in the personals. I flipped over the next page, more classifieds, mostly musicians trying to hook up with other musicians, *Garage/punk band seeks drummer for summer tour. Van=you get the gig* and the next page, which was all big ads for chat lines on one side and ads for escorts on the other.

And there she was. "Danielle," in a thin italic script, and then "Sexy, Discreet, Gentlemen Preferred" in regular typeface. Her hair was different in the picture, longer and looser and hiding half her face, the very picture of a coyly sexual come on.

The last person to see my father alive was a hooker. I felt, for a moment, as if I were inside a kaleidoscope, and all the complicated bits of my life, of Mike's life, were shifting, aligning themselves in a new pattern. But I was lost in the prismed mirrors amongst all the other bits of colored glass. I couldn't see what that pattern was, and my puzzlement took on a new shape.

Arnie Gossard showed up about the time I finished folding Mike's laundry. He knocked, but he was already in the house before I could make it to the front door, wearing a cap that said Titebond on the front. The shoulders of his jacket were wet with rain.

"I saw your car," he said. "Thought I'd see if you needed anything."

We sat in the kitchen, in the newly built-in breakfast nook, part of Mike's hundred thousand dollar remodel. The new cabinets and the nook and all the trim in the kitchen were done in a light-toned wood streaked with darker gray, very dramatic. "Hickory," Arnie told me when I asked, "it's what them that has to have the latest fashion gets." The nook had a view of the pasture, where the cattle were munching away on the grass even though there was a light rain falling.

"Jimmy and me spent all day yesterday fixing the fence," Arnie said. "It ain't pretty, but it'll keep them steers from wandering off. There's a couple that got away from us. They wandered on down into Scheele's place."

"Do we need to go get them?" I said.

Arnie was running his fingers along the edge of the molding at the end of the bench, stroking it as if it were a Stradivarius. "Not today," he said. "They'll be all right. Joe said he'd coax them into his corral if he got the chance."

Arnie's always been kind of a lump, a man with a body shaped like a fire hydrant and a face like a mole's, dark eyes set close together and big front teeth crowded into a narrow mouth. Mumsy likes him, but then Mumsy likes everybody. He got up and pulled open a drawer, and he bent himself over it and studied the way the front corner was put together.

"I could've built these for half what your dad paid," he said. He laced his fingers together in front of himself, and he cracked his knuckles.

"Why didn't you?"

"I wasn't asked," he said. Not a hint of how he felt about Mike snubbing him that way passed across his face. But the way he'd cracked his knuckles, that was Arnie trying to distract himself from the hurt he felt. He opened a cupboard and took his glasses off, studying the hinge with those myopic little eyes of his. "Your dad had to have that fancypants outfit in the city do the work. They do nice work, I'm not saying they don't, but they're spendy as all get-out."

One of Mike's steers stared at me from out in the pasture, chewing his cud, impervious to the rain. Where the pond had been was nothing but a stretch of mud. The creek took a turn it had never taken before when it got to the far corner of the pasture. There was a gap in the dike as wide as the county road, and the creek went right through it.

"It must've been hard," I said, "finding Mike out there."

Arnie closed the cupboard and put his glasses back on his face. "How you holding up, Ray?"

"So far so good," I said.

Upstream from the gap in the dike the creek ran through a culvert under the county road. A big piece of my childhood flowed through that culvert, the Gossard boys racing sticks down the creek with Michael and me, or making boats out of zucchinis from the garden when they got too big to eat. I always made up a story about what we were doing, the Spanish Armada, Lewis and Clark, German U-boats and American destroyers.

"Tell me what it was like," I said. "Finding him, I mean."

Arnie opened up another cupboard, and then another, and another. "Goddammit," he said, "I used to know where everything was in this kitchen." He worked his way around until he got to a cupboard next to where the fridge was built in. "Bingo," he said. "I knew this'd be here someplace." He had a bottle of bourbon in his hand. He got a couple of glasses out. "You want ice?"

"Sure."

The fridge was the kind where ice rattled right out of a dispenser built into the door. Arnie brought the glasses and the bourbon over to the nook and sat down. "Woodford's Reserve," he said. "This is top shelf stuff." He poured the glasses full, the ice crackling and settling into the bourbon. We raised our glasses and clinked them together.

"To your old man," Arnie said. The bourbon was smooth going down. "He may've been a son of a bitch," Arnie said, "but he always bought the best."

"You didn't like him much, did you," I said.

Arnie lifted up his cap and scratched the top of his head. His hair was so thin I could've counted each one. He looked at me over the tops of his glasses, trying to figure out if I was accusing him of something.

"It's okay," I said. "I didn't like him much, either." Arnie put his cap back on and grunted. He took a big sip from his drink and gave a little shiver that made him smile.

"It was raining hard yesterday morning," he said. "I was in my shop, and the rain on the roof was pretty loud, but I could still hear all those steers making a ruckus like they hadn't been fed yet. I hadn't spoken a word to your dad in the last six months so I let it go on for quite a while. Wasn't none of my business if your dad didn't get his chores done."

The second sip of bourbon went down even easier than the first. I don't usually drink in the afternoon, and I don't usually drink bourbon, but there were a lot of things I was doing that day that I don't usually do.

"When I come out of my shop," Arnie said, "I looked over to your dad's place to see if his truck was there, which it was. The cattle were all bunched up by the barn, mooing their fool heads off. Then I saw that the dike had collapsed, and I knew right then what the trouble was. So I hustled on over. Cut straight through the pasture calling out your dad's name the whole way. I figured I'd see him stuck in mud up to his ass."

Arnie drained half his glass in one long swallow, and then he set it down on the table and started turning it from the top like it was the dial on a washing machine.

"When I got to the dike," he said, "all I could see was mud. Looked like the water in the pond had worked its way underneath the dike, and with all this rain, the whole thing was just saturated top to bottom. You been over there to look?"

"No," I said. "I don't know if I'm ready for that."

"The mud carried him down the hill head first," Arnie said. "He was about two-thirds of the way from the top. On his back. Buried in a couple feet of mud, but all I could see was the tip of one boot sticking out. I figure he was on Scheele's side of the fence when it happened. The whole thing must've give way at once. The paramedics said he'd hit his head and probably knocked himself out."

You are supposed to feel something at a moment like that. Horror. Grief. A big sad lump in your throat. If you love your father, your body is supposed to be overcome, and if you hate him, shouldn't you feel some relief when he dies? Some respite? Instead, water kept flowing down the creek through the pasture. The cattle kept on grazing. Arnie poured himself another drink, a short one this time. He tipped the bottle my way, but I shook my head no.

"At least if he was unconscious," I said, "he wouldn't have suffered much."

Arnie took out a pocket knife and used it to scrape underneath his fingernails. "Look at that," he said. He held the knife out to me, showing me the tiny bit of dirt on the tip of the blade. "I've still got it under my fingernails," he said. He wiped the blade clean on his pants, and folded it back up. "Hell of a thing finding him that way," he said. "His mouth was full of mud."

Something stirred underneath my sternum then, an inkling of the price I would pay for losing my father this way. Not the price I was supposed to pay, not the tears of the bereaved nor the grief of a son who survives. No, this was something oily, something fetid and slick I would slip around in until I was covered in it like a second skin.

Arnie tossed down the rest of the bourbon in his glass, and he got up to leave. "Tell your mom to call me if she needs help with anything," he said. "I'll feed the cows until you figure out what to do with them. If you're going to sell the herd, you might give Kurmaskie a call."

"Is there enough feed in the barn?"

"You're good for maybe another month."

On his way out, Arnie stopped in the living room and looked at that enormous TV. His face was flushed, and he was swaying a little bit, and I had the feeling that the bourbon I drank with him wasn't his first that day. He pointed at the TV with his thumb. "You folks decide to sell that," he said, "you let me know."

"All right."

It struck me then, seeing Arnie in the doorway, his Titebond cap shoved back on his head, and the pouches of flesh under his eyes wrinkled and puffy, how old he was getting, and that he was getting old not slowly and evenly, but all at once, as if finding my father dead, with his mouth full of mud, had aged him far more than the mere minutes of actual time involved. We have spurts of growth when we're children, after all, so why not a spurt of aging on the other end of our lives?

Arnie's lips were pushed together under those tired eyes, such a rueful face, and he shook his head back and forth in a gesture of surrender.

"I'm going to miss the old son of a bitch," he said. "I truly am."

PICTURE ME PAINTED BLACK from head to toe, in a three piece suit with a Borsalino fedora planted on my shaved head. Neither dancing shoes on my feet nor flowers in my hands. I'm sitting on a box next to Mike's grave, elbow to knee and chin to fist, and I've held this pose for nearly an hour, a performance for an audience of none. Only this morning we all stood here and watched his casket being lowered into the ground. The mound of freshly turned earth is still covered with a strip of green outdoor carpet.

The Pioneer Cemetery in Logan's Prairie is a quiet place. It sits on a knoll with a grove of white oaks at one end, a nice place for a picnic if you're comfortable with all the headstones. Mike's headstone would come later, and it would say his name, Michael Truman Volpe Sr., and his dates, and beneath that, at Michael Jr.'s insistence, the words "Beloved Father," because I found it untenable to stand up and say I was in favor of something more accurate, like "Selfish Bastard."

All the old humiliations run through me, every slight, every small betrayal, all of the useless baggage I carry around with no place to set it down, and I move not a twitch while I replay every battle in that long war. Mike is so very quiet now, and the silence of sitting here is so instructive. While clouds move across the sky, their shadows sometimes passing over me, darkening the lawn and the headstones, and rendering deeper the black of my skin and my clothes, I have time to consider.

Consider this, for example. Mike wanted Mumsy to feel humiliated, and he wanted Michael to show everyone what a great sire he was, but from me, he could not be bothered to desire a thing. If I could have made myself into something that my father wanted to buy, then I could have been a part of his most excellent stuff, the way Danielle was. The way Michael Jr. was with his captain's bars and his dress blues.

It isn't from Mumsy that I get my flare for drama. My father spent the last evening of his life putting on an elaborate dog and pony show for his friends and associates, for his ex-wife and his two sons. He even hired an actress of sorts to play the role of his girlfriend. If he'd lived, I could have given myself the pleasure of exposing him for the fraud he was.

Only I know how truly desperate a man he was his final evening on God's green earth. Only I know the lengths to which he had gone to fool us into believing he had his life completely put back together. And knowing this is the only thing of his I have that belongs only to me.

AFTER I FINISHED COLLECTING Mike's things, I screwed up my courage and walked out to the pond. The gap in the dike was scary up close, as big as two or three dump truck loads of dirt, and the mud flow below it spread out like an apron down into Joe Scheele's place.

I worked my way down the mud flow to where Arnie found him. The mud was sticky and clung to my boots, making them clumsy and heavy. The creek poured down the slope, already cutting a new channel for itself. There were footprints everywhere, chopping the surface of the mud flow up and making shoe-shaped puddles. The mud was brown with a hint of orange. Even though they cleaned him up for the funeral, I'd rather think of him this way. For once in his life he was like me, his clothes, his hands, his face, every bit of him covered in a single color.

Sink Like a Steamroller, Fly Like a Brick

OF THE TWO AHLQUIST brothers, Todd and Jimmy, it was Todd who took illegal fireworks apart to make bigger bombs, Todd who got them involved in that business with the stolen tractor, Todd who went AWOL from the Army. Jimmy was the Boy Scout, the kid who charmed his teachers with homely little poems he wrote about them, the man who married a local girl and settled down on the family farm. But Jimmy was no straight arrow. It was Jimmy who saved up his lawn-mowing money to buy those illegal fireworks, and it wasn't like Todd had to ask him twice to climb out his bedroom window.

True, Todd stole the tractor, but Jimmy stood lookout, the both of them high on a pint of vodka and a Toronto Turn-Around they'd split. It was Jimmy riding on the fender as they raced through Renata at 2 a.m. just as all the bars were closing down, and it was Jimmy who told Todd to drive by The Ripsaw where they hooted and hollered and waved their arms around at the half-dozen loggers standing on the sidewalk having a last smoke before they went home to sleep it off. Todd cut a huge green John Deere donut at the intersection of First and Broadway, shot up First half a block and turned into the parking lot next to Fing Rivelli's insurance agency. They could hear the siren then, the county sheriff coming for them, and Todd tore through the alley, took a right into the parking lot for Cody's Motel, smashed through a stack of Ed McKinley's bird feeders and chainsaw-carved cedar lawn ornaments, drove through the parking lot of the hardware store. They caught the glowing red and blue pulse of the sheriff's lightbar bouncing off the buildings on Broadway like radar. The vodka mixed with the speed was hot ice in their veins, the moon was full, and they fully believed in miracles. They were flying, the night air cool on their faces, and nothing could stop them, not bullets, not barricades, and no shit-heel of a sheriff. Not even if God Himself appeared as a burning bush and blocked their path with a wheelbarrow full of King James Bibles. They would drive that tractor straight up the side of a cliff if that's what it took. Todd grabbed a crazy left on Fourth and drove across three or four lawns, leaving deep, wide tractor tire ruts behind them—they'd stolen the biggest, heaviest John Deere in the lot at Volpe's Machinery & Farm Supply—and he slowed down as they came under the hundred-year-old big leaf maple in Harold Johnson's front yard.

"Grab that branch, Jimmy," he yelled, "I'm going to try and lose the sheriff down by the river."

Jimmy didn't even stop to think how cartoonish and crazy this sounded, he just reached up and grabbed the branch and hauled himself up, and Todd raced away, mud flying from his tires, the sheriff rounding the corner from Fourth and falling in behind him a block and a half back. Todd took a hard right behind the Napa Auto Parts store, with the sheriff behind him and gaining, the sheriff's tires spitting gravel and his rear end fishtailing. It was a helluva splash, Todd told him later, Jimmy you should've seen it, he said, how he went cannonballing off the river bank twenty feet above the water, laughing his fool head off, and the flat surface of the river shot up around him, and that two-ton tractor sank like a steamroller while Todd set out swimming for the far side.

While everybody ran down to the river to gape at what had happened, Jimmy dropped out of Harold Johnson's big leaf maple and slunk away home. He climbed back in through his bedroom window, and he was in bed feigning sleep when the sheriff knocked on the front door. The loggers who saw them drive by The Ripsaw couldn't agree on how many people they saw windmilling their arms around and hollering to wake the dead. Some said one, some said two, and Mike Volpe, whose father owned Volpe's Machinery and Farm Supply, swore there were at least three, maybe four, because they had so many arms to wave. The sheriff knew Jimmy was on that tractor, but Todd kept his mouth shut, and the county DA couldn't prove a thing about Jimmy. The judge gave Todd a choice: two years in the state pen for grand theft auto, or make immediate restitution and do six months probation for reckless endangerment. Todd took the probation, and their father wrote out a check for five thousand dollars to Old Man Volpe.

Renata settled back down to its normal routine, nothing more exciting than the occasional brawls the loggers fought on Saturday nights. Old Man Volpe hired a scuba diver to hook a cable to the John Deere so he could winch it out of the river, sold the tractor to a John Deere dealer in Moses Lake, Washington, and ended up turning a nice profit on the whole deal. Todd got drafted the next year, and just before he was supposed to ship out for Vietnam, he went AWOL. Jimmy finished up his last year of high school, got a job at the mill, and moved in with Michelle Clemens. It was Jimmy who paid back their father.

TWO YEARS AFTER TODD went AWOL he showed up on Jimmy and Michelle's doorstep at 5 a.m. on a Sunday morning. He had a slack look on his face and a jar of bootleg quaaludes in his backpack. His hair was long and his clothes were filthy and he was full of wild tales about riding the rails from the Twin Cities down to Miami, running from yard bulls in Omaha and Kansas City, flying on LSD while he rode a hotshot over The Rockies.

Todd had a knack for finding the best drugs, and he was fearless when it came to mixing them. The best high, Todd liked to say, has the broadest base. Back when they were in high school, Jimmy tried everything with Todd. Mushrooms, acid, black beauties, PCP, some dirty white powder that Mike Volpe said was bona fide top quality mescaline—worth every bit of ten dollars a hit, Mike Volpe said with that how-can-you-doubt-me blue-eyed stare of his—but that dirty white powder tasted more like something to clear drain clogs, and it let all the smarts in Todd's head drain right out the bottom.

They let him stay in their basement for a month until Michelle got tired of coming home to find him 'luded up and ghost-faced, his mouth hanging open, shuffling into walls because he was so fried he missed doorways by a body width. She was four months pregnant and setting up the spare bedroom as a nursery, and she told Todd he had to find someplace else to crash.

Somewhere along the way to middle age Jimmy quit caring about the best high. He settled for a six-pack of beer and a baggie of Mexican pot after a day's work on the farm. There were too many chores to do, too many soccer games and band concerts and school plays to go to. The kids were gone now, but the story Jimmy told himself when he first pulled away from Todd, that he would raise his kids and then go back to chasing the perfect high, that story wasn't his any more. The past was over. They didn't hear from Todd for years.

JIMMY WAS DRIVING ALONG Burnt Springs Road after he checked on the shearing crew working the field he leased from Hildebrandt. His truck was running a little hot and he was thinking he should put some fresh coolant in the radiator. His mother, Richene, was in a hospital bed in his living room, recovering from a hip replacement surgery.

He was almost to the turn onto Gossard Road when he decided to stop in at The Viewpoint for a cup of coffee. There was better coffee at home, but he wasn't ready to face his mother just yet. He had to take her to a doctor's appointment later that morning, a post-op check-up for her hip surgery. He loved his mother, and she wasn't such a bad houseguest, but if he went home, he would have to sit with her while they drank coffee and listen to her chatter on and on about the day's news. She read the newspaper front to back every morning, taking it apart and folding each sheet into quarter-page squares and then stacking them in a shopping bag for recycling so that Jimmy had to buy a second paper for himself if he wanted to read it like a normal person.

Every day a new batch of bad things in the world, and every day Richene passed on all those bad things to Jimmy. There was a rapist loose in the woods east of Renata, armed and dangerous, and he looked like a bad man in the photograph, and he was a bad man, he did things too terrible to name to an eight-year-old girl. The police said not to approach him if sighted. A pair of suicide bombers had killed dozens at a mosque in Karachi, and what was the matter with those people? A piece of Antarctica the size of Connecticut had broken off and was drifting north, and still that fool in the White House didn't believe in global warming. Her neck was so stiff that morning that she could only look straight ahead, and Jimmy should be glad he didn't have arthritis yet, it would make him old before his time, only God knew how many good years he had left.

He was cold from the inside out, as if the morning's dew had settled on his bones. Maybe a Scotch whisky instead of coffee would brighten up his morning. Seven was way early for him to be drinking, and he didn't usually drink Scotch, but the way he'd been taking care of his mother the last couple of weeks, he figured he'd earned himself an exception.

The bar was empty. The barmaid was a woman with a permanently dissatisfied curve to her mouth and a frazzle of curly hair held back from her face with a hair band. She poured his shot and went back to the other end of the bar where she was studying a cash register tape. Jimmy put the shot glass to his lips, resting the smooth hard surface there a moment. This was so much more civilized than drinking it straight out of the bottle like he did back in the day with Todd. He tipped his glass back and drained his shot. The whisky burned all the way down but it left a sweet and sour smell in his nose that Jimmy liked.

The click of his mother's crutches on the hardwood floor had gotten him out of bed before dawn, an hour and a half since the last time he heard her get up. He'd slept hot, sandwiched between his wife and their two cats, and Michelle moaned when he left the bed and she pulled the bed covers in tighter to close off the rush of cool air into the warm spot he left behind. Jimmy pulled his sweat pants on. One of the cats hopped off the bed and followed him to the top of the stairs.

His mother's scalp was a shrill pink showing through her gray hair, thin and scattered with sleep. She had bad rheumatoid arthritis and her neck was bent forward with the weight of her head. Twenty years of Prednisone had eaten away her bone mass, turning her bones into white-edged silhouettes in her X-rays. She breathed loud enough for him to hear from the top of the stairs with each slow step. The belt of her robe dragged on the floor beside her.

"Ma?" Jimmy said. There was a pause in the slowly clicking progress she was making to the bathroom, but she didn't turn her head to look up the stairs at him.

"I'm all right," she said. "Go on back to bed."

Her voice was scratchy and thin, like the sound of a butter knife scraping the black off of burnt toast.

"You don't sound all right," he said. "When's the last time you took a pain pill?"

"I don't know," she said. She groaned when she brought her left leg forward, the leg she'd had the surgery on.

Jimmy started down the stairs. "Let me get you a pill," he said.

Richene grunted at him and kept moving. He stopped at the bottom of the stairs and watched her pivot on her right foot, making the turn into the bathroom. She got the door closed, and Jimmy went to the living room, where there were two dozen pill bottles on a table next to her hospital bed. She took four different drugs for her arthritis, two pills twice a day for her heart, a pill to help her hold her water at night, a decongestant for the phlegm that settled in her chest while she slept, more than thirty pills a day. She had a morphine patch she wore on her chest, all the Vicodin she wanted, and a hundred morphine tablets the surgeon prescribed for her post-op recovery. Jimmy opened up the Vicodin and shook out a pill. She didn't like the morphine, said it made her feel stupid. She'd told Michelle she didn't want to end up like Todd. All those drugs, the broadest base for the best high, and Jimmy had shuddered to think that once upon a time he would've been pilfering those pills for himself.

Jimmy eyed his empty shot glass. He was warmer now, and he should go home and put that coolant into his radiator. No end to the work he had to do to keep his farm going. Not that he was complaining, he made a good living off his Christmas tree operation, more money than he ever thought he'd have when he was starting out way back in the day. A second Scotch was not such a good idea.

But what the hell, he was an adult and he could do whatever he wanted. On second thought another Scotch was a very good idea. A great idea. Scotch whisky would sharpen his eyesight and improve his sense of balance. Richene would be impressed by the smell of Scotch whisky on his breath first thing in the morning. That nurse with those sly, Slavic eyes and those long slinky fingers would take him by the hand and lead him to an unused exam room where she would lock the door and push him up against the wall and kiss him hard on the mouth while she fondled him. He raised his shot glass at the barmaid.

"Another Scotch?" the barmaid said.

"With a coffee back," Jimmy said.

Might as well split the difference. Stimulants and depressants, the broadest base for the best high, he would drink that second whisky for Todd, wherever the hell he might be. Jimmy stared into the clear amber liquid in his glass and then drained his shot. He poured cream into the black coffee and watched it swirl around until his coffee was the color of mud.

THE NURSE WITH THE Slavic eyes wasn't there this time, and anyway, between the early morning whisky and Richene's constant chatter on the drive in, something vicious uncoiled at the base of Jimmy's skull.

The doctor was pleased with how well his mother was moving already. Her incision was healing just fine. More mobility would come, but not until he operated on her knee. Jimmy asked if they could have a wheelchair to get her back out to the car, and the doctor raised the steel wool strips that were his eyebrows and said, yes, surely, but the more she walked the faster she'd heal.

"I don't need a wheelchair," Richene said. "I can do this."

So they walked slow careful steps from the exam room to the waiting room, a hundred feet in five minutes, Jimmy at her elbow, nurses hustling by in the hall, Richene leaning heavily on her crutches. Jimmy's headache redlined to his forehead in ragged curves from the bony hinge where his head sat on top of his spine. Richene sat in a chair to rest while he went to bring the car around, her crutches leaned up against the arm of the chair.

When he came back, her eyes were scared white mice in the

corner of their cage trying to see out without being seen. She had a wrinkled tissue wrapped around her thumb and pulled taut. Bits of tissue were on her legs and on the floor in front of her chair. Her crutches had fallen on the floor.

"Is that Todd?" she said. She kept her voice down but there was pressure behind it, a sob swelling up like a blister about to burst. "Over there, by that door?" she said. She raised both her hands, her knuckles swollen and red, and several of her fingers bent at odd angles, as if they'd been broken and never set back straight. Her thumb poked up out of the tissue, and she pointed down the waiting room with it, her hands clasped and moving together. She turned her head to look but groaned, and turned it back so she was looking straight ahead again. "Oh God, I can't move like that," she said. "My neck."

"Todd your son?" Jimmy said. "My brother Todd?" Todd the missing, Todd who no longer showed up at family events, or called on Christmas, Todd whose front teeth fell out?

"Who else would I be talking about," Richene said. "Of course Todd my son." She pulled on the tissue wrapped around her thumb until it tore.

"He walked right by me," she said, "that's him, I know it's him."

The waiting room was crowded with old people, not a soul under sixty, except for Jimmy. The last time he saw Todd was six or seven years ago, and he'd looked all used up, deep creases in rows across his forehead and a lot of loose skin around his eyes. When Jimmy asked him where he was living Todd just shrugged and said, "Maybe I could come stay with you?" He was missing a bunch of his front teeth, his falsies had gotten broken or lost or stolen and he didn't have the money for a new set. Jimmy asked him who the hell would steal someone's false teeth, and Todd looked around to make sure no one was listening, and then he said, in a low conspiratorial voice, "I have enemies."

"He's with some woman," Richene said. She tore at the tissue in her hand and let the pieces fall to the floor. "Not that woman he married," she said, "some other woman. He's the red-haired one, the one with the stringy hair."

A man with reddish stringy hair stood in front of the receptionist's counter, a man the right height to be Todd, a man with a manila folder in his hand. A woman with tired eyes slouched behind him, nobody Jimmy had ever seen before. The man smiled at the receptionist. He had a full set of teeth in his mouth.

"I don't know," Jimmy said. Richene's eyes weren't that good—her cataract was growing back in the one—and Jimmy wasn't sure. He said, "Todd has curly hair." He felt for the lump in his pocket where he kept his headache pills. Over the counter stuff, but it usually worked. He'd get Richene settled in the car and then he could take his pills. He said, "Let's get you up."

"That woman," Richene said. "She called him Claude."

"Well then," Jimmy said, "it wasn't Todd."

Richene's eyes were fierce little prosecutors with a job to do now, pointing straight at Jimmy.

"He's a scoundrel," Richene said. "He's using your grandfather's good name for an alias."

Jimmy pulled her up out of the chair by her arms and got her set up on her crutches. She started toward the door with small gingerly steps, leaving the little bits of torn-up tissue behind, an archipelago of her anxiety on the carpeted floor. The glass doors slid back automatic and sure, something that worked the way it was supposed to. The car was right outside.

"He had some papers in his hand," Richene said, "and he covered his face so I wouldn't hear what he said about me."

Her voice was too loud now, and a woman who was just arriving at the clinic stared at her as she walked through the sliding glass doors.

"How do you know he was talking about you?" Jimmy said. The doors slid shut and they were outside with the white noise of the freeway a few blocks away. Someone in the parking lot laid on his horn and Jimmy winced at the spike of pain in his head.

"Why else would he cover his face?" Richene said. "I know it's him. Go talk to him."

"Let's get you in the car first." All Jimmy wanted was to take his pills and go home and lie down in a dark room. He was never going to drink Scotch in the morning again. He opened the car door. He wanted to pick up his mother's frail little body and set her in the car like a child who's fallen asleep but he didn't dare to with her hip surgery so fresh. It took her most of a minute to slowly sit down into the car seat and turn and lift her legs in, one at a time. When Jimmy turned around and looked back into the waiting room, the man with the stringy red hair was gone.

IT TOOK RICHENE HALF the ride home to calm down. She wanted to stop at Henry Thiele's for lunch, but Jimmy reminded her that Henry Thiele's was torn down fifteen years ago.

"I could use a good stiff drink," she said.

Jimmy did not rise to that bait. He let her talk herself out, going over and over the story, fixing each detail in her memory.

"He needs a good whack up the side of his head," Richene said, "walking right by me like that, looking right at me without saying a thing."

A year earlier Jimmy called up a lawyer friend of his and had her check the state prisons to see if Todd was there. Richene hadn't heard so much as a phone call from him in over two years then. He wasn't in any of the state prisons, wasn't on parole, wasn't in the federal system, and they decided not to check the other forty-nine states. Maybe Todd was dead, one of those bodies that gets found with no ID under a freeway overpass. Motor Vehicles had no record for him. If he was alive, he was off the grid.

Todd's last-known address, an address nearly ten years stale, was in one of those industrial parks, in a space with a big roll-up garage door and a little office in the front corner. There was a loft over the office where Todd slept on an old army cot. Behind the big roll-up door the space was piled high with pinball machines, police scanners, stacks of eight-track players pulled from junked cars, a sixteen-track mixing board, an old drill press, computers from the PC stone age, a rusty lathe, a golf cart that looked like it had been rolled. Everything stacked eight feet high with ragged aisles running between ragged rows, and all of it broken, all of it stuff Todd said he could fix and then sell. He showed Jimmy his prized possession, an AK47. He wanted four thousand dollars for it.

Jimmy held the gun and sighted down the barrel. The gun was a dark oily black, lighter than he expected, and the only thing in Todd's warehouse that actually worked.

"I'd trade it for a good truck," Todd said. He had a crooked grin, and with his curly red hair and his two front teeth missing, there was still something boyish about him, even with the skin sagging off his face. His eyes were wild with an exuberance not entirely his own and his gums were brown. He had a Casio keyboard in a thousand pieces on a cluttered workbench. He waved his arms around when he talked, and a couple of times Jimmy had to duck out of the way. "Three-quarter ton, four-wheel drive, decent tires," Todd said. He picked up a circuit board with a pair of needle nose pliers and held it up in the light. "There's silver on these boards you can recover," he said. "When silver hits eight dollars an ounce you can make big bucks," he said. He dropped the circuit board on the workbench and tossed the pliers at a tool box at the other end. He missed. "Or I'd take a step van," he said, "but only with a rebuilt tranny. Something I could trick out with a kitchen," he said, snatching up a flashlight and shining it in the corners to make sure no one had snuck up on them, "and then I'd be like, a cook on wheels."

There was no telling how another six or seven years of living would have changed Todd. At a red light Jimmy put his fingertips on his temples and squeezed his head. The headache pills were starting to kick in now. Richene was busy reminding him that Todd got married without even inviting her, just showed up on her doorstep with his new bride and introduced her, the two of them wearing matching bib overalls made of dark blue camouflage. Just imagine bringing someone in to the family unannounced that way, what was the matter with him?

In another fifteen minutes, they would be home. He'd get Richene settled, and then if he felt good enough, he'd go fix the clogged nozzles on his spray rig.

THE PHONE CALL CAME in the middle of the night. Michelle groaned and picked up the phone. She said hello, her tongue clumsy with sleep. Jimmy listened from his fetal curl in the bed next to her.

"Slow down," she said.

"Who is this?" she said.

"Where the hell have you been?" she said.

Jimmy's back was to her, but he felt Michelle tense up, and he rolled over and spooned his whole body next to hers.

"What are you on?" she said.

"She's been worried sick about you," she said.

"I can't talk to you when you're like this," she said.

She passed the phone to Jimmy. They both turned onto their backs. It was a moonless night and the room was as dark as it ever got.

"Todd?" Jimmy said.

"Jimmy," Todd said, "I got the good." Todd's voice was thick, the consonants a little slushy. "So good," he said, "it burned right through the baggie."

"Where are you, Todd?" Jimmy said.

"I got it all figured out," Todd said, "unified theory of

absolutely everything that matters. I'm slicker than a greased Jesus. I've been up for eleven straight days."

"Where were you yesterday," Jimmy said, "about 11:40 in the morning?"

"ArmorAll," Todd said, "spray it on, and poof, no more fingerprints."

"Todd, listen to me," Jimmy said.

"I love you guys," Todd said, "you guys are the only friends I got left."

A clatter came through the phone then, the sound of Todd letting go. The line stayed open. Jimmy pictured Todd in a motel room somewhere, passed out on the bed, the phone cord stretched across his body and the phone dangling onto the floor.

"Todd?" he said. "Todd? Wake up man, pick up the phone." He heard Todd cough, a choked off, gurgling kind of cough. He said Todd's name a few more times, louder and louder, until Michelle took the phone from him and hung it up.

"Terrific," Michelle said. "That's just marvelous. Todd's passed out some place and our phone line is tied up until he sleeps it off."

"I'm sorry," Jimmy said. He wormed his arm under Michelle's back and pulled her closer. She rolled on her side and draped her arm across his chest. "Did he tell you where he was?"

"No," she said. "He told me he was Mr. Clean. He said no one on this earth was keeping any papers on him."

"Do we tell Ma?" Jimmy said.

"Yes," Michelle said. "No," she said. "I don't know," she said.

Jimmy closed his eyes and let the dark wrap itself around them. They were safe in their bedroom, no bogeyman under the bed. Whatever Todd's story was, they would keep him at arm's length. They heard the slow click of Richene's crutches working her way to the bathroom.

"The phone probably woke her up," Jimmy said.

Michelle nuzzled her cheek into Jimmy's chest. "It's been good these last few years," she said, "not having Todd around. It's not like I've missed him."

"There was a time in my life," Jimmy said, "when I would've been jealous that I missed the party."

"Me too," Michelle said. "What do you think he was on?"

"Downers," Jimmy said. "He gets that mushy sound in his voice. You know him. He always liked a little something to smooth over the crash after he's been tweaking."

Michelle yawned. "Let's just tell her it was a wrong number," she said. "We don't want her getting all riled up."

"I'm wide awake," Jimmy said. He turned on his side and put his hand on Michelle's breast.

"Forget it," Michelle said. "I have to be at work early tomorrow." She kissed his forehead, and they lay there, their breath synchronized in the dark. Below them Richene's crutches clicked their way back across the house. It took Jimmy a long time to fall back asleep.

IN THE MORNING, JIMMY stayed in bed late, but he heard Michelle pick the phone up and say Todd's name several times. She cursed when she put the phone back in its cradle. He heard her talking to Richene for a few minutes before she left, and then the crunch of her tires in the gravel driveway. He dozed for a while, but he dragged himself out of bed before nine. He needed to change the oil in the tractor. His pickup truck still needed some coolant. The Bush Hog needed to be lubed. He would spend the day with his wrenches and his rigs, getting caught up on maintenance.

He was in the kitchen fixing lunch when the phone rang. Terrific, that meant Todd had finally hung up the phone. He finished spreading mustard on a slice of bread and picked up the receiver.

"James Ahlquist?"

"Yes."

"This is Deputy Coleman with the county sheriff's department."

"Okay." So Todd was busted?

"Do you know a man named Todd Ahlquist?"

"Yes. He's my brother."

"Mr. Ahlquist, I'm afraid I have some bad news."

Jimmy sat down at the kitchen table. Something lumpish and cold was expanding beneath his sternum. The sheriff didn't call to tell you somebody needed to be bailed out.

"Okay," Jimmy said, "tell me."

HE HAD A BOTTLE of bourbon he kept for emergencies in the cupboard over the stove. He got a couple of glasses and headed into the living room. The TV was on, that smarmy Regis character and his ridiculously cheerful co-host. Richene was working a crossword puzzle. She looked up when the glasses clinked against each other.

"Special occasion?" she said.

"Taken any pain meds this morning?" Jimmy said.

"I took a Vicodin earlier," Richene said, "about nine."

Jimmy poured her a short one and a taller one for himself. He set her glass down on the table next to all of Richene's pill bottles, drank half of his, and turned the sound down on the TV. He took Richene's hands in his, and he said, "I have something to tell you."

Her eyes floated off her face behind her thick glasses. It made him want to put his hands up and gently push her eyes back where they belonged.

"Todd," he said. He shook his head back and forth and pressed his lips together. "Todd's dead," he said.

"What?" Richene said. "No." Her hands began to shake so hard that Jimmy let go of them rather than try to force them to be still. She flapped her arms around and shrieked. A high wailing sound came out of her and sliced through Jimmy. She beat her fists on the bed. She grabbed her glass of whisky and downed it, set the glass back on the table, and stared at the jumble of pill bottles. Her lower lip quaked.

"How?" she said. The whisky had calmed her voice.

"An accident, it looks like," Jimmy said. "They found him in a motel room. It looks like he mixed some pills with some vodka. A lot of vodka, by the sound of it."

"The fool," she said, "my foolish, foolish son." Her face was full of failure, bloodless and pale and a wreck of wrinkles, a face collapsing in on itself as the news of Todd's death sank in. "How," she said, "did I ever raise such a goddamn fool?"

Jimmy leaned forward and gathered her bony little body into his arms. There were phone calls to make, funeral arrangements, the whole big mess of Todd's pathetic life to clean up. She shook with sobs, she wailed, she fought him to get loose. But really, holding on was the only thing that needed doing. He held on.

AFTER THE FUNERAL, JIMMY had Michelle drop him off at the river while she went grocery shopping. He scrambled down the bank on a steep path where he had to hang on to exposed roots to keep from sliding down willy-nilly. The river was slack there, the water backed up behind the dam just below town. Drifts of yellow pollen lay peacefully on the surface of the water, and the tops of the fir trees on the far bank moved gently back and forth. A red-tailed hawk circled in a thermal overhead.

The funeral had been open casket. Hardly anyone showed up, family mostly, and a few people who remembered Todd from high school. They hadn't been able to locate his ex-wife. Todd had a full set of teeth in his mouth, the same teeth he was wearing when the motel maid found his body. The autopsy found traces of amphetamine, and more than traces of morphine, methadone, and vodka. He was dressed in a brown suit the likes of which he'd never worn in his life. The funeral director sold the suit to them as part of the funeral package, a cheaply made thing with no lining and no pockets, only slits sewn shut where a pocket should go.

"I gather he led a troubled life," the funeral director said. Mr. Faber was a pink-faced man, freckled and bald, with an air of perpetual worry built into the lines across his forehead. Michelle and Jimmy both nodded yes at Mr. Faber. They waited for Mr. Faber to say something else, some platitude like "He is at peace now," or "His troubles are behind him." Instead Mr. Faber took his glasses off and polished them with a handkerchief. He hadn't pressured them when they chose the next-to-cheapest casket.

Jimmy found a flat stone and skipped it out across the surface of the water. They used to have contests to see who could get the most skips. Todd always won. He had great form, his leg stepping out like a pitcher's, and his arm snapping at the wrist just before he let go. Jimmy didn't cry at the funeral. He'd cried plenty when they went to view the body, and plenty more for the next day or so, but he was all cried out now. He'd stood in the funeral chapel and told everyone what a great brother Todd had been, how much he made everyone laugh, how much he liked to laugh himself. He left out the ugly parts. Everybody knew them anyway, and there was no point in a rehash of Todd's mess of a life.

"I'm lucky," Jimmy said. "The last words Todd ever spoke to me were 'I love you guys, you're the best friends I ever had.'"

He found a perfect skipping stone, thin and flat and just the right shape to fit in the long gap between his thumb and his forefinger. He threw his leg forward like a pitcher and skipped that stone out across the water, one, two, three big skips, and then a flurry of smaller ones, nine or ten altogether, a throw good enough to keep up with Todd.

A huge shadow sailed over him. He looked up, and there in the air was a John Deere tractor flying off the bank. Todd was in the driver's seat, a shit-eating grin on his face. He looked down and waved at Jimmy, and then he leaned forward, as if leaning forward would get that tractor farther out, maybe all the way across to the other shore.

He made it to the middle. The tractor cannonballed into the water like a brick through a plate glass window, smacking down hard, a glorious bellyflop. Water exploded up on both sides, great curtains of water shining in the sun. Above them a froth of water drops rose up even higher, sparkling with light and dropping back down, dappling the river like a fall of rain. The tractor sank and the surface of the water closed over it. The last Jimmy saw of Todd, he was swimming for the other side with long smooth strokes, making good time. No way was the sheriff going to catch him, not now, not ever.

To Walk Where She Pleases

RUTH, THERE YOU ARE. Aren't those roses lovely? Those pink ones have a lovely scent, you should pick some to take with you.

Come sit here beside me, I want to tell you some things. I've been sitting here thinking about the dead. Oh, don't look so shocked, a woman my age is close enough to dead it's only natural.

People don't talk about death enough, that's why it scares them so. It scared your mother, and she wouldn't let me talk to her about it. She told you I was crazy that day the two of you walked in on me when I was cleaning the garage after Lester killed himself. Only she chose her words carefully—dementia, senile dementia—and me barely out of my sixties that day. As if my own daughter could hide the truth of what she was saying with something other than plain English. As if my ears weren't as sharp as ever, and maybe a little sharper. As if a college education gave her the license to be condescending, never mind that it was our hard work, Lester's and mine, that put her through college. Vera always thought she was better than me, and a college education only made that worse. If I had it to do all over again, I would've sent Vera off on a mission to Africa and spent that money on remodeling the kitchen. Not that it isn't a tragedy that she died when you were what, fourteen? I know you loved her. As did I, Ruth, as did I.

At first I thought it was a mistake when she named you Ruth. Ruth is a serious name, a name from the Bible, but it is an adult's name, not a baby's name, or a child's name. But you were a serious child, even as an infant you had the sense of someone with an old soul. I was there the morning of your first day in the world, and it was me who dressed you the very first time while Vera slept after giving you birth. They say babies don't really see when they're newborn, but you were looking all around and taking it all in. You hadn't cried much. Very little fuss came out of you during the whole business, and when it came time to dress you I got the little shirt ready to pull over your head. You held your arm up and put it right through the sleeve. The first one could have been an accident, but then you looked right at me and held up your other arm like you had been doing this for years.

So Ruth has always suited you, I'll give your mother that one, and no one who knew you when you were little had the poor sense to call you Ruthie. We're alike in that way. No one ever called me Addie, not even my mother, it was always Adelaide. Such is the power of a well-chosen name. But Vera always called me Mama, as if she could make me less than I am with those two syllables. I am here to tell you that a daughter lacks that prerogative. I am here to tell you that Vera was not the only one who knew some words, either. Anyone who reads can have a vocabulary, and we have always been a family of readers.

You must have been twelve the year that Lester killed himself. Vera always said he took his own life, but I haven't got the time for such niceties. Dead is dead, and calling it something else never brought anybody back, so what's the point? But you were born in '49, I know that much, so you must've been twelve.

Nineteen sixty-one, my God what a year that was. Lester retired in '52, so we had nine years together where we could do pretty much what we wanted. Mostly what Lester wanted was to go fishing, and mostly he went alone because mostly what I wanted to do was garden. I don't know what happened to Lester. Why he had to kill himself. He didn't leave a note, and he was never much of a talker. Early on, when he was courting me, and the first years we were married, he wasn't quite so silent. And he was a good listener, that was one of the reasons I married him. But he was never the same after Ardennes. He saw things in those woods that he wouldn't talk about, and I suspect he did things in those woods that were even worse than what he saw. Shell-shocked we called it back then. We didn't have a fancy name for it like post-traumatic stress disorder.

A mess like Lester killing himself, I couldn't clean that up all in one day. That day in the garage must've been four or five months after. There was a layer of oily soot on everything in that garage, and I do mean everything. And I could still smell the exhaust. I felt like if I couldn't clean that exhaust smell out of the garage I was going to have to sell the house and move to The Whispering Pines, where everyone sits around and talks about their bowel complaints all day long. Can you imagine? At least Lester saved me from having to watch him die in a rest home, I'll give him that. There must've been half a tank of gas in the car, and of course he was too dead to turn the thing off. I know it sounds hard to say it straight out that way, but even all these years later I'm still mad at him for leaving me without even a word to say why. To sneak out of bed in the middle of the night so a person can go kill himself, if that isn't rude. Pure selfishness.

Vera thought it was Lester I was talking to in the garage tnat day. I still remember the pity in her eyes when she said "Mama, Daddy's gone. You have to let go." As if I were not in my right mind. But it wasn't Lester. Lester has never had the courtesy to pay me a visit since he died. I've been told, and on good authority too, the dead don't visit us much any more because they've forgotten how, but I think Lester is afraid of me, afraid to tell me whatever secret it is that drove him to it. Probably a woman involved in it somehow, although where a seventy-three old man with all the charm of a dried prune finds another woman to put up with him is beyond me. Unless he was paying some young tart for her time. But as tight-fisted as Lester was about money for everything except fishing poles, I don't hold that to be very likely.

No, it wasn't Lester. It was Sadie Gloss who was there in the garage with me, and now you'll probably call me crazy too. Sadie Gloss was an old Indian woman who lived around here when I was a girl. I took care of her back then, after she got caught up in the big fire, back in 1902 it was. She was badly burnt, but she recovered. We were very close, Sadie and I, and when she finally died, I grieved for her for some time.

She came to me one night about a month after they buried her. I saw her just as plain as I see the nose on your face. She told me not to feel so sad, that she was no longer hurting so much, and I shouldn't worry. And after that I would see her every now and again. She's never been fond of Lester, but when he went and killed himself, it was Sadie who came and took care of me in the dark of the night when no one else was here. I see her now almost every day, these last twenty years or so, and maybe you believe me and maybe you think I'm an old woman who's lost her mind. But all I can do is tell you what I know. It doesn't matter what you believe. About spirits, or the Bible, or Jesus. All that matters is how you listen, and if a spirit calls to you, then you are chosen.

Sometimes I don't so much see her as feel her close by. I hear the clank of the bell on the neck of her lead goat, and I know she's near. She likes foggy mornings because the fog is a balm to the scars she carries from the fire. If I got up early to take a walk, the way I used to do sometimes, she'd be there with me. She died walking along Burnt Springs Road, farther down that way, toward the turn to Gossard Flats, and she likes to take her flock of goats down there and then walk back up by here, to where her cabin was.

It's all in how a person listens. Sadie taught me that. Before she died she told me more than once that white people only listened with their ears, but her mother's people listened with their spirits. What a person hears depends on which world she walks in, and if all she knows is the world of things you can touch, then she never will hear the other world that is all around us, all the time. And you're not too old to learn how to do that. Once you get the listening figured out, then talking to the dead is no different than talking to your cat.

That day in the garage I had just come across my old pickle crock. Do you remember how you used to help me put up pickles when you were a little girl? That crock used to be Sadie's, and I was thinking I should put up a batch of pickles, and I would make the good dill pickles that Lester never wanted me to make because he liked his pickles sweet. That's when you and your mother walked in and I was talking to Sadie about where to get some cucumbers, because I hadn't put in a garden that year, what with all the fuss over Lester killing himself. Sadie has free range to walk where she pleases, and she had some ideas about who might have some extra cukes.

Sadie wants you to have this pickle crock. She wants you to have it because she sees the kind of person you are, the way you take care of the people around you. You're not like Vera was, all wrapped up in herself. It was being all wrapped up in herself that brought the leukemia into her blood. I know that sounds hard, and I don't mean that everyone who gets a cancer is all wrapped up in themselves. It's just that Vera's ambition was a way she poisoned herself. She was full of too much ambition, she had ideas about what a woman should be, and those ideas got between us in a way I never could get around. My own daughter, and I suppose I sound like I never loved her at all, which isn't true. Because she did some admirable things, Vera did. Teaching school is an admirable thing, and I'm sure in the classroom she wasn't so selfish, she was probably quite a good teacher because she took pride in everything she did. And she was a good mother to you, I would never say otherwise.

What I want from you now is a batch of pickles. Dills, made from this recipe right here. Use rock salt, and pick the dill from the patch along the edge of my garden, next to the raspberries. Get the cucumbers from somebody's garden around here, don't buy them from the store because they'll charge you an arm and a leg. That Jimmy Ahlquist down on Gossard Road, he knows how to grow a cucumber. Sadie says to go see if he's got any extra. Try and get them all pretty close to the same size, that's the secret to a good batch of pickles.

That's it. Just one more time before I die I want to taste a homemade pickle. And don't you go getting all weepy on me. Everybody dies, and look at me. I'm ninety-one years old and my bones are like peanut brittle. I've had a good enough life, and only the Good Lord knows how much time I've got left. Time doesn't mean so much in the next world, that's what Sadie tells me. But here, time is everything, and that's why we suffer so.

You just work on how you listen. You learn to listen for me, and you'll hear me. I'm not that easy to shut up.

As Men Will Do Unto the Least Among Us

SEPTEMBER 1902. IT WAS the smoke that first made Sadie Gloss look up. She was squatted down in Nordey's orchard, an old woman gathering filberts. For every hundred-pound gunnysack she weighed on Nordey's scale in his drying barn, she was allowed to keep five pounds. She stood up, the neck of the gunnysack still in her hand, and she sniffed the air. The smoke came at her from the swale above the Wadham back forty. Through the filbert trees she saw the smoke charge up the hill like a steam engine. It followed the fence line, and naught but a minute went by before she saw the flames. The fire followed the tall dry grass under the wooden rail fences.

Forty days and more since the last rain, and that nothing but a sprinkle that hardly settled the dust in the ruts. The orchard fence met the Hallock back fence, and from there the fire would follow the fence line up the slope to the woods where Sadie's cabin was, where she'd left the goats in their pen, figuring she'd be back by mid-morning to let them out. They'd pulled down a section of her garden fence the day before, and she wanted to get the last of Nordey's filberts before she commenced the repairs.

Sadie started up the side of Nordey's orchard with the gunnysack over her shoulder. The sack was too full to run more than a few steps at a time, and the weight of the filberts banged against her backbone with every step. The fire running up the fence line was already ahead of her when she dropped the gunnysack. The filberts spilled out on the ground, and she left them for later without so much as a glance back. She could run faster without it, and she ran until she reached the fence at the top of the orchard. The fire was spreading in both directions along the fence that separated the Nordey claim from the Hallock claim, coming straight at her like a lit fuse. She climbed the cedar rails and stood for a moment with her feet on the topmost one, holding her arms out for balance.

There was smoke in every direction. Long lines of flame boxed in the hay fields, the orchards, the rows of berry vines on their wire supports. It was the middle of September, too early for the leaves to fall, and the smoke rose high into a cloudless blue sky. A torrent of smoke rose where Nordey's barn stood. She could just make out the sound of them shouting. Farther off a column of smoke rose from the Bechtolds', and east of her from the Kopps place. To the north, Volpe's store looked to be on fire, or maybe it was his house. Served the old skinflint right, she thought, him so stingy with the salt pork he sliced off for her in trade for eggs.

A hot wind sucked all that was wet from inside her lungs, her nose, her mouth. The smell of it was sharp and made her eyes water, but the hot wind dried her tears before they could run down her cheeks. Everywhere around her was a distant roar, like the roar of water falling over a great precipice.

Her boots, newly handed down from Brother Gossard, were heavy on her feet, but she hurried on. Fire was headed for her cabin from two directions now; she saw the smoke charging up the hill from the Kiggins place, as if in a race with the fire from the Hallocks'. The wind was fitful as she crossed the Hallock hay field, air being tugged this way and that by the heat. The bleating of her goats came in snatches as the wind shifted direction. Her dress caught on something, and she ripped it free without bothering to see what. A wave of fire-heated air surged over her as she ran on. The closer she got to her cabin, the more the air stank of smoke.

Smoke swirled in dust devils made by the fire's own heat. Without her flock of goats, she'd have no money at all. Her neighbors wouldn't let her starve, but to have no money for kerosene so that she could read her Bible at night, no money for sugar to make jam with, nor salt to flavor her stew. Surely the Lord did not mean for her to have to put up with yet more deprivation.

Her legs ached from running so far uphill. When she cleared the top of the last rise before home, she saw the fire sprinting down the fence lines from two directions. The goats were still in the pen, milling about. She ran as fast as her creaky old legs would run.

The last fence was a wire fence. Hallock had given her the wire, left over from the fence he put up around his berry patch when the wooden rail fence grew too rotten to repair. He gave her the cedar posts in trade for a gallon of goat's milk each. The corner post was on fire, and the fire was spreading down the fence on both sides. The two strands of barbed wire she added across the top to keep her goats in came from the Kiggins place. There were tufts of goat hair flaring into flame all the way to the corner. A brace of rabbits ran past her without bothering to zigzag the way they would if a hawk's shadow had set them off. They ran so fast she felt old and broken down. But she was not broken down, not yet anyway, not if she could save her goats.

No time to make for the gate at the far end. She ran to the last cedar post that wasn't already on fire and started to climb. The goats were bunched in the corner of their pen, bleating piteously, their eyes scared as wide as they would go. The fire was six feet away when she put the toe of her boot into the net wire. Three feet away when she got to the top of her climb. Two feet away when she felt the tug on her dress that told her she'd caught it on the barbed wire. Ahead of her the flames had reached the goat pen and were working their way down two sides. The goats climbed on top of each other, trying to clear the top of the fence, the strong standing on top and pushing the weak down with their cloven hooves. Only her old billy goat stood and faced the flames, pawing the ground as if he might charge.

She tore at the dress, almost ripping it away from the fence, but the rip hit a seam and wouldn't rip any more. She jumped, and the dress held firm, so that she landed on her hands with her legs tangled up and hanging in the air. Fire caught on at the hem. Her hands were bleeding from the fall, but she clawed at the ground and pulled herself free, the seam finally ripping through. Her torn skirt hung behind her, still attached to the rest of her dress, and it was burning its way to her.

Sadie batted at the flames burning her skirt. She tried to rip away the cloth where it was torn, but the fire was too hot. Fire fell from the sky, bits of burning embers leaving trails of smoke behind them. She ran to reach the gate of the goat pen, but the flames ran up her back and caught on the long braid of her hair. She fell. Her hair was on fire. The heat made her scream in a voice not her own. It was the sound of the whole countryside screaming.

The goat pen was just beyond her reach. The big black and white nanny, her best milker, was running in frantic circles, the hair along the ridge of her back in flames. Sadie rolled on the ground, swatting at the flames in her hair. Deliver me Lord, she prayed, Sweet Jesus I am thy loyal servant. Her scalp smelled like scorched meat.

There was a water trough inside the goat pen. She pulled herself up to her hands and feet and lunged at the gate. Her hands caught the lowest rail, and she pulled herself to standing. She unlatched the gate, staggered through, and plunged face forward into the water trough. The goats ran past her, trampling the flames on the trailing edge of her skirt.

She climbed in and sank beneath the surface. The water was cool, the softest thing she had ever felt.

BY THE TIME THE fire reached people's yards, it was so hot that dry grass blackened at a distance of fifty feet. There weren't enough buckets nor enough people to man them to save much. People got out what they could and stood back and watched their homes burn to the ground. The volunteer fire crew from Renata never made it past the Llewellyns', the closest house to town in the whole Springwater grange. When it was all over, there were few buildings standing except the church, the manse, and whichever outhouses had been built in the middle of enough bare dirt to save them.

There wasn't so much as a grasshopper left alive in Hallock's hay field. Hallock picked his way through, avoiding the spots that still smoldered, wisps of smoke rising in the still September air. No birds called from the woods, nor did any rabbits startle out of the blackened grass. There was no buzz of bees seeking the last nectar of the season.

The fire had driven every living thing that could move fast enough across the creek, down below the Metzler place. It was the creek that had stopped the fire, that and a sudden shift in the wind that turned the fire back on itself. By the grace of Providence above, the fire had stopped, almost as suddenly as it began. Providence, too, that turned the fire away from the church and the manse, where everyone had gathered as if by instinct, coming with their buckets to save the one thing that belonged to them all.

Turkey vultures circled overhead, silent and vigilant, the first animals to return. Hallock saw a half dozen of them at the far edge of the field, converged upon some carcass. They flew off when he got close, stabbing for a last bite of what proved to be one of Sadie's goats when he got close enough to see. Her big nanny, the best of her milkers, and there was a loss they would all feel the sting of. The fence posts were blackened and smoldering. Sadie's cabin and her shed still stood, saved in part because her goats kept the ground bare in her yard, and in part because the Lord was merciful, and He had not let fall any burning embers on the roofs of her buildings, which were so old they were covered in moss half a foot thick.

He called out her name as he approached. There was no answer, but something pink and bony moved in the water trough inside the goat pen. There was a moan, audible only because the countryside, still in shock from the fire, was so silent around them. Several of her smallest goats lay dead in the far corner, their bodies so tangled around each other he could not tell how many, but the pink tongue of one of them stuck out of its mouth in a final bleat of desperation, now silenced. Hallock walked to the trough. He saw the bald top of a man's head, a blistery red, as if badly sunburnt. A hand gripped the side of the trough.

The eyes that looked up at him were crazed with pain. What Hallock saw at that close distance made him drop to his knees. This was no man, this was Sadie with her hair burnt off, and one side of her face charred black. The skin was seared off her shoulder, and a weeping red wound stretched down her arm. Dear God, he thought, Thou has shown me the fiery pit of Hell. What little his wife had scrounged from the root cellar for their evening meal spewed out onto the ground.

He rose up and reached his hand out to her, but she pulled hers away. Her eyes rolled back in her head and she started to slide down into the water, but when her nose went under she sputtered and sat up again.

"Sadie," he said, "it's Hallock. Can you keep yourself from drowning?"

She still had her boots on. He reached into the water and lifted one leg up, careful not to touch the burn down one side. The skin there was blistered, but it wasn't laid open and raw like the side of her face. The knot in her laces was shrunk tight from being in the water, but he managed to pull it loose and work her boot off. He got the second one off, and he set them on the ground upside down so that the water would drain out of them.

"Sadie," he said. He waited until her eyes found his. "I'm going to find something for your feet to brace against. Can you keep your head above water?"

Her eyes closed, but she gave one slow nod to him. Hallock ran to her cabin and pushed the door open. It was dim inside, the only light coming from the open door and the one window opposite. There was a large crock on the floor beneath the table where she kept her wash basin. It was full of pickles. He dumped the pickles into the wash basin, but they were too many, and half of them spilled out on the bare dirt that was the floor. Hallock left them, and ran back out to the trough.

Sadie's head was still above water. Hallock plunged the pickle crock into the end of the trough. He took Sadie's feet in his hands and placed them, first one and then the other, against the crock.

"Straighten your legs out, Sadie," he said. "Come on now, straighten your legs out." He pushed on her knees, and slowly her back slid up against the other end of her trough, raising her head until her chin was above the water level.

"I'm going to get help," he said. "I'll be back soon." A low sound from deep in her throat was all the answer she gave.

Hallock took off running for his house, or what was left of it. He ran so fast the turkey vultures didn't have time to startle from where they were feeding on the carcass of Sadie's goat.

SADIE'S BURNS HEALED A piebald red and white, the skin ridged and wrinkled in places, hairless and unnaturally smooth in others. Her face was the worst, if only because it was the most exposed to view. Her hair, where it came back at all, came back in frizzled patches, spread unevenly about her scalp. The Hallocks kept her in a three-sided shed until the weather got too cold, when they moved her back to her cabin. Their oldest daughter, Adelaide, a solemn twelve-year-old, stayed with her at night for the first month. They kept her wounds covered with honey to keep the infection out.

Sadie spoke little, not that she had ever been one for saying something merely to fill in the silence, and Adelaide took to reading to her, the Bible mostly, but sometimes she would bring a magazine from home, *Collier's*, or *The Saturday Evening Post*, copies of which were handed around from family to family in turn at church on Sundays. They could only spare enough kerosene to keep the lamp lit for an hour each evening, and then they would turn down the lamp and give themselves up to the oblivion of sleep.

The winter was a mild one, rainy and gray, with only one snowfall that stuck to the ground, and that one soon melted off. In the spring, Sadie was healed up enough to go back to work. The whole community commenced building in a frenzy, raising one barn after another. One-room shacks were built, later to be expanded into full-fledged homes. The sound of saws sawing and hammers hammering rang out from sunrise to sunset.

Sadie found work in two or three of the households. The Bechtolds had her come and wash their laundry and do other household chores, which freed up Mrs. Bechtold to be a carpenter's helper to her husband. Hallock gave Sadie a shovel and had her dig a root cellar. She was tough, even at her age, and used to being worked hard, but there were many who would have nothing to do with her, no matter how hard or how cheaply she might work. She was, after all, half Indian, which made her, with her dark skin and her Salish nose, an outcast from the beginning when she showed up in Springwater.

She took to covering herself with a long swath of dark cloth that she wrapped around her head, covering her neck and her face right up to the eyes. She did not own a mirror, but she had seen herself looking back from the surface of her water trough. That sturdy, hollowed out log had saved her life, but it now showed her the ruined flesh that was the side of her face. She was used to being ignored; even before the fire people often walked right by her without so much as a word of greeting. But this was different. On those rare days when she ventured into Renata there were many who would cross the street if they saw her coming so as not to pass her by too closely. Children thought she was bad luck, and some said she must be a witch. The old rumors of her dead husband were whispered about all over again, and told with particular relish to newcomers who had not heard them before.

The story was that she and her husband, both of them half-breeds, had lived in the coastal mountains, near a small town called Apiary, though some said where they lived was closer to Clatskanie. Back then she went by a different name, though none of the rumor-mongers knew what it was. Her husband worked her hard, and beat her whenever he suffered some humiliation at the hands of his neighbors for naught but the sin of being of mixed parentage. She had tired of his cruelty, they said, and killed the man one day after a beating the night before. They found his body at the bottom of a basalt cliff, and Sadie claimed he fell, and pointed to the broken shards of a whiskey bottle that caught the sunlight near where his body lay. Not everyone believed her, and there was talk of charging her for his death, and so she had moved east, and this was how she came to be in Renata, living under the name of Sadie Gloss.

Someone recognized her, or thought they did, and that was how the story attached itself to her two or three years after she arrived. By then she was living in the cabin up above the Hallock place. Hallock didn't believe the rumors, but there was nothing he could do to stop them. "There's only so much sand you can push uphill," was what he told his wife when the circulating rumor reached her ears. They took Sadie in because they saw no harm in it, letting her stay in the cabin they'd occupied until they built their farmhouse, and because they truly believed that what they did unto the least among us was also done unto the Lord.

Evenings, the summer after the fire, she went down to the creek after the sun went down and bathed herself in the cool water. The water soothed the tight feeling of her scars, numbing the pain that never went entirely away, and in the dark, when she let her head sink beneath the surface of the water, an ease came over her that was entirely absent from the hours she toiled with the washboard or the shovel. The roar of the flames and the stench of the burnt-over countryside finally left her alone.

After an hour or so in the water, she sat on a flat rock and let the water drain from her bare skin. She dressed herself, and wrapped the long strip of cloth around her head. Most thought she wore the wrapping to hide her scars, and that was true enough, but she covered herself in equal measure to keep her hands from touching the scars. There were ridges in the scars that drew her fingers there and would not let them go.

Most nights she would follow an old game trail from the creek back up the slope to her cabin, and then bed herself down. But there were some nights, when the moon was bright, that the sight of her cabin carried with it the sharp reek of burning hair, which made her think always of calves so rigid with fear they shat themselves as the branding iron was pressed into their hides. She saw in the shadows on those nights her big nanny goat with flames down the ridge of hair along her back, and she took a different trail, to the ridge road, and she walked out past the church and the manse and Volpe's store that was a little farther along. The road had always been called Springwater Road, for the many springs that surfaced on the south face of the high ground, but after the fire folks took to calling the whole area Burnt Springs, and the road became known as Burnt Springs Road.

Some nights she walked as far as the lane that led down to Gossard Flats, a distance of six miles and more from her cabin. Once or twice she saw someone out, walking along the road, carrying a lantern, walking the way the whites did, making enough noise with their steps in the night time quiet to be heard from quite a distance. On those occasions Sadie stepped into the shadows and made herself small, and she waited until she could step out and be entirely alone again in the moonlight. Just as the Lord Jesus had conquered death, the moon had the power to restore itself after it had been devoured each month by the darkness, and she left her face uncovered and open to his light. The moon calmed her fingers, and she kept her hands at her sides without having to fight the urge to touch the ridges that spiderwebbed across her cheek.

Walking back those nights she felt how old she was getting, felt the stiffness in her hips and knees that she knew was the rheumatiz. The rheumatiz was beyond the power of the moon to help. There were nights when it got so bad she laid herself down on the side of the road and slept, or tried to, because she could not make herself take another step.

VOLPE'S STORE WAS SPARED from the fire by virtue of the large area of bare dirt around it on all sides, and because rather than joining the others at the church, he and his boys climbed a ladder up to the roof and hauled buckets of water up with them so as to drown any embers that fell on the cedar shingles. He lost his barn, but because he was not a farmer the loss hurt him less than it hurt his neighbors. The store had long been a gathering place, and folks would stay a while because Peter Volpe had the gift of conversation and a comely wife who made the farmers' wives feel at home. He was known as a sharp trader, and someone who would press his advantage when he could, but there were none who considered him dishonest, and he had enough stature in the church's congregation to serve as sexton for the cemetery.

"Keep a tight grip on your coin purse when you go to see Volpe" was what many said about the man, but what was meant was that he never gave anything away for free, and that he could convince a body that he needed something enough to part with hard-earned currency, whether it be a new knife, or a pickled egg from the crock he kept on the counter, or something to be ordered from one of his several catalogs.

Every few months, Volpe drove his wagon and his team all the way to Stumptown to fetch more goods for the store. What was disastrous for his neighbors, the loss of their farm implements and their households, was a boon to Volpe. He had the wherewithal to purchase what was needed to make their lives possible, and the credit he extended to all, at a not entirely unreasonable rate of interest, made of him the man of means he had always aspired to be. The trip took some several days, exactly how long depending on the rains and the condition of the roads. He stayed with his younger brother, who was also a merchant, dealing in farm implements and machinery. He left his wife behind to mind the store with the aid of his sons.

While he drove those long rutted roads he did figures in his mind, adding up what was owed to him and subtracting out what he owed to his suppliers. He traveled with a pistol tucked into a cubby hole he'd tacked onto the back side of the wagon seat because he traveled with cash. Cash and credit and his good name as a man who paid his debts were all he had in the world, or so he told himself. The truth was rather different, because he owned the store outright, owned the house and some ten acres around it, and had a silent partner's stake in the log business that kept many afloat in Renata. He had approached the owners of the electric wires and the new powerhouse on the river to run a line up to his store, thinking the novelty would draw customers to him in the evening, but so far they had rebuffed his offer, having larger hogs to butcher themselves.

And so it was Peter Volpe who found Sadie Gloss's body lying next to the road as he made his way home from Stumptown one morning. He'd spent the night at Feldheimer's Ford, camped in a grove of trees there, and gotten an early start the next morning, crossing the river under the watchful eye of an osprey as the sun rose. Even from his wagon seat he'd had a pretty good notion who it was lying there. She was a dark lump of tattered cloth lying on the burnt over ground where there shouldn't be anything but tall grass and lupine. Volpe eased his horses to a stop and climbed down off the wagon.

She was on her side with her legs drawn up to her belly. She wore a man's pair of boots, well broken in, on her feet. There was a hole in one of the soles that she'd patched from the inside with a piece of leather. Volpe pushed her onto her back with the toe of his boot. A black beetle crawled across her forehead and scurried off as soon as he turned her. There was no question that she was dead. Her mouth gaped open and her tongue hung out to one side, speckled with dirt. He didn't need to touch her to know her skin would be cold. He went back to the wagon and got his gloves.

His boys came running when he pulled the wagon up to the store. There were no horses and no other wagons, and this made Volpe frown, for he valued the first sale of the day as a sign of how much profit might come his way, and always wished that it would come early, and bring more trailing behind it as the day wore on. His boys, Raymond and Samuel, knew better than to ask him what he'd got, but went instead straight to the back of the wagon to begin the unloading.

Raymond, the elder of the two, called out, "What's this?"

"It's that squaw who lived up to Hallock's place," Volpe

said. Samuel, only ten years old, took a step back. Raymond held his ground but drew his hand back. He was thirteen, and he had been about to touch the woman, but now he muttered some phrase that a schoolmate had told him would ward off the spirits of the dead.

"What you got her for?" Raymond said.

"She was dead by the side of the road. Vultures would have got her if I hadn't brought her along here."

Martha came out of the store and over to the wagon. Volpe took her by both hands, and they had a moment of silent communion as they always did when he returned, each grateful for the other's presence. "That poor woman," she said. "How did she die?"

Peter Volpe looked at his wife for a long moment. Her good nature was an asset of great value when it came to running the store. But she was like most women, prone to a sentimentality about how hard life was, and far too easy to convince that someone deserved some small bit of charity, when the truth was everyone had to face life's hardships with whatever fortitude they could muster. The better among us prosper, was what Volpe thought, and the lesser do not, and if this was not the Lord's way of ordering things then perhaps we should all give up on religion entirely and become accursed atheists.

"I have not troubled myself to examine her," he said. His wife knew this tone of voice, knew that it meant she should not ask another foolish question, but she went ahead and did it anyway.

"What will you do with her?" she said.

He turned away from her. "Get the wagon unloaded, boys." He grabbed a keg of nails and started for the store. As he passed Martha he said, "I could use some breakfast." She nodded without looking at him. Her husband was a decent man, temperate with whiskey and a more than able provider, but there were places in him hard and unyielding, and she had long since learned the art of not provoking him beyond a certain point. Never had he struck her, and it was that bargain between them that she strove to preserve. It wasn't until both her sons had loaded up their arms and started for the store that she came close enough to touch the hem of Sadie's skirt.

She was dropped into the corner of the wagon in a heap. Her neck was bent uncomfortably back, exposing the scars on the front of her throat. Martha gave the front of the store a quick look, and then she reached out with both hands and shifted Sadie's head forward so that her chin covered those scars, and she pulled the loose cloth of Sadie's head covering over her gaping mouth. The heft of Sadie's head was a surprise to her. At least her eyes were closed, the Lord be praised. May God have mercy upon thy weary soul, Amen.

Martha picked up a twenty-pound box of salt and headed back into the store.

After the wagon was unloaded and Volpe had tucked into his breakfast, and after Raymond and Samuel had reported back to him that his horses were put up and the harness was hung in its place with the other horse tack in their newly built shed, Volpe sent the boys to fetch the wheelbarrow. He put his gloves on, and he lifted Sadie's body and set it down in the wheelbarrow with the same care he would use for a sack of grain, no more and no less.

"Raymond," he said, "you help your mother mind the store."

"Yes sir."

"Samuel."

"Yes sir?"

"You come with me. I'll have your help with the wheelbarrow." Volpe chose not to notice the look the boys traded between themselves. He'd given the plum job to Samuel, who was the lesser of the two in age and less entitled, but Raymond was better with the customers, and dead body or none, it was the store that came first. And Samuel, because he was younger, would profit more from witnessing the way Volpe would deal with a man who was known to be soft-headed when it came to dealing with heathens.

Samuel picked up the handles of the wheelbarrow, ready to do his father's bidding. "Where to, Father?"

"Hallock's."

They set off. It was a fine morning, the dampness of the night before already cooked away by the risen sun. They walked down the middle of the road, on the high spot between the wagon ruts, the earth there well traveled and no longer blackened from the fire. The wheelbarrow bumped along, Sadie's body jostling and slowly settling lower, as if she were drawing herself into the smallest ball a body could be. Volpe was silent, his thoughts on what he was going to say to Hallock, and how he would say it. If the boy was spooked by the cargo he wheeled along he gave no sign of it.

Sadie's flock of goats, what was left of them, was loose in Hallock's lane, their presence announced by the low clank of a bell around the neck of the lead goat. Beyond the fence line the earth was still blackened where Hallock had not yet found time to plow. Two or three of the goats looked up from their browsings amongst the tufts of new grass and bleated as Volpe and Samuel passed them by. The lead goat followed them until Volpe turned around and shooed her off with a swat across her muzzle.

Hallock was sawing his way through a stack of rafters when they arrived. His back was to them, but something made him turn around when he finished cutting through a board. He'd ordered a large planer to replace the one he'd lost in the fire, but surely Volpe was not delivering his planer in a wheelbarrow, and surely not in person when he could easily have sent Samuel alone.

"Good morning," he called out, and he set his hat back farther on his head. Volpe waved to him in reply, and he and the boy bore down on Hallock with their wheelbarrow, as men will do when they have something serious to attend to.

"You may not think it is such a good morning," said Volpe, "when you see the news I bring." They rolled up the last few feet between them, and now Hallock could see the dark cloth Sadie wrapped around her head to cover her scars. He looked at Volpe with his lips parted to speak, and Volpe gave him a nod that needed no words to decipher.

"I found her down the road this morning," Volpe said. "She must've died in the night."

Hallock leaned in over the wheelbarrow. He pulled the cloth that covered her face down enough to see the scars on her cheek. He shook his head, and he pushed his lips together to hold back the tremor he felt there. He took his hat off and laid it down over her face.

"Had she been harmed in any way?" he said.

"I saw no sign of it," Volpe said.

The goats were working their way back up the lane toward the yard, bleating from time to time, and attentive to the doings of the men. Sam stood apart from his father, looking about, trying to guess the whereabouts of the Hallock children. One of the boys was his age, and they spent time together when their chores would allow it, but his father would not allow him to run off at a time like this.

His father being the sexton of the cemetery, he and Raymond were used to dealing with mourners and funerals. Their familiarity with the dead began after the bodies had been prepared and laid in their coffins, and sometimes, when the bodies were awaiting a service in the church and the coffin had not yet been nailed shut, the boys would sneak in and take a peek. The newly dead were a different matter, and Sadie Gloss, being a heathen, was something altogether new. Sam was content to stand, and listen to the men, so that he could report back to Raymond everything that happened.

"I'll have the missus prepare her for the burial," Hallock said. It appeared to Sam, already at his age something of an expert in the ways that mourners held back or released their emotions, that Hallock cared for the dead woman as if she were a close relative.

His father looked straight at Hallock, with the direct and accusatory gaze he used when he'd caught a man sticking a knife from the display case into his pocket. "You do whatever you think is right," his father said, "but when you're done with that, don't bother bringing her up to the church. I won't allow a heathen to be buried in the sanctified earth."

Hallock smoothed his hair back, although anyone could plainly see it was in no need of smoothing. He said, "Where am I supposed to bury her then?"

His father set his shoulders square, as if he were readying himself to put up his fists and defend himself. "You bury her wherever you like," he said. "You can burn her for all I care. Finish the job that the grass fire started. She's a murderess, and a half-breed heathen, and she'll rile up the spirits of the good folk who are buried in our cemetery. I won't have that."

Sam was behind his father a pace or two, his insides a-trembling at the prospect that a fight would break out. He made himself perfectly still, and perfectly small, and he directed his gaze away from the men, so that if his father happened to notice him, he would think he was attending to other things. Although it was everywhere dotted with fresh green growth, the blackened earth spread out around them on all sides.

Hallock rocked back on his heels. He was not known as a fighter. Things might be going differently if they were at the Kiggins place. Mr. Kiggins had gotten into a brawl with some pipe workers down in Renata the year before and had spent the night in jail.

"There's no proof beyond mere rumor that she killed her husband," Hallock said, "and if I remember the way the story was told, the man deserved it, if it is true."

"A man's got a right to beat his squaw," Volpe said, "if she misbehaves."

The way Hallock shook his head was as if Sam's father had said something shameful. "Not in these modern times," he said.

The two men regarded each other, both of them resolved beyond persuasion, but neither willing to be the first to raise his fists over the matter. The lead goat gave out a long bleat, drawing Hallock's gaze away from his father's. There would be no fight to report back to Raymond.

"I will not have it," his father said. "I will not have a half-breed heathen buried in the sanctified earth."

They left then. His father would send one of them down for the wheelbarrow later. The goats crowded past them as they started up Hallock's lane, following the low clank of the bell on the lead goat. When Sam turned to look, they were gathered around the wheelbarrow, with Hallock stroking their heads. Even though the morning was bright and full of promise, their bleating sounded mournful, and bereft.

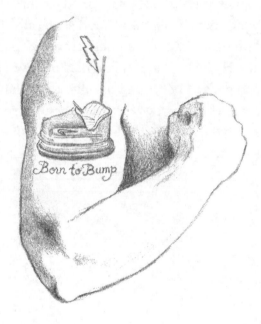

A Simplified Map
of the Real World

UNCLE LENNY ALWAYS SAT in his car listening to the ball game after Sunday dinner, but we were not allowed to go anywhere near him because Grandma always told us not to, unless we wanted to be sent to bed early with no dessert. This would have been July because it was always July when we stayed at Grandma and Grandpa's, and this particular Sunday afternoon would have been in 1960, the year the Pirates won the World Series, so it was the summer I turned nine. I'd been baptized and confirmed the summer before because I had reached the age of eight, the age when Mormons are considered old enough to be held accountable for the difference between right and wrong.

There were six ways I knew Uncle Lenny was different. One, the tattoo on his forearm. Two, his red hair. Three, Uncle Lenny wasn't married, so there was no Aunt Somebody to go with his Uncle Lenny when we said hello. Four, his car, a '39 Buick the color of Concord grapes that he kept shiny as a new coin. Five, he was the only one of my aunts and uncles who was allowed to sit in the driveway after Sunday dinner. Six, Uncle Lenny never went to Church.

Sunday dinner was always roast beef or roast pork from beeves or hogs that Grandpa raised right there on the farm. Grandpa said the blessing, we passed the dishes to the left like clock hands turning the hours, and when dinner was over you took your dish into the kitchen. My mother and the aunts helped Grandma clean up, the men sat in their starched white shirts and their ties in the parlor, and the children were allowed to play outside, but not anywhere near Uncle Lenny in his car. The game we played most was hide and seek, but if enough cousins were there, and if we could convince enough of the girl cousins to play, we played kickball. It was kickball that sent me running to Uncle Lenny's Buick, chasing a ball that my cousin Ted kicked clear over my head for a home run.

Uncle Lenny's arm rested on the open window of his car, and it was the arm with the tattoo on it, a heart with a dagger pierced through it and strange words written on the blade. There were drops of blood dripping off the tip of the dagger, and this was the arm I called the scary arm, but only to myself. Uncle Lenny did not wear starched white shirts on Sunday. He wore cowboy shirts in dark plaids with pearl buttons that weren't buttons at all, they were snaps. So there were seven ways I knew that Uncle Lenny was different, but even though I was almost nine that day, and old enough to be held accountable for the difference between right and wrong, I didn't always know what I knew, and because the ways Uncle Lenny was different were not something my family spoke of except in whispers, the only words I had were my own, and my own words were not always enough.

The ball rolled to a spot right in front of the Buick's front tire, and when I picked it up there was Uncle Lenny, smiling at me, his shirt sleeve folded carefully back to just below the elbow the way he always did. "Hey Spud," he said, he called all the boys Spud, and the girls he called Puddin'. His red hair was combed in a big wave that swept back from his forehead and he had big ears like all of the Lingstrom men do, and lines across his forehead like my mother's. The sun had colored the skin on his face to a deep reddish brown and his skin had that same roughened look of human leather that Grandpa had, the weathered look of someone who works outside, a look so different from my father, who worked in an office building with papers that were both too important and too dull to explain to me. The words La Herida de Amor written on the blade of the dagger, and my sister, who was older and took Spanish, said the words meant the wound of love.

The ball I held was a dimpled red playground ball. I held it out to Uncle Lenny by way of explaining why I had broken the rule about bothering him, and Uncle Lenny's hand raised up off the shiny steel of his car and he motioned me closer with his fingers. I stepped forward, drawn in by the bright blue of his eyes as much as his come-hither fingers, and Uncle Lenny took the ball in one hand and held it like a baseball, his fingers were that long. He tossed the ball up a few inches and caught it. He did this several times. My cousins were yelling for me to get back to the game, but I smelled something almost exotic, something unthinkable, and smoke was rising in the car next to Uncle Lenny, a bluish smoke, and it was at that exact moment that it came to me why Uncle Lenny sat out in the driveway after Sunday dinner. My parents didn't smoke because the Word of Wisdom told us not to, and none of their friends smoked for the same reason. People smoked on TV shows sometimes, tough men and bad guys and sometimes even bad women, and there were commercials where smiling people who must be good people smoked while they sat under a tree next to a beautiful lake with a sailboat on it, but no one in my own life ever smoked. Yet here was Uncle Lenny sitting in his car smoking, and even though he kept the hand that held the cigarette down where I could not see it, I knew that he was breaking the Word of Wisdom right there in front of me.

Uncle Lenny tossed the ball back to me. The ball bounced off my chest and I almost dropped it, but I caught the ball with my hands and felt those red dimples as something soothing and cool against my palms. Uncle Lenny winked at me and it was the friendliest thing, the smile on his face the same smile that was in the photograph of him on the buffet in Grandma's dining room. That row of fancy framed photographs of my mother and her six brothers and sisters, with Grandpa and Grandma's wedding portrait in the middle, a look of serious purpose on their faces, for they were Latter-Day Saints. It was a look that ruled me until I began to come to my own understanding of the world, and the way things truly are.

I CANNOT REMEMBER THE exact moment when I learned all of this, but Uncle Lenny ran away with a carnival when he was seventeen. Probably there was no exact moment, because the things I knew about Uncle Lenny were things that were whispered by the adults when they thought they were alone, things they would not say if they saw one of us, in which case they gave each other a look that meant they would talk about it later. But I knew that he never finished high school, that the carnival came through town and took him away, and when he came home years later he had that tattoo on his arm. Only sailors and Hells Angels wore tattoos, I heard them say, and that left it up to me to figure out which one Uncle Lenny was, and for a time I believed that the carnival he ran off with must have sailed away on a ship to foreign lands.

What was loud and clear was Grandma, who said we were not allowed to go anywhere near Uncle Lenny's house. Not that Grandma's rule was enough to keep us from riding down the road he lived on. We rode our bikes everywhere on those summer days, and Uncle Lenny's was only twenty minutes away.

Mostly we rode our bikes down to the little store at the cross-roads to buy candy and pop, or into Renata to play on the playground at the school, or to the county park to catch crawdads in the creek. We rode in packs of five or six. Grandpa kept a small fleet of bicycles in his equipment shed and there was always a gaggle of cousins around because we came from such a large family of Mormons who believed it was God's plan that they multiply the number of Saints in God's service. We knew where all the best hills were, the places where you could pump the pedals hard and feel the wind in your face and coast the farthest. The best of those hills was the long hill on Hollyhock Road, and if you bent yourself low into the pull of gravity and coasted without wobbling until your bike would coast no farther, you ended up in front of Uncle Lenny's driveway. As far as Grandma's rules went, it was simply a matter of interpreting what the words "anywhere near" really meant.

Children though we were, we all of us knew that if you got too close to Uncle Lenny you were crossing the line that held us all safe within the bounds of Church and family. It was whispered that Lenny drank coffee and beer, things forbidden by the Word of Wisdom the way tobacco was forbidden. Even though he came to Sunday dinners, and even though he was my mother's brother, he lived outside those bounds, and so we were all afraid of him, afraid that whatever it was that made him run away with the carnival would rub off on us. This was not something I had words for, but a dread that I knew in my bones.

And yet, in the summer I turned twelve, the year the Dodgers swept the Yankees in the World Series, there came a day when we coasted down the big hill on Hollyhock Road, the whole gaggle of cousins and my sister and I, and instead of pumping my hardest, I hung back. When even cousin Jessie, who was only seven, was in front of me, I put on my brakes and let the others ride on ahead. I got off my bike as if I were going to pick a few blackberries, although it was too early in the summer for them to be ripe. The others waited for me at the bottom, but I waved them on, shouting that I would catch up, and off they went around the turn in Hollyhock Road that took them out of my sight. Only then did I ride my bike the rest of the way down the hill, and when I got to Uncle Lenny's driveway, I turned in.

His driveway was lined with cedar trees on one side and a fence on the other. The fence sagged between the posts and the posts themselves were old and gray, but it didn't matter because Uncle Lenny kept no cattle. He grew hay, but not grass hay like the other farmers around Renata, his hay was oat hay, and he sold it for a high price every year to a man who bred racehorses, and it was whispered that Uncle Lenny sometimes made bets on those horses, another sin against the Word of God. There was a hum of machinery in the air, but not the clank and grind of farm equipment, this sound was more like the hum of electricity. It put me in mind of the power station next to the dam on the river just below Renata, or the laboratory of Dr. Frankenstein in that creaky old black and white movie.

The driveway ended in a patch of gravel big enough to park several cars. Uncle Lenny's old Buick was there, shiny and round and twenty years out of date. His car was so different from the cars my parents and my other aunts and uncles all drove, newer cars with boxier lines and two-tone paint jobs. There was a cement walkway from the edge of the gravel to Uncle Lenny's front door. Both sides of it were lined with old license plates, rusty old things from states I'd barely heard of, exotic states like Tennessee and Oklahoma and Saskatchewan. The world was vast, and if you only knew how, you could get there from here, and bring back artifacts that proved you knew the way.

I went up to the front door and knocked. I was old enough by then to know that Uncle Lenny was probably not a Hells Angel, but the feeling inside my chest was as icy as a popsicle straight from the freezer on Grandma's back porch. In another month I would be twelve, and I would be ordained as a deacon into the Aaronic Priesthood of the Church of Jesus Christ of Latter-Day Saints. I would be ordained by a laying on of hands by Elders in the Church, my father among them, men who had themselves been ordained into the higher priesthood, the Melchezidek Priesthood, and once ordained, I would pass the sacrament on Sundays. Great things were set before me, a path was laid out that I should follow. My Uncle Lenny had set out on that path, but when he was seventeen he strayed, and he had never found his way back. Nor was he even looking for the way back, because having once strayed, Uncle Lenny had found another way to walk in the world.

I knocked on his door, and I waited, listening to that faint electrical hum from somewhere back behind the house, wanting in that moment only to see what was there in my uncle's house, how a man who did not go to Church and had no wife or family might live. Or not even that much did I know. I went there with no plan at all, no thought in my head as to why. It was the whisper of blood that called to me, an ache in my bones that needed to know something I could not even name.

No one came to the door, even after I knocked a second time. I went around back, following the sound of that hum. Out back was a barn, a mammoth wooden structure painted ox blood red. There were two sliding doors covering an opening big enough to drive a hay wagon inside with a tall load of hay on board, and room to spare. A smaller door the size of a human being was cut into one of the big sliding doors, and that door was open. The sun was so bright I was squinting, and the rectangular opening of that door was dark enough that I could see nothing inside the barn until I stepped inside.

It took a few moments for my eyes to adjust. The barn had a wide alley running down the length of it, with stalls for horses and rooms built along both sides. The front end of a tractor poked out of one of the horse stalls. There were no horses or other animals, but there was a smell that was sweet and sour at the same time. At the far end, there was a bare light bulb hanging down on a wire from the darkness above. The hum was coming from down there. I was old enough to be held accountable for the difference between right and wrong, but I couldn't see what would be wrong about going down there to see, except that Grandma had expressly forbidden us to go to Uncle Lenny's. And yet there was something dishonest about that rule. They taught us in Sunday School that we should be obedient, but they also taught us to be kind. They taught us that families were so important that they would be kept together even in heaven. Uncle Lenny was my mother's brother, he was family, and why would we stay away from him on earth when we would be together in heaven? What could be more unkind, for heaven's sake?

And so I advanced into the dark interior of the barn. Dim shapes lay in the stalls as I passed them, things I could not name. Some of them looked like farm equipment and some of them looked like something else, strange pod-like shapes, and something like a giant teacup. I kept going forward, the hum growing louder, and then, halfway down the length of the barn, from the far corner and off to the side, a blue glow, an electrical sizzle, and then a shower of sparks.

"Damn," I heard someone say, a bad word, a swear word, but not so bad as saying God damn, which was taking the Lord's name in vain and the breaking of one of God's commandments, but it was Uncle Lenny's voice saying it, and he sounded more surprised than angry, and so I kept on going forward. Even my mother said damn sometimes when she was especially vexed, like she was the time we ran out of gas on the way to Church. Forward I went, until I was close enough to that bare lightbulb to see Uncle Lenny's back. He was hunched over a strange piece of machinery, something on its side and as big as a kitchen table, but metal, with wheels sticking out of it. My uncle had a wrench in his hand, but it was not the hand of the scary arm, and that helped me find the courage to speak.

"Uncle Lenny?" I said.

Uncle Lenny's whole body jerked, and he turned his head to see me and he said "Jesus Christ," and that was definitely taking the Lord's name in vain, for Jesus Christ was nowhere in that barn and His name was not to be said aloud in that way.

"Cal?" Uncle Lenny said, "Is that you?"

"Yes," I said. Uncle Lenny stood up, his eyes big and round and the barn too dark to see how blue they were. The way he held the wrench in his hand made the tool seem like a natural extension of his arm.

"Whoa, you gave me a start there, Spud." He let out a big breath of air, and then his head shuddered back and forth like a cat's does when you touch its ears. "What are you doing here?" he said. "Is everything all right at the folks'?"

"Yes," I said. I pulled my cheek in between my teeth, a habit I have when I'm nervous. There was a cigarette lying on a post with smoke rising from it. Something inside me felt crooked, and I did not know if the way to straighten it was to leave or to stay.

"Okay, good, that's good," Uncle Lenny said. He had his forehead pulled up from his eyebrows, and that made his whole face into a question, and I knew he wanted me to say what it was that had brought me over there, but I had no words to tell him.

"What's that you're working on?" I said.

"This?" Uncle Lenny said. "Why, this here's a bumper car, Spud. You ever been to a carnival?"

"No," I said. There was a carnival every year in Renata when the Fourth of July happened, but we were not allowed to go because it was a frivolous waste of money, and a place where juvenile delinquents congregated, and because they sold cotton candy there, which was nothing but spun sugar and pink food dye and would only lead to us having more cavities in our teeth than a tree full of woodpeckers. Instead Grandma made homemade ice cream and gave us all sparklers and we stayed home for the holiday.

"Well," Uncle Lenny said, "that's a crying shame." He set the wrench down on the edge of the upturned bumper car. He stared off at something behind me for a while, rubbing his hand across the bottom of his face. Then he let his hand drop to his side, and he smiled that smile he had that made you wonder what all the whispering was about, because there was nothing but friendliness in his face.

"Well Spud," he said, "we just might have to do something about that."

He had me come over and look at the bumper car, and he told me he was fixing it for a man who owned an amusement park. He told me he'd learned how to fix all kinds of things when he worked on the carnival, and now that he lived in one place, they sometimes brought him carnival machines that were broken for him to fix up. "I'm a pretty fair mechanic," he said. "I can fix darn near any carnival ride you care to name, but bumper cars are one of my specialties."

He showed me how he'd rigged up a special place to work on bumper cars there in the barn, with a special floor and a special ceiling covered with sheets of steel, because bumper cars worked off of electricity that went from the wheels up through a pole that touched the ceiling.

"This one here," he said, "the motor was burned out, so I had to rebuild it." He showed me his workbench where he had another motor pulled apart, and how he was putting new wire brushes in it that helped the electricity get where it needed to go. We tilted the bumper car back down on its wheels, the two of us working together like men, and Uncle Lenny telling me to bend at the knees so that my back would not go out. Then he had me sit in it, and I held the wheel in my hands like a man driving a car, and I was tall enough to see the way in front of me.

"You push on that pedal to make it go," he said, "and you

steer it with the wheel. We're going to test this one out, but you have to be careful not to run it off the edge of the steel floor. We'll aim it at the back wall there, and you can run this car straight at it, and all that'll happen is you'll bounce off. Wait'll I flip the switch, and then give it a go."

He walked over to a big switch mounted on a post, and when he switched it on, sparks came from the ceiling above my head where the pole touched it. "Don't worry about that," he said, "that's normal." I put my foot on the pedal and pressed it down, and the car jerked forward. It scared me and I pulled my foot back, but then Uncle Lenny told me to go ahead and bump that wall.

I held the steering wheel tight in both hands and I pushed down on the pedal. The wall was right in front of me, maybe six feet away, and I drove straight into it. I wanted to drive slowly and carefully into the wall, easing the bumper car into it, but the bumper car seemed to have only one speed. It crashed right into the barn wall and bounced off. The wall did not come crashing down, the bumper car was not broken, and no one was looking at me like I had done something wrong.

"Good one." Uncle Lenny had the biggest grin on his face. He gave me a thumbs up sign, and he came over and pulled the car back and told me to take another run at it.

I could not believe it. I was to crash the bumper car into the barn wall again. Surely there was a rule against crashing cars into barn walls. This was like breaking all the rules I'd ever been taught and how could there be nothing wrong with that? Uncle Lenny was behind me, and he laid his hands on my shoulders, and he whispered something in my ear that was like he could read my mind.

He said, "You are born to bump, Cal. All of us are."

The way he said "You are born to bump," it was like a new kind of rule, a commandment almost, a commandment that said what you were supposed to do instead of telling you what not to do. A thou-shalt, instead of a thou-shalt-not.

And so I bumped, and I bumped, maybe another twenty times, and after each time, Uncle Lenny pulled the bumper car back to the front edge of his parlor, he called it a parlor, the same word Grandma used for her front room. And each time I crashed into the barn wall, it put a smile on my face, better than homemade ice cream, more fun than sparklers, happier than riding full tilt down a hill that never ended.

But it did end, because Uncle Lenny looked at his watch and said, "We better go call the folks and let them know where you are." He switched off the electricity to his parlor, and he had me climb out of the bumper car. He opened a metal box on the post above the switch, and he pulled a big handle down, and the hum in the barn stopped and the lightbulb hanging down on the wire got brighter.

"I don't want folks worrying," he said, and he laid his hand on my shoulder and we walked down the alley all the way to the door. Along the way Uncle Lenny told me what all the stuff he had was, a popcorn popper with a big glass box to catch all the popcorn, a roller-coaster car, a car for a carnival ride called The Cyclotron and another for a ride called The Mad Tea Party, a Model A Ford that needed a lot of rebuilding. One stall had another '39 Buick covered up with a tarp. He called it his parts car.

"You've never ridden in my Buick, have you, Cal?" he said.

I had not. We were halfway to the house, the sun bright in our eyes and making us both squint. The warmth of his hand still lay on my shoulder, those long fingers of his wrapped lightly and easily around the top of my arm.

"Well Spud," he said. "We just might have to do something about that."

We went into the house through the back door, and soon enough I knew several more ways that Uncle Lenny was different. The back porch had a washer and dryer in it, nothing special about that, and at first his kitchen wasn't too different, except there were dirty dishes stacked in the sink and crumbs all over the counter where his toaster was plugged in. But when he closed the door to the back porch, there was a big black and white picture of a man with a cigarette hanging down from his mouth, and he was looking right at me from the picture, and he had hair combed back like Uncle Lenny's. Uncle Lenny followed my eyes to that picture and he said, "James Dean, the greatest actor who ever lived."

We went into the dining room and there was another big black and white poster on the wall, a man with full lips and a look in his eyes that was far away and hurt, a look like La Herida de Amor. Uncle Lenny told me this was Montgomery Clift, and that he was another great actor, and not to listen to anyone who said different.

Instead of a buffet like Grandma had, or the china cabinet my parents had in their dining room, there was a strange boxy looking table on steel legs that I did not know the name of, so sheltered had been my life. It was tall and had a glass cover and at one end it had a picture of Daisy Mae from the L'il Abner comic in the Sunday paper, Daisy Mae with those long legs of hers and that blouse so full of her chest.

"You've never seen one of those, have you, Spud."

All I could do was shake my head no. The colors were bright, and as I got closer, I could see that the table had something like a game board on it, a 3-D kind of game board with mushroom-shaped pegs sticking up and pictures of Pappy Yokum and L'il Abner, and the whole table was slanted so the far end was higher than the near end.

"That's a pinball machine," Uncle Lenny said. "It's a game. Here, let me show you."

He reached underneath the table and then lights came on, and the machine made a sound like a doorbell, and the numbers next to Daisy Mae's head changed to all zeros. Big shiny steel balls popped up in a chute on one side. Uncle Lenny showed me how to shoot the steel balls up a long alley and how to use the flippers. He held the table in both hands so he could reach the buttons that controlled the flippers with those long fingers of his, and he played that table with his whole body leaning forward, bumping it with his hands so that it shook a little on those long steel legs, and getting that shiny steel ball to go back up the table with the flippers so he could score more points. He racked up a lot of points before the ball finally dropped down between the flippers and disappeared. He told me to go ahead and finish the game, and he showed me how to reach under the table to the button that made the steel balls come back for a new game.

"Have fun," he said. He went into another room and I heard him dial the phone. I shot a couple of pinballs while he talked on the phone and I scored a few points, but my balls went straight to the bottom and the machine said Game Over. I heard Uncle Lenny talking, and I knew he was talking to Grandma because what he said was, "Ma, I don't need your permission, just let me talk to Loretta." Loretta was my mother.

I could have reached under the table and pressed the button for a new game, but all I really wanted to do was listen. I could tell Grandma didn't want to hand the phone over to my mother because Uncle Lenny was saying things like, "I don't know why you're putting up such a fuss, Ma." He wasn't letting his voice get angry but he wasn't giving up either. I had never heard anyone talk about me like this, like I was someone to be argued over, but finally he must've gotten my mother on the phone, because he said "Hello Sis," and he said "yes" several times, and then he said, "I'll have him home by dinner time." I reached under the table then and pushed the button for more balls. I shot one pinball into the game and I fiddled with the flippers but I let the ball go through without even trying. Then Lenny said this:

"I may be the wild one, Sis, but I'm not the devil, okay?"

He listened on the phone for a minute, and then he laughed

and said goodbye. He came back into the dining room and he said, "Come on, Spud, we're going to a carnival."

THAT WAS THE SUMMER between sixth grade and junior high school, and in the fall, after the Dodgers swept the Yankees, President Kennedy was shot. In junior high school, I had Mr. Dermout for social studies, and Mr. Dermout was Dutch but not from Holland. Mr. Dermout grew up in Indonesia, and he was in a Japanese prisoner of war camp when he was a boy, and when he told us stories about growing up in Indonesia, he would pull down a map and show us where Indonesia was. The map was called A Simplified Map of the Real World, a map with different colors along each country's borders instead of just lines. Each country had only one city, or maybe two cities if it was a big country like the United States or China. Mr. Dermout always clicked his tongue when he pulled down that map, and one day when I asked him why, he said it was because the world was a complicated place, and we should have maps in our classroom that showed more.

There were no carnivals or amusement parks in the world that my parents had carefully constructed for me, no pinball machines or cotton candy, no bumper cars. There was school all week long and Church twice on Sunday, and there was the certainty of being a Latter-Day Saint and knowing God's plan and how to get to heaven. No one had tattoos and no one smoked. There were no loose cannons, which is what my father said about Lee Harvey Oswald, the man who shot JFK. Lee Harvey Oswald was a loose cannon, and Jack Ruby was an even bigger loose cannon, because when he shot Lee Harvey Oswald we were all of us watching it on television, and it was real, not something made up like *Peter Gunn* or *77 Sunset Strip*. My mother put her hand over my eyes, but I pulled away from her, and I watched, and though I had no words for it, I could feel then what Mr. Dermout meant when he said we needed better maps.

Riding in Uncle Lenny's Buick was like nothing I had ever done before. I got to sit in the front seat, which wasn't that unusual, but the car was so tall inside, and it had that same tobacco smell I remembered from that first time when I knew he smoked. Uncle Lenny drove with his window rolled down and his arm resting on the window opening, and before we left he took a pack of cigarettes out of his shirt pocket, and he shook the pack to make a cigarette pop up, and he stuck it between his lips.

"You don't mind if I smoke, do you, Spud?" he said. He waited for me to answer and I said no, because how could I mind when he was taking me to the carnival? We set off, driving down his long driveway, and I remember looking back at his front walk with those license plates lining both sides of it. I asked him if he had been in every one of those states.

"You bet I have, Spud," he said, "most of them more than once." He steered that big '39 Buick around with one hand on the steering wheel and his cigarette in the hand that rested on the open window. "It's a big world out there," he said. "You ought to go see it when you're older." He put his cigarette to his lips and drew the smoke in, and then he looked at me with those bright blue eyes of his, and even though he kept calling me Spud, he was talking with me like I was just someone he knew, instead of a little kid he was telling what to do.

"Look here, Spud," he said. "I don't want to tell you what to think, okay?"

"Yes," I said.

"Or what to believe," he said. He put a lot of weight on that word "believe" when he said it, and I knew then that what he meant was the whole Joseph Smith story about the Golden Plates and the Book of Mormon. He meant going to Church twice on Sunday and the Aaronic Priesthood and the Melchezidek Priesthood and the Word of Wisdom. He meant all the things that made our family different from other families that weren't in the Church.

He pointed his cigarette at me like he was a teacher with a piece of chalk in his hand, and he said, "You figure out for yourself what you believe, okay?" He put the cigarette to his lips and drew more smoke in then, and his lips got all squinched up like he had a bug in his mouth, and then he stubbed that cigarette out in his ashtray like he was squishing that bug. Smoke came out of his mouth.

"Just don't go taking up this tobacco habit," he said, "it ain't worth it. It's too damn hard to quit." He threw the cigarette butt out the window.

"Lecture's over," he said. "Let's go have some fun."

THE CARNIVAL WAS IN an amusement park all the way into Portland, and there was a ferris wheel and a roller coaster and a lot of other rides with names like The Octopus and The House of Thrills. Uncle Lenny said I could go on any of them I wanted but how about we start with the bumper cars. We walked by booths where you could shoot guns at targets that popped up or throw darts at balloons or try to knock down those steel milk bottles with a baseball. Uncle Lenny said not to waste our money on any of those, and he led me to a wooden building like a big shed that was open on one side like Grandpa's equipment shed. We got in line and watched while people drove their bumper cars around inside it. The only light was from the sun, but it was enough light to see how people were just crashing into each other with their bumper cars. Every so often some sparks would come from one of the poles that connected the bumper cars to the steel ceiling. There were kids out there and grown-ups too, and everybody was smiling and laughing and they went around and around this part in the middle that was like a low dock with old car tires at the ends to bounce off of.

When we got to the head of the line, Uncle Lenny nodded at the guy who ran the ride, and the guy nodded back like maybe they knew each other but maybe not, and then Uncle Lenny pushed his shirt sleeve all the way up so his shoulder showed. This was his other arm, not the scary arm, and his shoulder was white above the line where the sleeve of his T-shirt ended, and on that white skin he had a tattoo that I had never seen before. He showed it to me, and then he showed it to the guy who ran the ride, and that guy gave him a big grin. The tattoo was of a red bumper car with yellow lightning bolts coming off the top of the pole. Underneath the car it said "Born to Bump," and this was how much Uncle Lenny loved bumper cars, the way his face got all crinkly around the eyes when he showed me his tattoo, and him wanting to have that picture on his arm forever. Uncle Lenny leaned in and told the guy his name and said he was the one who'd rewired the main switchbox last year, and how was it working, and the guy waved us both through without taking the money Uncle Lenny held out to him.

Uncle Lenny laid his hands on my shoulders and guided me to a bumper car on the far side of the parlor. "It's just like the one in my barn," he said. "Just remember that if you steer the wheel too far, it'll be sideways and you won't go anywhere. But don't worry about it, you can't screw up out here."

No one in my family was allowed to say "screw" like that. I wasn't exactly sure why. No one had ever explained it to me back then, only that it was a vulgar word that shouldn't be used that way. The way Uncle Lenny said it, it didn't sound like a vulgar word, it just sounded like something to say that nobody should get too excited about. He got in the bumper car closest to mine and put his hands on the wheel, and then he got this grin on his face like he did when he showed me his Born to Bump tattoo.

When all the bumper cars had people in them, the guy who ran the ride told us all to go in the same direction and not to have head-on collisions. He reached down and pulled a brush out of a bucket, and he made a stripe of grease across the steel floor. Uncle Lenny leaned over and told me I should drive across that line of grease, it would make my car go faster. Then the guy who ran the ride stepped on a big button on the floor, and all the cars started up.

Uncle Lenny took off right away and got ahead of me. Somebody crashed into me from behind. I got pushed forward, and I had my foot down hard on the pedal that made the car go, and I crashed into a car in front of me. There was a girl in that car with long blond hair and braces and she gave me a great big grin and then crashed into somebody else. People were crashing all around us. I could see Uncle Lenny up ahead crash into the side of a bumper car that had a man in it, and they both just laughed. This was about the craziest thing I had ever done, smashing that bumper car around with all these other people who were doing the same, and everybody laughing and trying hard to hit each other. I got closer and closer to Uncle Lenny, bumping my way to his side, and when I hit him, it was full bore ahead and right into the side of his bumper car. I hit him hard enough to bump his car a good half a foot.

He looked at me with the whole wide world in those wild blue eyes of his, that grin of his spread all across his face, and he gave me a thumbs up.

I gave a double thumbs up right back at him.

I REMEMBER WATCHING A television show with my parents one night, maybe *The Ed Sullivan Show*, and this would have been the spring after the summer that Uncle Lenny took me to the bumper cars, and after President Kennedy was shot. A man came on in a suit that looked like a matador's suit because it had so many sparkles and sequins on it. He sat at a piano with a candelabra, and he played that piano like it was the whole orchestra and he was the conductor. My parents watched him play, and when he was done, he stood up and smiled this huge smile, and then he bowed from the waist. And then my father said something that I did not understand at the time, he said, "Talk about light in the loafers."

My mother laughed a little, a nervous kind of laugh, and I was looking at the television trying to see the man's shoes, to see where the lights were. Loafers I understood, because I had Florsheim loafers that I wore to Sunday School and I liked them because they slipped on and off so easy. But they never showed the man's legs while he stood there with this great big smile on his face, and then they went to a commercial.

And then my father said something that didn't seem to fit, something that made me pull my cheek in between my teeth. He said, "When's that brother of yours going to find himself a wife?"

My mother said nothing while the commercials ran. When the show started up again, and I thought maybe my mother wasn't even going to answer the question, like maybe she hadn't even heard my father say it, she said, "He just hasn't found the right girl yet."

My father looked at her over the tops of his glasses the way he looked at me when I forgot to take the garbage out. He said, "I don't think it's a matter of finding the right girl."

We watched the rest of the show, and my parents didn't say any more about Uncle Lenny or anything else. I went to bed after the show was over, but I heard them arguing later that night. It was scary hearing them argue because they never argued. The sound of them came up through the heater vent in my bedroom floor, and most of it was too soft to catch the words, but I heard my name and Uncle Lenny's name more than once, and it seemed strange to me that I was being argued over again, and that again I had no words to understand why.

The next morning my father told me at breakfast that we

weren't going to make the long drive to Grandma and Grandpa's that July, we were going to Disneyland instead.

I knew what Disneyland was, of course. We watched *The Wonderful World of Disney* on TV, and Disneyland was better than any carnival because it had all those cartoon characters walking around, and because my father told me it was. A whole wonderful world of fun was mapped out at Disneyland, and my father was taking us all there, and we would stay in a hotel right next to Disneyland and eat in restaurants all the time. The world was a big place, and we were going to see some of it.

It was years before I saw Uncle Lenny again.

Vortex

PICTURE AN EMPTY DUMP truck in a hay field, engine idling, and the hay field is filled with parked cars. It's late August, 1970, and Nixon is president. Half a million U.S. soldiers are in Vietnam, fighting a war they will not win. Four students have been killed by the National Guard the previous May at an anti-war demonstration at Kent State University. The hay field is in Oregon. The hay field is full of parked cars because fifty thousand people have shown up for the only state-sanctioned rock festival in the history of the United States.

All of this is true. The governor of Oregon, Tom McCall, has sanctioned the rock festival because the American Legion is holding its national convention twenty-five miles away, in Portland, and radical elements of the anti-war movement have promised to confront the American Legion in the streets. They are looking to even the score for Kent State, for Chicago, for the war and Nixon and his attack dog, Vice President Agnew, who will speak at the convention. They are looking for blood to repay a blood debt. McCall, even though he is facing an election in November, has the brilliance, the audacity, to perform an act of political jujitsu. He allows a small group of hippies to organize something they call Vortex, A Biodegradable Festival of Life, to draw off the crowds of hippies that the anti-war radicals want for their street protests.

All true. The dump truck is in the hay field to shuttle people from their parked cars to Vortex. The dump truck has been pressed into this kind of service because Vortex has been organized, just barely, in less than six weeks, and because it is already there, at the park. Most people get tired of waiting for shuttles, which are too few and too infrequent, and they walk in with their sleeping bags and their backpacks, but the people we are concerned with are among the lucky few who get a ride. They are thirty-nine-year-old Lenny Lingstrom, his nephew, Cal Rasmussen, who is nineteen, and Ruth Sauerberg, the twenty-one-year-old daughter of his neighbor and best friend, Gene Sauerberg. They are not hippies. Lenny and Ruth live across the road from each other, less than five miles from the park where Vortex takes place, so they are here as tourists in their own backyards, and Cal, who appeared on his uncle's doorstep the day before with a tale of woe, is along because he doesn't know where else to go. They climb into the back of the dump truck with their picnic basket, their cooler full of beer and soda pop, and their blankets for spreading on the ground.

The dump truck sits idling for a moment, but they are soon joined by a dozen or so hippies who have ridden out to Vortex in an old milk truck with faded lettering on the side that says Milk from Contented Cows. On the way out, they have smoked several joints and they have mooed contentedly and they have giggled until their cheeks hurt. They have drunk half of the contents of a jug of wine into which one of them has crumbled twenty hits of orange sunshine. None of them will remember much about this day when they are middle-aged except that they were here, and they got really, really high, and it was maybe the biggest, stoniest party they ever went to. They pile into the back of the dump truck and they see the three straights, Lenny and Cal and Ruth, and they smile at them. But they are thinking what are these people doing here? These tourists, these straights who wouldn't know the difference between macramé and macrobiotic, between window pane and Jefferson Airplane, between the Grateful Dead and the *Tibetan Book of the Dead*. They are on the bus, this dump truck is the bus, but are they really On the Bus?

They settle in, hippies and straights, everyone with their backs to the walls and their stuff in the middle, and the jug of wine is passed from hand to hand, some of the milk truck crowd taking big slugs of it, and some of them little sips, for they are old hands at this, and they know their limits. The jug is headed around the circle to Lenny Lingstrom, and some of the hippies are wondering if they should tell the straights what is in the wine, but when the jug reaches Lenny the dump truck revs its engine and they set off for Vortex. The engine noise is too loud to talk over, and so nothing is said as Lenny takes a swig off the jug. The wine is cheap and more than a little tart, and Lenny, who has always been a beer drinker, makes a face that gets the hippies all laughing at him. Lenny shrugs and smiles back at them, he knows he's made a funny face, and then he holds the jug out to Ruth, who shakes her head no, but she takes the wine jug and passes it to Cal.

Cal has never tasted wine. Cal is a Mormon and he has never tasted alcohol of any kind, nor has he smoked tobacco, nor had sex, beyond the hours he's spent making out with the two girls he went steady with in high school. He got to first base with one of the girls, or maybe it was second base, because the truth is, Cal's not really sure about that whole sex-as-baseball thing, he's never really cracked the code. He has shown up at his Uncle Lenny's because he thinks Lenny is the one person in his family who will understand, who will help him get out of the trouble he is in. He was supposed to leave for Provo, Utah, the next day, to study Portuguese, because he has been called to a mission in Brazil, but he has decided he cannot go. He's afraid this means he will not be with his family in heaven when he dies, so he's not ready to try his first taste of wine, not with the prospect of spending eternity in Outer Darkness staring him in the face. So he passes the jug to the hippie girl who is sitting next to him, who smiles at him and takes a slow sip. She passes the jug on, but all the while she is looking at Cal with a look that makes Cal wonder what the secret code for virgin is, and how she can read him with such ease. It is a look that makes his insides run hot and cold at the same time, and he looks away, and what he sees are Ruth's toes. Ruth is wearing flip-flops, and her toes are long in a way that makes him want to trace their length with his finger, and he is wondering what in the world he has gotten himself into.

The dump truck takes them down a long hill, and when it stops, they get out at the edge of a large meadow. There is a stage at the far end, and the meadow is filled with people who are standing, or sitting on blankets, or throwing frisbees, or batting beach balls around above their heads. Some people are sleeping in sleeping bags even though it is nearly noon and there is a loud buzz of laughter and talk. Someone is flying a kite that looks like a dragon. It's the politics of a day at the park instead of the politics of billy clubs and tear gas.

The hippies from the milk truck, all of them feeling the effects of the orange sunshine, get out and wander off like kittens who have just opened their eyes. High above them a jet plane crosses the sky, but they are too loopy to pay it any mind. The girl who sat next to Cal takes a long look at Lenny, wondering if she should say something to him about the wine, but she figures he didn't drink that much. He won't even notice, she thinks, the effect will be subliminal, and she will be right about that.

VICE-PRESIDENT SPIRO T. AGNEW, Ted to his friends, is in his private cabin aboard Air Force Two, with his wife, Judy, and they are minutes from landing when the pilot comes on the intercom.

"Sir, the park is below us, on the left side, next to the river."

The river flashes below them, and next to it are big splotches that look like some kind of mold. "My God," Judy says. "There must be a hundred thousand of them." The road out to the park is one long line of cars that stretches for miles. It doesn't appear to be moving at all.

Agnew was briefed the day before by his chief of staff, Stan. It was all McCall's doing. He'd met McCall at a governor's conference a few years before. Impressive man, steely eyes, and well over six feet tall. You had to hand it to him, he'd gotten all these miscreants to gather in one spot with this crazy idea, a spot far from where the radicals wanted them to be. There were National Guard troops stationed nearby, just in case trouble broke out.

"It's closer to forty thousand," Agnew says. Forty thousand spoiled brats who never had a good spanking when they needed it. "But don't worry about it, Stan says there's only one way in to that park. And one way out." That was the best part of McCall's plan. He'd picked the park for that very reason. If it came down to it, the National Guard would take the road and hold the bottleneck.

"Forty thousand," Judy says. "That's still a lot."

"They're nothing but a mob," Agnew says. "They're not even citizens, not in any real sense of the word." They didn't vote, didn't pay taxes, and you'd never get a campaign contribution out of a single one of them.

His wife continues to stare out the window. She's sitting across from him, facing the rear of the plane, her legs crossed neatly at the ankles. She reaches up and touches her hair, her fingers checking for any lock of it that might be out of place. She's good that way, careful that she always looks well put together. There are always photographers around, now that he's speaking his mind more, carrying the president's water.

"They're all on drugs, aren't they," she says.

Agnew nods. That's the part of McCall's plan that troubles him, letting the hippies get away with their drug use. Not a single cop in the crowd, not even a few undercovers to line up some arrests for later. He has his doubts about McCall. He's not sure McCall has the stomach to pull the trigger if it comes to it.

"For every one of them," Agnew says, "there are two parents back home who are our people. Part of the great silent majority, just as horrified as we are."

He looks out the window of the plane one last time. Nearly noon, local time, and they're hardly stirring at this hour. Worn out from their all-night drug party, they're as insignificant as an ant hill. Now would be the time. If they get out of hand, you crush them like bugs.

He would have to remember this. Not the kind of thing to put down in writing. But if the need arose, throw them a party and then come in with the troops. At dawn, when they're too groggy to resist. Arrest them, take them all out in one clean, surgical operation.

Six more years of shining Nixon's shoes. It will be different when it is his turn. Spiro T. Agnew has the stomach for it, by God. For that and more.

OUR THREE TOURISTS WORK their way along one side of the meadow, where it begins to slope up to form the bluff above, and this affords them a view of the mass of people who fill the great grassy space before them. They find a flat spot on the edge of the crowd, about halfway forward to the stage. The men spread the blankets, and Ruth opens up the picnic basket. She's made fried chicken and potato salad, her mother's recipes, and as she takes out the Tupperware containers, she remembers her mother lying in her bed at the end, her face the color of unbleached cotton.

She takes out the plates, speckled blue enamel camp plates that her mother's mother gave as a wedding gift, and she feels she's touching her mother when she touches them. She puts a chicken breast and a thigh on a plate for Lenny, and a leg and a wing for Cal, and a big scoop of potato salad for each of them. She's left plenty of chicken and potato salad at home for her father, and her younger sister, Mary, who is fourteen and who stayed behind only because their father insisted. How it pained her father to say no to Mary, she saw it in those sad old eyes of his, but he was doing his duty the way he thought best, doing what he believed the girls' mother would have done.

I have done what you asked, Ruth thinks, I have done my duty, I take care of him every day. Seven years since her mother died. Seven years that none of the words—daughter, sister, mother, wife—have quite fit the person she's been. She's kept house for her father, and mothered her sister, and she's never had much time for boys or friends. She fixes herself a plate, with a smaller scoop of potato salad, and the back of the chicken because it's the piece nobody else ever wants, and she takes a modest forkful of potato salad and lifts it to her mouth. The potatoes are perfect, not boiled, but steamed the way her mother taught her, and the dressing has just the right tang. Her mother would be proud.

"Looky there," says Lenny, and he points by tilting his head to one side. Here comes a hippie girl in a long skirt with a design straight off a flying carpet and threads of gold woven through it. She carries a parasol so old and of such delicate fabric it appears to be made of paper. Her hair is long and wavy and light brown, hanging well past her shoulders, and she wears nothing but the skirt and a pair of sandals with tire treads for soles, and there are her breasts, right out in the open, for all the world to see. Cal's mouth falls open, and Lenny is staring right at her as she walks up, and even Ruth is slow to take her eyes off her naked breasts. She stops right in front of them and shades her eyes, her back to them as she looks out across the crowd. Then she turns and faces them all. "What a fine, fine, super-fine day it is," she says, and her smile is broad and without a trace of irony, as if she is perfectly content to have them all look at her fine, fine, super-fine breasts, is that not, after all, what the gods made breasts for?

Ruth, brought up by her mother to always offer food to a stranger, to always do what will put people at their ease, says, "Would you like a piece of chicken?"

The hippie girl looks at Ruth, and she waves a lazy hand in the air, and on her thumb and on each of her fingers are rings of silver, as if she is some tribal princess from the deserts of far-away Araby. "Oh, no thank you," she says, "I'm a vegetarian," and then she turns, her skirt aswirl around her, and she strolls on, twirling her parasol. She is twenty feet away before it registers on Ruth that the woman has tufts of hair sticking out from under her armpits.

"Who'd a thunk," says Lenny, and he has that wry curl to his lips, so much in the world is funny to Lenny, but not in a way that makes him laugh. Ruth opens the cooler and gets out a beer for Lenny, and a root beer for Cal, and she has to nudge him with the soda can to pull his attention away from all that bare skin.

"It's not polite to stare," Ruth says, and she is smiling at Cal, but when his face turns red she says, "I'm sure she wouldn't walk around that way if she really cared." There is gratitude for more than the soda in the way Cal says thank you.

"Well," says Lenny, "I don't believe I've ever met a vegetarian before."

"Me neither," Cal says, and it's Cal who chortles first, but they are all laughing before they are done. Ruth allows herself a long look at Cal, at the way his eyes crinkle up when he laughs, and the slight upturn at the end of his nose, and how there's something elfin about that, as if he were capable of mischief, if only he knew it.

"She's right," Ruth says.

"How so?" says Lenny.

"This really is a fine day," Ruth says. "A super-fine day." Anything could happen here, Ruth is thinking, anything at all.

LENNY FEELS RESTLESS, NOT an unusual thing for him, but something he has learned to live with. He is a life-long bachelor, a man who spends his days tinkering with machines and his evenings reading *Popular Mechanics* and drinking beer. He has the lean body and the callused hands of a farmhand, although the only farming he does is to raise a single crop of oat hay each year that he sells to a racehorse breeder, and this makes him enough money to pay his mortgage for the year, and it makes him different from all the farmers around him, who grow grass hay because that's what they've always done. He lifts weights to keep the fat off, and in 1970, lifting weights is one more way that he is different. He has always been different, a little peculiar is the way his Ma put it. She defined him with that word "peculiar," and used it to keep from delving any further into the exact kind of peculiar that he was. He was still trying to sort out whether it was her not being able to name the kind of peculiar he was that made him such a loner, but he has always been someone who kept his feelings to himself. He has never said "I love you" to another human being, not because he hasn't felt love, but because the occasion has never arisen.

Ruth and Cal are chatting away about songs on the radio they like, and bands Lenny has never heard of. They're sniffing each other out like two dogs at a fire hydrant, he thinks, what a nice surprise that's turning out to be, and maybe just the ticket for Cal. They barely notice when he announces he's going out for a little ramble.

It's been seven years since he's seen Cal, except for a quick handshake at his Ma's funeral last fall. It was cruel what his sister had done, her and that scripture-quoting husband of hers, keeping Cal and him apart all those years. He could only guess what they said about him, their voices hushed, what ridiculous things they suspected. He might be peculiar, but he wasn't that kind of pervert. Never had been. He spent half a day with the boy, and it never crossed his mind to be anything but an uncle to him. Six brothers and sisters, and not a one of them had the decency to ever speak a word to him about it. It's how they all were, even Loretta, the boy's mother, he'd been closer to her than any of them when they were growing up, but the whole damn family never talked about anything that didn't have the church's official seal of approval.

He lit a cigarette and sucked the smoke in deep. At the funeral he could tell there was trouble brewing between Cal and his dad from the way Loretta told him that Cal was going to the state school instead of BYU. Cal's old man was a BYU man all the way, and he'd done a mission in Indonesia or some damn place, bringing that whole cockamamie Joseph Smith story to the heathens there. Golden Plates with sacred hieroglyphics, magic spectacles to translate them, and the resurrected Christ come to the new world to preach the gospel to the Indians, who weren't Indians at all but one of the lost tribes of Israel. What a crock. Loretta had those tight little wrinkles all around her lips, and even though she was smiling that dental hygienist of the year smile of hers when she said it, those wrinkles got tighter than a banty rooster's asshole when she talked about how well Cal was doing at the state school.

The whole family together at the funeral for the first time in all those years, and it wasn't the time to tell Loretta how wrong she was about him and the boy, not with Ma all laid out there in her casket. They'd done a nice job on her hair, but they'd put a shade of red on her lips she never would've wore when she was alive. He was never going to have to look into her eyes again and see her pretend she wasn't disappointed in how he turned out.

He didn't miss that, he surely didn't. She'd died last

November, sitting in front of the television watching the news. The doctors said it was a bad valve in her heart that killed her, but he knew different. It was the sixties that really did her in, what with the long hair and the drugs and the free love. Ma hated rock and roll, said The Beatles were the Antichrist, and she said the draft dodgers ought to be lined up and shot. Small wonder then, that the news she was watching when she died was all about how a hundred thousand radicals had marched on the Pentagon.

CAL AND RUTH SIT happily on their blanket, eating their fried chicken and potato salad, and watching the crowd in the meadow. All that wild hair on all those wild-looking people in the meadow, grown-ups with bottles of bubble soap blowing bubbles like kids on a summer day, and Ruth knows that funny-looking cigarette those people two blankets below them are passing around must be pot. The words sound funny in her head, pot, she says to herself, smoking pot, why is it called pot? She's never tried it, but from the looks of things, it does not turn a person into a slavering dope fiend on the spot, and who knows, today might be the day. There is something about this day, this boy Cal, this Vortex, that makes Ruth feel reckless, and when he starts wiping his hands free of the grease from the fried chicken, she reaches over and takes his hand. "Let me help you with that," she says, and at first she uses her own napkin to wipe his fingers clean, but the grease is sticky, and they have no water, so she pulls his finger to her mouth. His fingernail is clean and carefully trimmed, his finger is an irresistible morsel around which she wraps her lips, his firm first finger sliding easily between her soft lips, and she applies the slightest bit of suction to his finger as she pulls it back out of her mouth. For a moment they are both too surprised to move or to speak, and she thinks maybe she has ruined her chance with him.

"I'm shocked," he says, and his face is indeed wide-eyed

with shock, but his grin is wide under the upturned tip of his nose, and there is delight in his eyes. "Who are you?" he says, "and who taught you these strange manners?"

"I'm shocking," she says. "I'm Ruth Shocking Sauerberg," she says, laughing and giddy. "Pleased to meet you." She's not the least bit shy, for once in her life, and she takes his middle finger between her lips, watching his face this time, and he is watching his finger disappear between her lips, and as she sucks it into her mouth his eyes go cross-eyed, and that makes her laugh so hard she has to quickly pull his finger out of her mouth, and lie back on the blanket. He bends over her then, and she offers him her finger, still shiny with chicken grease, and he takes it into his mouth and sucks it clean.

"No one taught me," she says. "Do you think I'm awful?"

"Awfully nice," he says, "and that's awfully corny, isn't it, you must think I'm an awful idiot."

"Oh no," she says, and then they are quiet for a while, both of them wondering what you say after you've had someone's greasy chicken finger in your mouth. They stay that way, lying on their backs close enough to touch but not touching, the haze in the sky above them thinning as the day heats up. Ruth has her eyes closed, and the sun through her eyelids makes the world inside her head a fuzzy orange glow, and Cal shades his eyes with his hand because it gives his hand something to do besides ache with the need to touch her. A hawk floats across the sky, its wings still and its body held aloft by the warm cushion of wind, and Cal feels the earth spinning on its axis, how we are all held in place by gravity and will not go flying off.

LENNY IS OUT IN the middle of the crowd, and here they are, there must be twenty thousand hippies in this meadow, and all they're doing is having the best damn party of their lives. All around him people are talking and laughing, lying back and letting the sun soak in, kissing and holding hands. No crime in any of that, unless you want to get pissy about the people next to him who are passing a pipe around, and he knows from the greasy sweet smell what it is they're smoking. He'd tried it once, back when he traveled the carnival circuit and it took him through Tucson, where a bunch of them went out in the desert in an old pickup truck. They built a fire and passed a bottle of mescal around, fire water made from cactus juice, and one of the crew brought out a couple of marijuana joints and passed them around too. It made his head buzz from the inside out, and his skin felt like it had so many nerves in it he could feel the weave of the cotton in his undershorts. He'd gone off after that with one of the men into a little arroyo away from the others, and they looked up into the Milky Way, and got so lost out there amongst the stars that the earth where they were fell right away. The man's rough callused fingers touching him as soft as a kitten's tongue tracing the curve of his ear, and Lenny's lips found the other man's, and in that arroyo they'd given each other a little of what they could never get from a woman.

The smell of marijuana is all around him in the meadow, and it isn't long before someone passes him one of their marijuana joints. He's far enough away from the blanket where he's left Ruth and Cal that he takes a puff before he passes it on. He walks on, and pretty soon a beach ball floats down out of the sky in front of him, and he gives it a whack that sends it spinning back up into the air, where it catches a little breath of wind and takes off on its own crazy course until it floats down again and someone else bats it on. His head feels as light as that beach ball. Every here and there is a woman with her top off, soaking up the sunshine. He feels the part of him he calls his motor revving up, but it's not the bare-breasted hippie girls that run his engine hot. What has his motor revved are all the long-haired men in the crowd with their shirts off.

Their lean young bodies draw him on, the rosy circles of their nipples aglow in the sunlight. There is a shimmering quality to the sunlight that is burning through the haze above, an aura of rainbow-hued brightness surrounding everything he sees. Their white skin is luminous. Their lean and muscled bodies bend and stretch, and he wants to touch them, all that bare skin calls to him the way a magnet calls to steel. Their lips are apple-red and delicious to the eye, their faces are framed with hair that hangs long and straight or erupts in wild curls. There are thousands of them, and they are Buffalo Bill Cody on horseback, Grecian athletes on the side of a vase, Marlon Brando on a motorcycle, James Dean racing to the edge of a cliff.

Lenny walks among them with mirrored-lens sunglasses hiding his own peculiar hunger. He wears a cowboy shirt in a light blue plaid, snaps instead of buttons, the shirtsleeves rolled back. He has a tattoo on his forearm, a heart with a dagger pierced through it, and the words La Herida de Amor on a blood-red ribbon below. His hair is short and he has a farmer's tan underneath his shirt, his arms browned up past the elbow and a yoke of color at the front of his neck, but the rest of him is palest white, and he is sure if he took his shirt off, they would laugh at him for being a hick.

A frisbee comes sailing right at him, and he catches it with one hand, and there, fifty feet away on the edge of the crowd, a man with the wild curls of Harpo Marx and a red bandanna around his neck is waving at him with both arms, yelling, "Here man, throw it here."

Lenny throws the frisbee, something he hasn't done in a dozen years or more, but that quick flick is there in his wrist, never forgotten, and the frisbee sails true, all the way back to Harpo with a red bandanna, who catches and yells a sound that is pure joy. And Lenny is part of it now, a stranger, true, and yes this is a strange party, but he is not in a strange land, this is his piece of the country, by God, and he belongs here simply because he is here, and not hiding back at his house with a loaded shotgun waiting for some hippie to try to steal his tomatoes.

Not hiding the way his best friend Gene is, scared by the rumors their neighbors are spreading, that after Woodstock the hens way out in New York laid rotten eggs and the cows gave milk that smelled of patchouli oil. That the men have fleas and carry foul diseases and will carry off their daughters like gypsies, that Vortex is the governor's very own Pot Party & Naked Orgy, it is Sodom and Gomorrah come right here to Renata, and anyone who set foot near it was going straight to Hell, do not pass Go and do not collect your federal crop subsidy check on your way out of town.

Lenny reaches the edge of the meadow, where a broad path leads down to the river, and people are coming and going. He follows them into the trees, and in the shade there he takes off his sunglasses. Here, along the edge of the path are young men sitting on blankets, a long ragged row of them on either side. "Mescaline," they say, "Owsley," they say, "Double dome grape barrels." Lenny doesn't know exactly what all the words mean, but he knows, from the evenings he's cruised through Washington Park, they are selling drugs that will let loose in the mind a tornado that carries you all the way to Oz, as long as you survive the trip without having a house land on you. Only here it's not like in the park, where the men say the words out of the sides of their mouths as they pass by. Here they're doing it right out in the open, and as he goes deeper into the woods Lenny thinks what would that be like, to feel safe enough to be seen, to not have to pretend.

RUTH PULLS A COUPLE of Cokes out of the cooler, and when she offers one to Cal, he hesitates. Coca-Cola has caffeine in it, and is forbidden by the Word of Wisdom, and he has not yet missed the deadline. If he left now he could still get back home in time to catch the plane to Utah. His father would give him the worst talking-to of all time, and he would have to face the great devouring brown-eyed maw of his mother's disappointment.

He could do that, he supposes, but the Elders will be watching him so closely to see if he is still worthy, he will have to be so perfect in his every thought and every act to prove he isn't going to slip up again. What a long, tedious, holier-than-holy slog his life will be if he goes back now.

Ruth takes his hesitation as a silent request for another beverage choice. "Would you rather have a beer?" she says. "I'm sure Lenny wouldn't mind."

"Good heavens no," Cal says, "I can't have a beer." From the brief look of hurt that crosses her face he knows he's said it too harshly, and without even thinking he has launched into it, his whole long tale of woe, beginning with how sorry he is to have spoken that way, and then moving on to what it means to grow up in the Mormon church, to be a Latter-Day Saint, and all about the Word of Wisdom. And then he tells her about Joseph Smith and the Golden Plates, and how he has believed this story his whole life, but now, the more he thinks about it, how no one ever saw the Golden Plates but Smith himself, how Smith set himself up in a wagon with a curtain drawn across the middle, and dictated his translation of the Plates to Oliver Cowdrey and Martin Harris, and then buried the Plates again in the Hill Commorah, and it all seems so convenient, and what does she think, because the Book of Mormon does exist, you can't deny that, and is it any less fantastic to think that a boy of seventeen with no education to speak of really made up the whole thing?

"I have to figure this out," he tells her, "because I'm supposed to go to Brazil and convert people, and how can I convert people to something if I'm not even sure it's true?"

She's a little frightened by all this, not what he says so much, but the way he says it, like it's all a matter of life and death. But there's something about all the heat he puts into it that leads her to want to calm him, to lay his head in her lap, and she strokes his brow until he talks himself out. He talks on and on for a long time, such a rush of words spilling out of him, and it makes the world around them fall away, until the crowd of people around them are nothing but background noise. And all the while she soothes his fevered brow with the soft touch of her fingers. When he finally stops, when the great boil of his religious dilemma has subsided, she stands up. She puts her hand out to him.

"Come on," she says, "let's go for a walk."

WHEN LENNY EMERGES FROM the woods, he is near the river, and there are teepees and tents scattered here and there in another, smaller meadow, and a circle of drummers pounding out a primal beat. Half-naked children who've never had haircuts are running around in packs. Everyone is smiling, and as he works his way down to the river he sees a man leaning against a tree. And wonder of wonders, this man is not a hippie, but a tall lanky man with short hair, dressed in blue jeans and a shirt with the sleeves rolled back. He has the thick-muscled forearms of a man who works with hand tools. Motorcycle boots just like the ones Lenny has on his feet, his blue jean cuffs rolled just so, and at the distance of twenty paces, it's almost like Lenny is looking in a mirror.

If we cared to investigate this tall lanky man, we would discover him to be a pilot, a crop duster from the wheat country east of the mountains. He's always had a wild streak in him, and just a few months ago, when a fellow he knew in high school, one of the boys who went off to Vietnam and came back a whole lot crazier than he was before, when that fellow offered him fifteen thousand dollars to fly an airplane full of marijuana fifty feet off the ground through an arroyo on the Mexican border, the tall lanky man said, "I'm your guy." That same wild streak has brought him to Vortex, looking for something that is hard to find in the wheat country. The man's fingers give Lenny a come-hither, as if he's been there waiting for him, and he puts a hand rolled cigarette to his lips and lights it with a shiny Zippo.

"Have some of this," he says, and there is that greasy sweet smell again.

"Well, well," says Lenny, "a marijuana joint," and this makes the man smile at Lenny, what a funny way to say it.

"I do believe," says Lenny, "this is the very thing that Ma warned me about," and he takes the joint and sucks down hard on it. Take that Ma, I am here on God's green earth with ten thousand freaks and there ain't a goddamn thing you can do about it because you are gone mama gone, all the way gone. Take that Loretta, your darling boy Cal has come to me with his troubles, and he's got no more use at all for your wacky cult religion, and I will show him how a man can live his life without it.

They smoke the marijuana joint together, and they watch the people drift by, and it is not long before Lenny knows that this man is peculiar the way he is peculiar, because when a hippie man comes strolling up the path from the river totally buck naked, with mud smeared on his legs and his chest, they are both staring at his privates, swinging there between his legs for anyone to see. They are both staring, and they both catch each other staring, and when his new friend says, "My my, full frontal nudity, what a treat that is," they both know.

"I'm Luke," his new friend says, and when they shake hands they're in no hurry to let go. Soap bubbles keep floating by with little patches of fractured light captured in them. The path from the river produces more naked people, hippie chicks with muddy breasts and hippie men with muddy asses. A pregnant hippie has mud all over her bulging belly, and like all of them she seems to have faint traces of rainbow light streaming behind her, although when Lenny tries to look straight at it, the rainbow streams disappear. Luke pulls another marijuana joint out of his shirt pocket, and he waves it back and forth at one of the naked hippie men, who comes over with his hair in a wild tangle on both sides of the big grin on his face.

"Have some of this, brother," Luke says, "and tell us what the deal is with all you naked people and all that mud."

They share the marijuana joint, and now Lenny's head is buzzing from the inside out like a thousand beehives, and his grinning mouth is stretched so wide his cheeks hurt. But when they are done they follow the hippie man's beautiful muddy ass to the most righteous mud bath, down that trail and off to the left, with a mud slide right into the river, and all the way there Lenny and Luke are shedding their clothes and letting that fine, fine, super-fine sunshine soak right into their skin.

BACK IN PORTLAND THE Legionnaires are gathered in a huge auditorium, and Vice President Spiro T. Agnew stands before the cheering crowd, giving them exactly what they want. He grips the podium with both hands and leans into the crowd. "This government," he says, "this country, backed by the stalwart soldiers of the armed forces of the United States, will win the war in Vietnam." The Legionnaires' response is raucous, this is what they came for, to hear a government leader tell them that the country they fought for in World War II is still the home of the brave and the land of the free. This, and the free booze. It wouldn't be an American Legion convention without a boatload of free booze. They clap their hands together for Agnew, for the blood their soldier brethren bled, for the greatest goddamn country on earth, for the sheer joy of filling that big hall with their own big noise. For Spiro T. Agnew the sound of their clapping hands is the warm wind of political grace lifting him toward the presidency in 1976. Six more years of this vice-president crap, and then the country's his.

The best lines in the whole speech are the next ones. "America will never back down," he says, "to a godless gaggle of conniving communists." Alliteration, he thinks, who'd have thought a cheap trick like that was the key to success. He raises his hand and points a precise finger at the streets outside. "No picayune pack of puerile protesters," he says, and he pauses as the Legionnaires rise to their feet, for drunk though they are, they still know that alliteration is their cue. "No picayune pack of puerile protesters," he repeats, poking the air with his precise finger on each of the p's, "will sway the president from proudly prosecuting the war as he sees fit." He waits while the Legionnaires applaud, and yes, thunderous is the right word, cliched though it might be, and as he bathes his ambition in that warm sound he is thinking this: if only you could see me now, Ma, they love me. God how they love me, and if a graceless, power-grubbing shlub like Nixon can get himself elected, then I'm going to take this country as sure as there's bulletproof glass on the president's limousine. Ma, I'm going to do you proud.

As THE AFTERNOON WEARS on, Cal and Ruth are out in the middle of the meadow, and a band mounts the stage and starts into a long lazy blues jam. The crowd rises to its feet, and there is a general movement toward the stage, and in the push of people Cal is separated from Ruth. He turns and looks for her, and she is there, her sweet smile finding him from a few feet away. He reaches his hand out as they work their way back to each other, and she takes his hand with hers, and it is a long time before they let go.

Vortex is a circus happening all around them, a carnival, a mardi gras of laughing freaks and dancing folk. The band is picking up speed now, the bass walking a bluesy figure down the scale, an electric guitar solo soaring out over their heads, and underneath is the rhythmic thump and crash of drums and cymbals. They amble through the crowd hand in hand, weaving their way through the meadow, and she is leading him to the stage, where people are packed in closer and everyone is dancing. He is talked out, and she has no answers for him but the comfort of her touch, her fingers clasping his, and when they can go no closer to the stage without pushing, she lets go of his hand and faces him, and she lets her body begin to sway to the music. He is shy at first, shuffling his weight from one foot to the other, but Ruth closes her eyes and gives herself up to the beat. This is her day to set aside her duties. A sinuosity overtakes her, her shoulders and hips moving in counterpoint, her arms undulating, and this is the dance she has done alone in her room, after her father and sister are asleep, her record player turned down low so as not to wake them, one of the only pleasures she has allowed herself all these years since her mother died.

Watching her Cal is struck by how her face, too long and narrow to be pretty, is aglow with the afternoon light, the face of someone carried away from this world of striving and woe. He wants to feel what she is feeling, and the music works its magic on him, he feels the blues of his own life, the sorrow of being a disappointment to his parents, and the sacrifice of all the wicked fun he has given up to be a Latter-Day Saint. The pulse of it moves his hips, and he raises his arms and he lets his head drop back. He faces the heavens above, and he knows then. Forget Provo, forget going on a mission, forget doing all the things his parents want him to do. He will dance with this girl, he will grow his hair out, he will ask his Uncle Lenny if he can stay on a while. It is his life to live.

He's not here on this earth to convert the heathens. He's here to become one.

THE MUD BATH IS a tent rigged out of clear plastic with a lot of naked hippies packed into it, and a lot of talk about the world they see coming, a world of peace, of living off the land, of barter instead of money. Lenny and Luke are next to each other, thigh to naked thigh, and it is here that Luke asks about Lenny's tattoos.

"I know 'Amor' means love," Luke says, "but what's 'Herida'?"

"'Herida' is wound," says Lenny, and they are so close to

each other their lips could meet if only they leaned forward a bit. No one is paying them any mind, but Vortex, even with all that pot and all those naked hippies running around, even with all those folks tripping on psychedelics with the power to turn grown men into babbling babies, Vortex is not an orgy, and most definitely not a place where a man can kiss a man in public.

"The wound of love," Luke says, "don't I know it." The wound of love is in his eyes for Lenny to see, that same hurt look he's caught reflecting back at himself in a store window after some nameless encounter in the laurel hedge up at Washington Park. Luke touches the tattoo high on the shoulder of Lenny's other arm, tracing the outline with his fingertip.

"This is what?" he says. "A bumper car?"

The feel of Luke's fingertip on his shoulder is about to rev his motor to a level that will get them in trouble, so Lenny shifts over a little, breaking the contact. He lets his eyes drop to his crotch and then rise back up to Luke's, so that Luke will know why.

"I ran away with the carnival," says Lenny, "back when I was a kid. Worked my way up from roustabout to mechanic. When one of them carnival rides breaks down bad enough, I'm the guy they call."

The hurt in Luke's eyes has given way to something else, something playful, and this is the best part, Lenny thinks, the flirting, because what comes after is never enough. All he really wants is to take Luke home with him, to slip between the sheets of his own bed with this man, something he has never in his life done.

"I'm a pilot," Luke says. "I like working on my own airplane."

He's not just good-looking, Lenny thinks, he's a fellow with some wit. "I like working on my own machinery too, but I like it even better when I can get me some help."

"Is there someplace we can go?"

God, the impossibility of it all. If Cal hadn't showed up

when he did, they could just leave and go back to his place. "Not during the daylight," says Lenny, "there's too many people around."

"How long till dark do you figure?"

"Too damn long."

It's well past dark by the time they make it back to the blanket. Ruth and Cal aren't there, but the cooler and the picnic basket are right where they left them. Lenny pulls a couple of bottles out of the cooler.

"You want a beer?" he says to Luke. They're both sunburnt from walking around naked in all that super-fine sunshine. They spent a long time in the mud bath, but when they got tired of waiting for the sun to go down, they slid down a muddy chute into the cold river. The shock of the water was like the shock of the kiss they shared later, walking back through the woods in the dark. They might have gotten farther than that kiss if someone hadn't come crashing through the woods near them, babbling like a baby. Lenny wanted more, and at the same time he wanted to wait, to stretch this out, because this was different. They knew each other's names.

Luke holds his beer against his forehead, using the ice-chilled glass to cool himself down. "You ever think you'd be a nudist for a day?" he says. "That was wild, man, just wild."

"I never," says Lenny. "Not in a million years." They clink their bottles together. "To Vortex," says Lenny.

"To Vortex," says Luke. "I never had a sunburn feel so good."

They settle themselves on the blanket and look out over the crowd. There's a band on stage, and people dancing in a big dark mass, but further back it's all people standing or sitting around. There's a lot of whooping going on, a lot of partying. On the way through the crowd they couldn't get ten feet without somebody offering them a pull on a wine jug, or a pipe, or a marijuana joint.

"Lenny," Luke says, "I'm dizzy. I need to lay down."

"Go right ahead," Lenny says, and Luke stretches out on his back with his head in Lenny's lap. It's dark enough that no one is paying them any mind at all, and Lenny lets his fingers stroke Luke's forehead, to soothe his fevered brow. His fingers drift down across Luke's cheek, and he traces the outline of his lips.

"What are we going to do?" says Lenny.

"I don't know." Luke's voice is lazy, as if they have all the time in the world. "My truck's parked up there in one of those hay fields. I got a sleeping bag."

Not at all what Lenny had in mind. He sees Ruth and Cal then, making their way back to the blanket. It's dark, but he's sure it's Ruth, with Cal trailing behind her. He pulls his hand back from Luke's face, and Luke says, "What is it?"

"My nephew, and my neighbor, the people I told you I came with."

Luke sits up, and they are side by side, their hands almost touching. Lenny feels their whole day together fall away from them. They were so brave, walking around naked together, letting the backs of their hands brush each other. In the mud bath there was a moment when Lenny had his head leaned on Luke's shoulder.

To not have to pretend. Luke straightens, his back rigid. "Relax," Lenny says. "You're just somebody I met in the crowd."

Luke gives him a sidelong look. "You ever done this before? Introduce somebody like me to somebody who knows you?"

Lenny lets his little finger slide over on the blanket until it touches Luke's hand. One little stroke in the dark, nothing anybody can see.

"No," Lenny says, "but we just might have to do something about that." His Ma was dead, and he was sorry she had to die for this to happen. But she had taken her peculiar definition of him with her to the grave, and he was not sorry for that. "There's a first time for everything," Lenny says.

For just a moment before Ruth says hello to them, he feels Luke's little finger hook together with his. She was a good woman, Ruth was. Maybe she would keep his secret. Maybe she could help him explain it to Cal.

Anything was possible. Anything at all.

Trish the Freaking Dish

PATRICIA EVANS WAS FIFTY-SIX, and she had never been in a protest before, but this new minister, Pastor Flint, he made it feel so important. Those lovely blue eyes of his held the clarity of someone sanctified, even from across the room, and the very idea of a Saturday workshop on the American Holocaust, well, it was pretty thrilling. She would be an instrument of God's will, they all would.

Pastor Flint's handwriting on the white board was bold and vigorous, and his fingers flew as he wrote down the terrible statistics. Forty-five million abortions since 1973, and ninety-nine percent of them done for the mother's convenience. Forty-four hundred abortions a day, and each one of them a murder. Pastor Flint stood front and center before them, and he looked each one of them right in the eye. A shiver ran up Patricia's spine when his eyes fell on her. She took her husband, Rick, by the hand. She wanted him to feel her excitement too.

"These so-called doctors are getting rich to the tune of seven hundred million dollars a year," Pastor Flint said. He spoke without notes, the man obviously lived and breathed his subject. "They are protecting wicked old men who prey upon young girls, who seduce them into the sin of fornication, who get them pregnant and then bring them down to the killing clinics where they can pay to have their sins covered up."

She gave Rick's hand a squeeze, and when he looked at her, she pointed at Pastor Flint with her eyebrows. Look at how tall and straight this man of God stands. What a ramrod of the Lord he is.

"The clinics keep their secrets for them, breaking not only God's law, but the state laws about reporting statutory rapes. These are secularists," oh, how clearly Pastor Flint pronounced that difficult word, "yet they don't even obey their own secular law. They do this because they're greedy, and those wicked old men are only too happy to pay them so they can go on sinning." Such a command of the facts. Here was a man who could stand and deliver.

They made signs. There were twelve of them—the number was a sign of the Lord's favor, Pastor Flint said—twelve who volunteered to join the protest, and they gathered at the tables at the back of the Sunday School classroom. The very next day, after church, they would stand together on the streets of Renata, and they would let everyone know that these were Christians who stood shoulder to shoulder against the sin of abortion. Rick was busy writing "Abortion Is Mean" on his sign. Patricia looked at the white board, where all the slogans were written, and she wrote "Abortion Is Murder" on her sign. But then a voice in her head said words that were better than Rick's. Better than anything on the white board. Words from God that said it best for her.

She took another piece of card stock and wrote on it. Then she stapled both pieces of card stock to her stick. She held her sign up for Pastor Flint to see, and she flipped it around so he could see both sides. His smile when he saw her sign was full of promise. Pastor Flint knew her in ways that old Pastor Selfridge never had. Her sins were forgiven in that smile, especially the sins of her wicked youth. Yes, she and Rick had engaged in the sin of pre-marital relations. Her mother had gotten her the birth control pills, and she had been weak enough to take advantage of them. And not just with Rick. There had been two others with whom she shared her favors, just to spice things up. Well, three if you counted what she and that boy did in the closet of the choir room without even taking their robes off. She never got caught, although Rick had been suspicious. But that was all a long time ago, and she knew when she told Pastor Flint all of her sordid past, they would kneel and pray together, and she would be washed clean.

He held her gaze from across the room, the very air between them crackling with the presence of the Holy Spirit. When Pastor Flint put his hands together palm to palm and raised his eyes to heaven, Patricia joined him in a brief moment of silent prayer. He crossed the room and took her sign in his hands. "Patricia," he said, "you are bold in the service of the Lord. The minions of Satan will sit up and take note when they see this sign."

He held the sign up for everyone to see. Everyone was nodding their heads at her, and they began to clap their hands together in praise. She was bold in the Lord's service. Even Rick was impressed. She leaned in close enough so that Pastor Flint could hear her above the noise of the applause.

"Call me Patty," she said.

"Patty," Pastor Flint said, just for her to hear, "this is a very strong message. Let me give you one bit of counsel. We can hate the sin, but we must never hate the sinner."

Her heart was filled with the Holy Spirit. What a man of God Pastor Flint was, he could see right into her. He was much younger than Pastor Selfridge, but he held the wisdom of the ages in his gaze. His breath was minty, and clean-smelling, and he saw that the distinction between sin and sinner often escaped her.

He was there for her. She would follow him anywhere. They had declared war on the Evil of Abortion.

RUTH SAUERBERG SAT ON her deck with the Sunday paper spread around her, and her second cup of coffee steaming on the arm of her chair. One of her cats lay purring in her lap. The crossword was finished, and soon she would drive down to the Shop 'n' Save for her weekly grocery run.

There were puffs of clouds in the air that morning, hanging low over the foothills of the mountains. There were clefts in the foothills that held them like a baby nestled into a green bosom. All that vibrant green of the forested hills, it never failed to make her happy. She'd bought this house on the edge of the bluffs for the view. The town of Renata sat where the river came sweeping out of its canyon in a big bend, and the valley widened out into farmland. All the old part of Renata was wedged between the bluffs and that bend in the river, a neat grid with half a dozen streets running each way. It was a quiet place most of the time, especially on a Sunday morning, when everybody was either lazing about like her or gone to church.

A line of six or seven cars appeared below her, on Broadway. They came from up here on the bluff, from the neighborhood behind her where the schools and all the churches were. At first Ruth thought it must be a funeral because they had their headlights on, but then they all angled in and parked between Third and Fourth, and they got out of their cars, and they were carrying signs. They spread out in a line in front of the bank, situated so that if you were going to go to the Shop 'n' Save you were going to have to drive right by them.

It wasn't the first time they'd had protesters in Renata. Renata might be a small town, but it was no different than anyplace else these days. They had their peace rallies, and the Support Our Troops folks all wore red T-shirts on Fridays. Back in the eighties environmentalists faced off against loggers. This bunch was probably the Support Our Troops crowd, because the peace activists mostly drove hybrids, or Subarus like Ruth, and these people were all in minivans and SUVs.

Ruth put her binoculars to her eyes, but the signs were too far away to read. At fifty-five, her eyes weren't what they used to be. She'd get a good look at them when she went down the hill to do her shopping.

THE FIRST THREE SIGNS said "Lord Forgive Us And Our Nation," "Jesus Forgives And Heals," and "Adoption, The Loving Option."

"Oh my God," Ruth said. She sank back in her seat, a little less eager to be seen gawking at them, and she hit the buttons to roll up her windows.

An anti-abortion protest, that would stir things up. There'd never been one of those in Renata. And it was a little odd—who were they trying to reach? It wasn't like you could get an abortion here.

It would be easier if they were outsiders, because then you could ignore them and maybe they'd go away. But it was Burdine Lopate from the phone company, and Ron Machado who drove a propane delivery truck, and Tim McIlvoy who taught history up at the high school. There was a young man she didn't recognize in a white shirt and red tie, holding a sign that said "I Survived The American Holocaust." He stood with his head bowed, as if he were praying. What a crock, a public display to try to shame folks into seeing things his way.

The last two people in the line were the Evanses, Rick and Trish, still a couple thirty-five years after high school. Cheerleaders for the narrow-minded, they were whispering to each other and waving their signs like this was a big sale or one of those fund-raising car washes. Ruth pulled up to the stop sign and Trish looked right into Ruth's car and thrust her sign forward. The look on her face is so hateful it's like she's caught a cannibal dumpster-diving behind an abortion clinic.

Her sign says "Abortion Is Murder." Then she flips her sign around, and the other side says "Friends Don't Let Friends Have Abortions."

And now you get it. You had an abortion once, and Trish the Freaking Dish is the only person on God's green earth who knows about it. This is about you.

RUTH TURNED THE CORNER and pulled into the Shop 'n' Save lot. That sign had sent her over a cliff. Thirty-four, no thirty-five, years ago she had met a boy at that rock festival at McIver Park. Cal Rasmussen, he was Lenny Lingstrom's nephew. A sweet boy, but all mixed up about his religion. They went out for a few weeks. She'd given him a copy of *On the Road*, and he took off hitchhiking before they could admit to each other that maybe they were falling in love. She found out she was pregnant a couple of weeks after he left. He would have come back if she'd had a way to find him. He was that kind of boy.

But she didn't really want him to come back. He wasn't ready to be a father, any more than she was ready to be a mother. She'd moped around for a few days, scared, her mother long dead and her sister too young to help. She was twenty-one, a grown-up, but she still couldn't bring herself to tell her father what she'd gone and done. And then she ran into Trish the Dish at Sluggo's, the drive-in.

All through high school everybody knew Trish was doing it with Rick Evans. She used to brag about how she was on the pill and she could screw all she wanted and never get caught. So it was Trish she went to, and Trish who knew somebody who knew somebody, and that was how she ended up thirty miles away in the city, in a medical clinic in a downtown building on a Friday evening, having an after-hours abortion.

And now, here was Trish the Dish all grown up, and all these years later she was outing Ruth. And she calls herself a Christian. What a crock.

THIS WAS SO EXCITING. All these cars driving by. Patty loved it when they honked their horns. Rick was on one side, and Pastor Flint was on the other. She loved it when they did things together, like waving their signs in unison, or this thing that Pastor Flint came up with, where they bent their knees, and held their signs out to the left as a car approached and then slowly swept them to the right as the car went by.

Some people tried to ignore them, and this bothered her. Their message was so important, didn't everyone understand that millions of lives had already been lost, and millions more were at stake? They had to try and reach everyone.

"We'll pray for them," Pastor Flint said. "Right here, on the sidewalk." He bowed his head, still holding his sign, but he stood in silent prayer. This was wonderful. Patty saw how one of the people in the next car gave Pastor Flint the sign language for "I love you." Surely that was a sign from God.

"Rick, let's pray with Pastor Flint," she said. Her arms were getting tired from all the sign-waving. Rick looked at her sideways the way he did sometimes when he was perturbed with her. What was it this time? Surely he wasn't still mad at her about the chicken enchilada casserole she fixed for Pastor Flint. What was the man supposed to do, take a break from saving the lives of the unborn so he could cook? It wasn't her fault he was good-looking and single.

"Yes," Rick said, "let's pray." He was talking out of the side of his mouth in a voice low enough that Pastor Flint couldn't hear. "Let's pray that you don't forget who the number one man in your life is."

"You mean Jesus?" Patty said. Oh, gosh, had she really said that out loud? Rick turned and waved his sign right at her, his face meaner than any abortion ever was. They had been married such a long time. He had absolutely no sense of humor these days, and she was sick and tired of his petty jealousy. She could not help it if she was still attractive, that was one of the Lord's blessings to her, and it wasn't her fault that Rick had let his belly get so big. He could sleep on the couch tonight, it would serve him right.

A green Subaru station wagon drove by just then. What was it with those people? The people who drove Subarus now all drove hippie buses in the sixties. They were the pot-smokers and the left-wingers who think the war is a big mistake and that killing babies is just fine. She would show this one what God's wrath looked like. She made her face as mean as Rick's had been, and she thrust her sign out.

Take that, ye minion of Satan.

THEY RAN INTO EACH other in front of the video store a week and a half later, after the second Sunday of the anti-abortion protest. Ruth was coming out with a subtitled Italian film that had recently won the Palme d'Or at Cannes, and Patty was going in to return a copy of *The Passion of the Christ*.

"Oh, hi," Patty said. They went to high school together, now what was her name? "It's been ages. How have you been?"

The smell of Trish's perfume was so sweet it made Ruth's wisdom teeth ache. And she was so perky, the two-faced bitch. She had the look of a real estate agent trolling for referrals. Her hair was fluffed and sprayed into a mass of curls that framed her face, and her nails were painted to match her lipstick. She wore a gray pantsuit with a subtle stripe in a lighter gray.

"I'm fine," Ruth said, "never better."

"Me too," Trish said. She held up that stupid movie with both hands like she was selling a box of cereal. "We've just had a showing of this at our church, have you seen it?"

Ruth shook her head no. How could this woman pretend like nothing had happened?

"We have this wonderful new pastor," Trish said, "Pastor Flint. He's full of energy. That's him over there in my car. I'm giving him a ride home."

Pastor Flint smiled at them and gave a little wave of his hand. Mr. I-Survived-The-American-Holocaust in his starched white shirt and red tie. And now the two of them were conspiring against her. This was really unbearable, the way the two of them were acting so innocent.

"Didn't I see you both in front of the bank on Sunday?" Ruth said.

Trish's curls bounced as she nodded her head in a vigorous yes. A sweaty Jesus, his eyes raised to heaven, stared back at Ruth from the movie case in Trish's hands. "Pastor Flint is here to help us restore Christian values. We have to let people know that abortion is a sin."

A sin. If abortion is a sin, if abortion is murder, then no doubt driving a friend to have an abortion must make Trish an accessory. Hypocrites. Why couldn't they let the past alone?

"Where did you come up with that slogan on your sign?" she said. It was probably this new pastor who came up with it. Trish wasn't that smart.

"Oh, it just came to me," Trish said. "The Lord works in mysterious ways." Mysterious ways, yeah, right. Her smile was insufferably smug. Well, if Trish the Freaking Dish was going to try to get away with being coy about this, there was really only one remedy. She might as well come out and call a spade a spade.

"You're not going to admit it, are you," Ruth said. "You're not going to admit that you made that sign specifically about me."

That finally broke through her facade. She looked genuinely surprised. What a performance.

"What are you talking about?" Patty said. She looked over at Pastor Flint, but he was watching a couple of boys skateboarding across the parking lot.

"I'm talking about you driving me down to that clinic," Ruth said.

"What clinic?" The skateboarders hopped up on the

sidewalk in front of the video store, but one of them stumbled off his board and nearly fell.

"Oh, my gosh," Patty said. Ruth, this woman's name was Ruth. "You mean, way back when we were kids? I haven't thought about that in thirty years."

"Right," Ruth said. "That sign has nothing to do with me."

"It doesn't. Oh Ruth, you must be hurting so bad. I didn't mean it that way." Pastor Flint said that people like her often suffered from post-traumatic stress disorder. It could take years, even decades, to show up. Her sign had been the trigger. She had to help this woman. Ruth needed to grieve for that baby. They could pray together, with Pastor Flint. Oh, that would be wonderful! They could do it right now.

"You should come and talk to Pastor Flint, he has the most marvelously compassionate way of talking about this. He feels your pain, Ruth, he really does." She reached out and put her hand on Ruth's arm. Ruth stared at her hand as if a giant spider had dropped out of the sky.

"Are you out of your mind?" Ruth said.

How rude, Patty thought, and no, it's you that's out of your mind. It's called PTSD, but we can help you. "Ruth, I'm so sorry to have been the one to trigger all this for you, but you have to grieve for that baby you—" she'd almost said "killed," but fortunately she'd stopped herself in time, "—for that poor little lost soul." She pulled on Ruth's arm, the poor woman so desperately needed what they had to offer, but Ruth jerked away.

"What makes you think I haven't grieved?" Ruth said. Her voice was harsh, threatening even, and she was jabbing her finger at Patty.

"Of course you have," Patty said. Pastor Flint had said that one of the symptoms of PTSD was sudden outbursts of violence. Ruth might have a gun in her purse. Patty took a step back, she could run into the video store if Ruth did something crazy. She could hold up *The Passion of the Christ*, surely that would stop a bullet under these circumstances. "But have you gotten down on your knees and asked for God's forgiveness?" she said. "We could do that together, all three of us."

Ye gods what a nutcase Trish had turned out to be. "You actually have the nerve to invite me to pray with you after what you've done?" She started for her car. There was no reasoning with these people, they were lunatics.

"But I haven't done anything," Trish said. "You've got it all wrong."

Ruth slammed the door of her car shut. This was personal now. There was a brief moment, before she pulled out of the parking lot, when she considered driving right up over the curb and smashing Trish into the plate-glass window of the video store. But there were too many witnesses. She could have cheerfully killed that pipsqueak Pastor Flint, but those two boys on the skateboards had nothing to do with this.

THE FOLLOWING SUNDAY, WHEN Patty and Pastor Flint arrived at the bank, she'd made herself a new sign. "Honk If You Hate Abortion," she'd written, in cheerful green letters, and on the other side "Kill Rapists, Not Their Children," because having two different slogans was kind of her trademark now. Rick was at home watching an "absolutely critical" Mariners game, but Pastor Flint was with her, and most of the other regulars were on their way. They were all a little disappointed that no one else in the congregation had joined them, but Pastor Flint said that perhaps this was the Lord's way of testing their faith. She lugged their lemonade jug and her sign down the street to the corner she'd come to think of as her personal Outpost For The Unborn. Pastor Flint carried his Bible and a couple of canvas chairs. Three hours was a long time to stand on the sidewalk without a break.

They turned the corner and there was Ruth, across the street. She was holding a sign that said "I Had An Abortion."

As soon as she saw Patty she glared at her for a moment, and then flipped the sign around. On the other side it said "Do I Look Like A Murderer To You?"

"Oh dear," Patty said, "this is what you warned us about. She's lost touch with reality." Pastor Flint nodded, and the way his lips were pressed together was so compassionate it made Patty feel better immediately.

Across the street two more women arrived. They were carrying signs too, with the same thing written front and back as Ruth's. A few minutes later, another woman came, and they kept coming until there were close to twenty of them. They held hands, the whole long line of them, and they sang "Amazing Grace," but to Patty's ear, they were a little off-key.

Pastor Flint came over to Patty. He had come to rely on her at times like this, and she loved being there for him. It had happened so soon after they met, and surely this was yet another sign from the Lord.

"Our prayers have been answered," Pastor Flint said. "This is the best thing that could have happened. We'll get the media here now. The rest of the congregation will step forward to support us."

On Patty's side of the street they numbered nine. Pastor Flint gathered them in a prayer circle. They all knelt together on the sidewalk, and Pastor Flint raised his eyes to heaven. There was a look of transfiguration on his face, a look of complete and utter joyfulness. Patty was by his side, holding his hand, and as they all raised their eyes heavenward, a voice in her head said words that she knew came directly from heaven.

Divorce Rick, the voice said, and cleave unto Pastor Flint.

Conflations of a Hard-Headed Yankee

THE CAT, A CHOCOLATE Siamese, headed down the path from the back door to the barn. Verne stopped and watched her run, an animal with a purpose. He was up early with a to-do list in his pocket and the widow Faricy on his mind. The widow Faricy was a woman who valued promptness, and he was due at her house for dinner that night at 6 p.m. He had weeds to pull in his vegetable garden, some pepper starts to plant, a pile of mulch to put around the lettuce and the spinach. He had peonies to cut for the widow's carnival glass vase, and a trip into Renata for a trim from Don the barber. He had an engagement ring in a velvet box on his dresser.

A western tanager called from the big leaf maples beyond the pond, and another answered from deeper in the woods, their calls fluty and liquid. Yellow slants of early morning sunlight broke through the trees and lit a patch of mist that hung over the water. The pond was his wife's favorite place on earth, and her ashes were there, in the silt at the bottom. He was glad he'd never told the widow Faricy that, glad she didn't know there were bits of Evelyn's bones so close to his home. Their home, if she was willing.

His mulch fork and the wheelbarrow were in the barn. He undid the latch on the door and stepped into the dark. There was the metallic tang of gas and solvents from the row of cans he kept on a shelf just inside the door, and as he stepped farther in, the faint smell of old cedar. He breathed the smells deep into his lungs, and then he pulled the string hanging down from the bare light bulb and lit up his workbench.

His cat was on the floor, her tail switching back and forth, hunting. She was a good hunter, and since Evelyn had died he'd taken to marking the cat's kills on the calendar. Evelyn wouldn't have liked that, but she'd been dead for two, almost three years, and Verne was getting on with his life. He rubbed the deep groove on his ring finger where he used to wear his wedding band. If he wanted to track how efficient the cat was at doing what came naturally to her, he was free to do so, just like he was free to wash his work clothes along with everything else, never mind if he spilled a little gasoline on them.

The cat crept forward, attuned to some distant rustling that Verne couldn't hear. It was then he saw the spilled over jars of screws, his carefully sorted hardware dumped out and scattered. Damn that cat. The chocolate colored tip of her tail disappeared around a corner, almost as if the force of his thought propelled her.

He let a big, exasperated breath of air out. One of the best things about retirement was the way he was getting caught up on things. The hours he'd spent standing here, happily sorting through an old coffee can full of screws, washers, nails, assorted nuts and bolts, putting like with like, tossing out what was too corroded or stripped or bent to be of use any more. His hand tools hung on the wall above the workbench. His power tools were in bins on the shelf below, the saws in one bin, the electric sanders in another, the drills in a third. Everything in its place.

There was nothing for it but to clean up the mess in front of him. He started with a tipped over jar of wood screws labeled 3/4"-1 1/2" ph. "Ph" was Phillips. He had a separate jar for slot heads in those sizes. Thank God he didn't have any arthritis, like the widow Faricy did. His fingers were still nimble, and he used his forefingers to quickly sort through the pile, making sure there were no strays from other jars mixed in. He scooped the pile to the edge of the workbench and let them drop into the jar.

The light changed at the other end of the workbench, at the edge of what he could see. He pushed his glasses tighter against his nose and turned his head to look at the sunlight where it came through the glass of the old windows set high in the barn wall. The light rippled, as if it traveled through water, and then a largish splotch of light began a tiny, tight shaking, like fine sawdust around the edges of an electric sander. The splotch detached itself from the beam of light, and it began to swell, brighter at the core, gelatinous, quickening with a movement that light had no right to make. Verne's ears rang, the sound coming from a place deep inside his head. The shimmer drifted closer. His mouth was dry as dust.

"Evelyn?" he said. His voice was all breath, the raspy sound of dry leaves crumbling. The rise and fall of his chest would not slow down, and the ringing in his head got louder as the thing approached. For a brief moment it had a surface like skin, it had Evelyn's hair pulled back tight and then erupting into a wild bun on top, it had her wide cheekbones, her squared-off jaw, her lush full lips. Her hand was palm up, and she was pushing the forefinger of her other hand into it, turning the finger as if she were squashing a bug, a gesture she used when she talked about her father's wild streak, and the way her mother had tried to tame him.

Her lips were parted, mumbling perhaps, or trembling. The tremble spread, and the surface was all vibrating particles again, wavicles of light spreading out thin, thinner, thinnest. The wild strands of her hair drifted away from her head, her eyes became empty sockets, and then the sockets merged and her face melted away like vapor into a lab room fan. She was gone.

His knees felt weak. He leaned against the workbench, his knees collapsing underneath him like sand falling into a hole, and he sank to the floor. This was the second time he'd seen her. The first time was in the middle of the night, more than two years ago, in the hallway between their bedroom door and the bathroom of their old farm house. Her hands were raised, and she waved them back and forth and began to turn in a circle. Seeing her had brought him to angry sobs. She'd left him, and now she was making fun of his loss, dancing the hokey pokey. He'd written it off to grief, a trick of his sorrowed mind. He'd pushed the memory as far back in his head as it would go. It wasn't a memory he had any interest in examining.

He didn't believe in God or heaven or angels. Never had. He didn't believe in ghosts either. So it was something inside him that had gone wrong. Something he wanted to fix.

His cat slinked in through the open door. She came straight for him across the floor and rubbed the length of her body against his leg. He lifted her and felt the weight of her, the solid undeniable fact of her existence, and then he set her down in his lap and stroked her head.

Cats only had one life, and spirits were for the weak-minded. He'd taught high school science for thirty-seven years, and now that Evelyn was gone, he didn't have to tolerate this kind of thing. Evelyn may have believed in things that couldn't be proved, but that was an argument they'd long ago decided not to have any more. If he was seeing things that weren't there, it was hallucination, nothing more.

The cat dug her claws into his pants, their sharp tips prickling his skin. He pulled on her ears, massaging them between his thumb and finger, knowing full well this would make her dig her claws in deeper. At least this was a pain he understood.

When he let go of her ears, she looked at him and widened her green eyes. Her claws retracted, and her ears fluttered in a feline shudder.

"Go catch a mouse," he said.

She walked away with her tail straight up, twitching at the tip, the way she did when she was pissed at him for not letting her out at night.

He stood up and went back to sorting nuts and bolts into jars.

HE MISSED EVELYN, THERE was no denying it. The loss was sharpest when a great blue heron stood on the shore of the pond at the edge of their woods looking for fish, or when a coyote trotted across the yard just after sunrise, or when the deer browsed by in the evening. They both loved living in the country, loved the wildlife and the garden and the quiet, and this was the life they shared for better than four decades. Most days now that note of loss was just one birdcall in a morning full of birdsong.

Theirs had been a marriage of opposites, everyone said so. Evelyn was the free spirit, the dancer, the one who did the talking for both of them when they were out with friends or people from the schools. Verne was her hard-headed Yankee, the one who needed proof rather than faith, the one who could learn the steps but who could never really dance the foxtrot. Salsa dancing, one of Evelyn's passions for a time, was beyond him. He gave up after two lessons, saying he could never move his hips that way in front of other people.

What they shared was the outdoors—the garden, the wildlife, hiking and camping. Verne knew the names of everything—plants, birds, even the rocks were named things for him. He could name every flower they saw on a hike up to the top of Dog Mountain, or name the stars in the night sky. He made her a devotee of field guides, of life lists, of hiking the same forest trail in different seasons.

He was the planner, and she the one who reached over, took his day planner out of his hands, tore that day's page out and wadded it up into a ball that she tossed over her shoulder.

"Let's go skinny-dipping instead," she said.

And they did just that—their pond was right there, out back of the house where no one could see. After that, skinny-dipping became one of the words in their private language, a word that meant let's go buy some ice cream, let's go for a drive in the country and see where we end up, let's turn somersaults in the front yard. At first he humored her only because her delight was so great. But over time he learned to surprise her, to get up in the morning and announce that he'd arranged a substitute teacher that day so they could go mushroom hunting, or hike to a waterfall, or spend the day in bed. He brought her flowers and told her it was because the birthmark on the back of her neck looked like a bouquet. She smiled, and asked him to kiss her there, and then unbuttoned her blouse.

He was the frugal one, the one who saved and re-used and recycled, the one who took things back to the store if they weren't right. Evelyn was the one who bought on impulse, who maxed out her credit card, who once bought a brand new dress for a party and paid five hundred dollars for it when they were struggling to make their car payments. This was early in their marriage, the year he was student teaching, and she worked as a checker in the grocery store.

At the party a man they didn't know cornered her in the kitchen and said that dress made him want to kiss her. She said no thank you, collected Verne and told him they were leaving. In the car, when she told Verne why, Verne said he understood why the man made a pass at her, look at how low the neckline was cut.

"So you think I led him on?" she said. They were both a little drunk. There was an edge to her voice that Verne should have recognized.

"I didn't say that," he said. The dress was clingy and black and revealed the upper curve of her breasts. He was looking forward to watching her take it off when they got home, the way she would reveal the smooth white flesh of her upper thighs as she lifted it up from the hem.

"You implied it," she said. "You think this is my fault, because I spent so much on this dress."

"That's a separate issue," he said. "You're always conflating things." He might be a little drunk, but he wasn't going to let her get away with mixing things up the way she always did.

"It's all the same thing," she said. "Sex is power, and money is power, and which is it that bothers you more? Is it him making a pass at me, or is it the money I spent?"

He knew better than to answer a question like that. When he pulled into the driveway Evelyn got out before he even shut the car off. She grabbed the filmy fabric of the dress at the hem in both hands and had it up and over her head before Verne was out of the car. She took a cigarette lighter out of her purse, and she held the dress by the shoulder straps at arm's length. When Verne stepped toward her she stepped back, shaking her head at him.

"Fire," she said, "there's nothing like it for ritual cleansing."

She snapped flame from the cigarette lighter and held it under the hem of the dress. She lit it in three places, as careful as if she were lighting candles on an altar. The flames ate holes in the clingy fabric, turning it into heat and smoke and ash. Whatever synthetic fiber it was made of burned like a torch. She was in her bra and panties and nearly as tall as Verne in her high heels. She dropped the burning dress on the ground between them.

Christ, he thought. No pair of thighs was worth this.

"Conflate that," she said, pointing at the dress. It sizzled on the grass, burning blue-hot like plastic. Light from the flames rippled across her face. Her squared off jaw pushed out at him. All Verne could think of was the credit card bill that was coming, and how crazy Evelyn could get, the caroms of her moods shifting in neck snapping ricochets.

He slept on the couch that night. In the morning she knelt beside the couch and asked him how he wanted his eggs.

"Scrambled," he said. He sat up. "I'm sorry," he said. "I shouldn't have said anything about your dress last night."

"What dress?" she said. Her lush full lips spread across her face in a wide smile. "I remember a ritual, I remember a fire, but I don't remember anything about a dress."

She leaned in and kissed him, and as they kissed, her hands drifted down to his thighs. They never spoke of the dress again.

THE WIDOW FARICY WAS a different sort of woman. She was practical and frugal, like him, and she would understand the care he'd put into finding the right diamond, in how he'd gone back four times to bargain the price down, and still spent over a thousand dollars on just the stone. An orderly sort of woman, someone who liked her habits and routines. They walked together in the mornings, Tuesdays and Fridays. They had dinner together on Saturday nights, and went to church together on Sundays. He kept his utter lack of religious belief to himself, and thought of the church as a social service club, nothing wrong with that. Her kisses on those Saturday nights hinted that she was capable of desire, perhaps even of passion, but when he let his hands drift up her sides to her breasts she pushed them away. She let him know early on that she didn't hold with premarital sex, that marriage was a sacred vow, and that if he wanted to keep company with her, he'd better accept her the way she was.

He could do that, he decided, because his urges weren't so urgent any more. They had grief and loss and survival in common, and at his age, that was a lot more important than sex. He was after companionship this time, not some youthful hot-headed desire for flesh. Gone were the days of pushing

Evelyn up against a tree in the middle of the day like animals in rut—something else they'd shared, the way lust could overtake them and then leave them breathless and laughing at what they'd done. If Evelyn was a woman who saw sex at the root of everything, the widow Faricy was a woman who believed in the contentment of order, the comfort of everything having its assigned place, the wisdom of God's law. He didn't have to believe in God to go along with all that.

HE ARRIVED AT THE widow Faricy's house precisely at 6 p.m., and she rewarded him by presenting her cheek for a quick kiss. She wore the cinnamon red lipstick he'd admired once, and a green dress. She didn't like him kissing her on the lips when her lipstick was fresh. She took the peonies he'd picked for her and put them in the carnival glass vase. The thick smell of roast pork came from the kitchen. The table was set with her best china and the linen napkins.

Verne felt the ring box in the side pocket of his sports coat. There was a part of him that wanted to get right to the proposal, to cut through anything that stood between him and the thrill of what he was about to do, but he held off. He had a plan, and he would stick to it. Dinner first, and then their postprandial game of cribbage. He would let her win. She would suggest that they watch a movie she'd rented, and he would say yes. But first he would get the champagne flutes and the bottle of champagne she had in her fridge, the one he'd brought a few weeks before, the one she'd insisted they save for a special occasion. Now, he would insist.

"Verne," she would say, "what's gotten into you?" A mysterious smile would be his only answer. He would take a ceremonial sip from his glass, set it on her coffee table, on a coaster of course, and then drop to his knee. A few words about what a lovely, sensible woman she was, elegant and practical at the same time, and then he would produce the ring. She would smile, blush perhaps, she would say yes—how could she say anything else?—and then he would slip the ring on her finger. She would take his hand and draw him up off his knees, and they would embrace on her couch. It was possible, he had decided, based on the two or three heartbeats' time before she pushed his hand away from her breast the Saturday before, that he might even be allowed to touch her there.

Things went according to plan right up to the moment when he dropped to his knee. His knee gave out on the way down and his leg twisted. His knee hit the corner of the coffee table, and delivered to him such a fierce twinge of pain that he thought he would faint. He ended up on both his knees with his head buried in her lap, moaning. The widow Faricy gave out a yelp and dropped her champagne glass on the couch. She pushed his head back with both hands.

"Verne," she said, "I'm shocked. Do you think you can have your way with me after a sip of champagne?"

Verne reared back, desperate to get his weight off his throbbing knee. His mouth hung open, and he grabbed the widow Faricy's thighs and tried to pull himself up, his thumbs buried together in the tight space where her legs joined. Her perfectly combed hair with its careful flip forward on either side of her face trembled.

"You're hurting me," she said.

His knee felt as if he'd driven a ten-penny nail into it. He gripped her thighs even tighter and tried to raise himself to his feet. The widow Faricy yelped again. She picked up the glass of champagne, which still held a finger's worth of liquid, and she tossed the champagne into Verne's eyes.

"Ahhhh," Verne yelled. The champagne stung him. He let go of her to rub his fingers in his eyes, but that put his weight on his knee again, and the ten-penny stab of pain sharpened. He fell over on his side. He held his knee in both hands. He rocked from side to side and blinked back the tears.

"Goddammit," he said, "it's my knee."

His ears were ringing. The widow Faricy stood over him, but when he opened his eyes he saw Evelyn's face, and she was shaking her head. "I'm sorry," she said. "I can't let that woman trap you."

"What?" he said. He closed his eyes tight and shuddered. When he opened his eyes, he saw the widow Faricy.

"What did you say?" he said. He gripped his knee as if holding it tight would stop the pain.

"I said I thought you were trying to grope me."

"Grope you?" he said. Anger functioned, for a brief moment, as his analgesic. "Damn you, woman, do you think I'm some pimply faced teenager at a high school dance?"

The widow Faricy's mouth tightened, and she held one hand with the other, her knuckles a row of red, swollen bumps in front of her belly.

"I'd appreciate it, Mr. Verne Regner," she said, "if you'd stop swearing at me."

The tight wrinkles around her mouth made her whole face older, made it a school marm's face, the face of a woman who had never known the pleasures of the flesh.

The drive to the hospital was silent.

HE LAY IN BED the next morning with the cat curled next to him, his peripheral vision fuzzy at the edges. The pain medication was wearing off. His mouth was dry, his bladder was full, and he was still in the clothes he'd worn on his date.

They sat in the waiting room the night before, he and the widow Faricy, on separate couches. He sat with both hands wrapped around the spike of pain in his swollen knee, sweating. She sat with her knees together and her hands folded into her lap. A television mounted on the wall gave them an excuse not to speak, but at one point, during a commercial break, the widow Faricy leaned in to him and said, "I think you've bruised me." Her eyes gave a quick downward look to her lap, and when they came back up, she forced her lips into the smallest of smiles.

Her thighs were not the only thing bruised. She had to know that he was about to propose to her when his knee went out. Maybe he should say something to her. He could take the ring out and tell her about the cut and clarity of the diamond, and how he'd talked the dealer up a grade in color for the same price. A practical approach to the subject of matrimony. But then a nurse appeared with a wheelchair, and he went off to a little cubicle without the widow Faricy.

He watched the soft heave of breath going in and out of the cat, and he reached out and stroked her between her ears. She opened her eyes for a moment, yawned, and went back to sleep. The dull ache in his knee was growing sharper. He reached for the bottle of pills next to his bed, but he had no water to take them with. It was strange what pain could do to the mind, the way pain had made him hallucinate Evelyn's face. He'd even heard her voice, all garbled up in the widow's. She was that much a part of him, woven so deep into the fabric of his mind that a vision of her appeared, warning him. And what a piece of work the widow Faricy turned out to be, tossing champagne in his face, thinking all he cared about was her body. She should be so lucky. And the way her mouth got all tight like that, like a sphincter, that wasn't a hallucination, that was real.

It was a struggle getting out of bed, but once he was up and had the crutches underneath him, he was able to get around. He took two of the pain pills because the label said "Take one every 4-6 hours as needed for pain," and he damn well needed two. Going to the bathroom had been a bit tricky, but he managed the business without falling over. The crutches and the immobilizer on his knee made him an old man.

He sat down at the kitchen table with his leg straight out

in front of him. The word "widower" hung over his thoughts in big dark letters made out of smoke. He was hungry, but the only thing he could imagine doing about it was opening a can of tuna fish and forking it straight into his mouth. The cat came in and hopped up on his lap.

"Just the two of us," he said. He'd been talking out loud to the cat ever since Evelyn died, and all too often he heard himself say something he used to say to her. He'd thought forty years of marriage had taught him something about women, but the only woman he understood was his dead wife. He was an old man who lived with a cat, a man who ate tuna fish right out of the can, a man who had nothing better to do than sort nuts and bolts on his workbench. He stroked the cat down her flanks until she was purring.

The western tanagers were calling to each other from the woods. They were too small to see at this distance, but they sounded like a pair. He got his crutches and pulled himself up, a little easier this time. The warm buzz of the pain pills was starting to kick in. He hauled himself to the back door, nearly tripping when he dragged the crutches over the threshold, a three-legged man in a two-legged world.

There was the barn, the hundred-year-old cedar boards weathered as dark as coffee. Halfway there the path forked, and one branch led to the pond. He was gaining confidence on his crutches with each step. He worked his way to the edge of the pond and stood shading his eyes with one hand, searching the maples for the tanagers, but he couldn't find them. His eyes weren't what they had once been, but if he waited long enough, the tanagers would start singing again, and he would find them that way.

He let his hand drop, and it brushed the lump in his pocket. The ring was still there, in its box. He fumbled with the flap on his sports coat pocket and got the box out. He took the ring out of the box and held it up so he could see the diamond sparkle.

All that money spent on a ring. Foolishness for a man his age. He should take it back. Buy something practical. He'd always wanted a pressure washer. There was a lot a guy could do with a pressure washer.

Doubling Down

BROOKE HAD A NICE buzz going and a glass of merlot in her hand. Her calves were killing her, but it was nothing that a half hour of yoga wouldn't fix. She'd worked the afternoon shift at The Kitty Palace wearing chunky platform heels and not much else, and she'd closed the place down the night before. Friday nights and Saturday afternoons were good, especially after the first and the fifteenth, the payday pulse in a pole dancer's cash flow. Half a dozen lap dances for her regulars, and then one old wheezer hit up the ATM next to the lap dance lounge and paid her for four straight songs. She made three-ten in tips, and a hundred at video poker after she got off her shift. Another week like this and she'd have her Visa bill caught up.

Outside it was a cold November day going dark. She sat in her Italian leather armchair, watching the room grow darker. Soon she would get up, fix a little dinner, take a hot bath, do some down-dog until her calves stretched out. She had her sweats on and the heat up, and nobody to tell her what to do. She was sitting sideways in her armchair, cradled in it the way some men liked to hold her. Big men mostly, because she was petite, and they liked to pick her up in their arms. If she nestled in and gave them one of the Jane faces it fed the feeling of power they got. The whole trick was letting them feel powerful without giving them any real power.

Three thousand she'd spent on that chair, at an upscale boutique in The Pearl. Leather dyed the color of a green curry, but when the sun shone it had a blue cast to it, as if the chair had invited the sky down for a visit. The frame was made of steel tubes with a brushed nickel surface, strength concealed with elegance. Leather so soft it was like something a mother would buy to wrap her baby in.

Headlights played across the dark room from a car making the corner to turn onto her street. They cut the room in half, cold halogen light above, darkness below, her face caught in those high beams for a moment like her face in a spotlight, and then they moved on. Time to close the drapes, but first she was going to have another hit. She swung her legs around and set her merlot on the coffee table. She tapped out her pipe and filled the bowl again. Feed the buzz, and the rest would take care of itself. She sucked in a lungful and choked back a cough.

If she did another six weeks at the Buckeye Ranch, she'd have enough money to put twenty percent down on one of those condos her daddy was selling. Or a duplex, Daddy was right, investment property was the ticket out. Positive cash flow. Pay off her Visa, no more expensive toys, no more spur of the moment vacations to that lovely little resort in the Caymans, not until she had that duplex bringing in some straight money. Six weeks in Vegas, eight weeks tops. She was that good.

She took another sip of the merlot. She would show her daddy. She'd get out of this shitty little house in Felony Flats, where there weren't any sidewalks and the grocery store had bullet holes in the window. Daddy only wanted the best for her, he was sweet that way. He wasn't going to find out the truth about her trips to Vegas, not even Justin knew that. The money was so much better down there, and everything was legal. But

God, the look on Daddy's face when he found out she wasn't a cocktail waitress. And her mother, who turned absolutely white. It was worth it, that train wreck of a family dinner, to see her mother so shocked. But still, screw Justin for telling them where she really worked. Her brother was such a wanker. Screw him and his fancy computer networking job. She was young, she was beautiful, and she could take care of herself, so screw all of them.

Her new TV was right in front of her, fifty inches of plasma screen with a credit card remote. She loved how sharp the picture was. Look at that pool of water, the way it reflected those trees, and then those ripples. So lush. The picture was so clear it felt like she could reach her hand right in and it would come back wet. Maybe she was living in Felony Flats with the white trash and the Asian gang bangers, but Justin didn't have anything this nice. Four grand on sale, and when she got caught up on her Visa bill she'd have the whole thing paid off. Worth every penny, and she'd talked the salesman down another hundred with some cleavage and her pouty lips.

Men were so easy. Such fools, really, she could dance money right out of their pockets. Look them in the eye, show them some pink, and give them a Jane face. It worked every time.

The pipe was still in her hand. As she reached for her lighter another set of headlights swung across the room. One more hit and she'd get up to close the curtains. The headlights did their usual sweep from side to side. But then they swept back the other way, and this was wrong, this had never happened before. The headlights came straight at her. The front of the truck crashed through her picture window and drove straight into the room. Straight through her TV, straight through her coffee table, glass flying right at her. Straight into her chair. The back of the chair cracked when it hit the back wall. A chrome ram's head glared down at her.

She had a truck in her lap. The horn blared and did not

stop. Hot engine smell. The bumper of the truck crammed up against the arms of the chair. The frame sticking out through ripped leather.

A shard of glass the size of a shoe stuck out of her chest, right between her breasts. God she had great tits. Blood flowed down her front. It made her shiver. She passed out.

DADDY PICKED HER UP from the hospital in a new yellow Hummer. This was the first good thing she had seen since the accident.

"Nice car, Daddy."

"I thought this might put a smile on your face." He was a handsome man, silver-haired, his face wide and pleasantly ruddy, with high cheekbones. He opened the door for her. The running board was as tall as her knees, and when she tried to step up, she felt her stitches pull a little.

"Ouch," she said. "Help me up, please?" She leaned her head against her Daddy's chest, and he put his arms around her. She'd doubled up on her pain meds as soon as they got the prescription filled.

"Here you go, princess," he said. Daddy was so easy. He bent down and put his arm under her knees and picked her up. His body felt warm against her. She could stay like this a long time. He lifted her up and set her on the seat.

"Oh Daddy," she said. "You're such a sweetie."

Nice carpet on the floor and digital instruments in a padded dash. Where Catholics put a Saint Christopher her father had a Betty Boop in a slinky red dress with the tops of her perfectly round breasts sticking out and a classic Jane face. Her eyes were wide open and round, framed top and bottom with curved eyelashes, the eyes of a woman pretending to be a girl. They were eyes that said, "Oh sweetie, you believe me, don't you? This is my very first time."

They drove to her house so she could pick up a few things.

Her plasma TV was face down on the carpet, busted in two, and the curry green leather of her chair, that baby soft leather, was stiff with her blood. She was bruised and cut up, and she was going to have a monster of a scar down her front where the glass had sliced her, but none of her bones were broken. At least the old wheezer who'd driven through her front window was dead. There was some justice in that.

She was going to stay with her parents for a while. Her mother had insisted. She absolutely had to come stay with them while she recovered. The repairs to her house weren't even started, and it would be nice to have someone to change her bandage every day.

Still, to be stuck out in Renata, she wasn't sure this was going to work. It had been a long time since she'd spent more than an afternoon around her parents. Daddy could be handled, but the Jane faces didn't work on Marlene. Not much of anything Brooke tried worked on her mother the last couple of years. Her mother didn't handle attitude well, and Brooke had been replaced in her mother's affections by her Barbie business. Marlene had a website, and a room full of Barbies, and she sold her Barbies on eBay.

"I made a nice little bundle on a new subdivision in Sunnyside," Daddy told her. His hands caressed the steering wheel. "This is my reward."

His fingernails were manicured. His smile was confident, as if the world owed him things, and he knew it. She'd seen that smile on men at the rail, watching her dance. Men who thought if they tipped her double they could take a few liberties during a lap dance. But those kind of liberties didn't come that cheap, not with her.

The back seat was the size of a hot tub. They cruised along above the traffic, looking down on lesser vehicles. The Hummer was bulletproof. There was nothing she was afraid of. Not even a truck could kill her.

"Nice seats," Brooke said. Real leather. The padding on the armrests was thick. There was nothing military about the inside of the car, everything was done in the name of luxury. Daddy had Johnny Cash on the stereo and it sounded like Johnny was right there, in the back seat.

It was a forty-minute drive to Renata. She pressed a button and the seatback reclined. She leaned back into the plush leather and closed her eyes. Her pain meds were really kicking in now. A hundred and eighty-seven stitches down her front to close up the wound. She was feeling dozy. She was going to be out of work for a long time.

She woke up when the Hummer slowed down to make the turn off the main highway. Her father reached over and touched her cheek with the back of his hand. "Let me show you something," he said.

They drove past the high school, where she'd had quite a reputation. Daddy bought her a Mustang convertible for her sweet sixteen, and once she had a car, there was no stopping her. She was suspended a month after she was Homecoming Queen, caught in the back seat of her Mustang by her biology teacher, Mr. Regner, with a boy, and half her clothes off. They were cutting class, and there was a baggie in plain view on the console between the front seats. The boy sprang off her like a terrified kitten when Mr. Regner leaned in the open window and told them to stop. Mr. Regner got a good look at her breasts, and Brooke had seen the jolt of lust in his eyes before he turned away.

She'd worked it all out, though. Mom wanted to send her to therapy, to drug rehab, to some ridiculous wilderness boot camp for wayward kids, but she talked Daddy into letting her work in his office instead. It would give her something to do after school and on weekends, she argued, and she'd work for free to pay him back for all the trouble she'd caused, and they would know exactly where she was. She was grounded—she could only drive the Mustang to school and to his office, and she wasn't allowed to date for months afterwards, but she'd proven to her mother that she was Daddy's little princess. It was worth it.

"Does Mr. Regner still teach here?" she asked.

"I think he retired," her father said. His fingers tightened on the steering wheel. "Why do you ask?"

They were a block past the high school now, headed for the ridge above town.

"Just wondering," she said. After her freshman year in college she came home for the summer to work in Daddy's office again. The week after the last day of classes at the high school she happened to drive by and see that there were only a couple of cars in the lot. One of them was Mr. Regner's. She pulled into the lot and parked at the far end. The halls were shiny with fresh wax and her heels clicked along like she owned the place. She found him in the little room off his classroom where he kept his stuffed animals and other supplies. There was a nutria, an owl with its wings spread, a beaver with long yellow teeth, and a coyote with its ears perked up.

"Hi, Mr. Regner," she said. He turned, and coffee sloshed out of his cup when he saw her. He had pretty eyes, brown with flecks of gold in them like mica. "Verne," she said, "it's okay if I call you Verne, isn't it?"

"Brooke," he said. He had chalk dust on the front of his slacks. "What are you doing here?"

"I saw your car in the lot," she said. She took the three steps that brought her close enough to him to smell his aftershave. "I came to say hello."

"Hello," Mr. Regner said. He was an old guy, older than her father, but she knew things about older guys that she didn't used to know. Her biology prof had needed some help deciding to let her drop her field studies class, and she let him teach her what kind of help he liked best.

"It was an impulse," she said. She bit down on half her

lower lip, and let it slide ever so slowly back out. She said, "I'm very impulsive you know."

She put her hands on his belt buckle. He looked past her to his classroom door. She pulled the end of his belt through the buckle.

"Don't worry," she said, "I locked the door."

His hand trembled when it touched her breast through her clothes. She liked the shine of his gold wedding band there. His pants dropped to his ankles. White briefs underneath. She was homecoming queen all over again. She dropped to her knees. He didn't last five minutes. That's how good she was.

"Why?" he said, when she was finished, the same look on his face as the wide-eyed barn owl he was standing next to.

"Don't ask why, Verne," she said. "There is no why."

She left him standing there with his briefs around his ankles and his mouth wide open, the perfect exclamation point for her high school career. She'd gone back to the state university in the fall, but by the time spring term rolled around she was cutting all her classes and flunking out. Her parents cut off her money, but with looks like hers, she didn't need an education to get a job. She'd waitressed and been a hostess, she'd sold lingerie in a store at a mall, she'd even worked in a bookstore for a little while. All of it was shitty money for shittier work.

Some random guy she dated took her to a strip club one night. She watched how much money men put on the rail, did the math, and went back for an audition the next day. Something she'd learned in her introductory psych class clicked for her when she was on stage, and she put that one little bit of her education to work. Basic behaviorism: the mind was a black box, nobody knew what was in there, not in any scientific sense. All a person could do was observe the behavior, correlate stimulus with response, time how fast the rat ran the maze. If she twirled upside down and naked on a pole, with loud music and colored lights sliding across her bare skin, men put money on the rail for her. Stimulus and response, as simple as that.

She worked on her moves, and she learned how to work the guys who came back again and again for a tease. The money she made at the rail came in ones and twos, but lap dances were the cream. She moved to the city, where there were more strip clubs than there were McDonald's. She was a bad girl, a wicked, wicked girl, and everyone wanted her.

By the time she landed at The Kitty Palace she had her signature move down, where she rolled back on her shoulders, reached her feet back over her head with her G-string around her ankles, and tied a knot with the flimsy little piece of cloth around the pole. That one brought the fives out at the rail.

She had a small posse of regulars who followed her from club to club. They were married guys in their fifties mostly, guys with dumpy wives at home who wouldn't give them what they wanted. She liked the gleam of their wedding rings and the way they squirmed when she spread her legs and gave them a Jane face. She liked saying no to them when they asked if she did private shows. Only in Vegas. Never shit in the water you swim in.

"This is what I wanted to show you," her daddy said. His ruddy face was smiling at her as he turned the Hummer into a new development on the edge of town. The streets and curbs were in, and there were light poles with wires coming out the top but no lights yet.

"A hundred and forty-plus lots," her father said. "I'm going to make a bundle out here. This whole town is about to pop wide open. New houses, new schools, new parks. New businesses. Lots of opportunities for somebody to make something of themselves."

So that's what this was about. Daddy was trying to plan her future again.

"Just what kind of business do you think I should start?" she said. "What is it that all these fine new Renatans can't live without?"

"You were always good with animals," Daddy said. "Maybe a pet grooming business?"

"I was good with animals when I was a little girl," she said. "I don't even have a cat any more."

What was it with her parents? She was twenty-three. She wasn't going to move back to the podunk town she grew up in and start some random little business.

They worked their way out of the development and started up the road to her parents' house. The road was curvy. Her stomach was queasy even though the Hummer was so big it was like riding in a limo around those curves. Daddy drove it with one hand, as easy as if he were driving a golf cart.

"Have you considered going back to school," he said, "or getting your real estate license?"

Christ, this again. Ever since she dropped out of college Daddy kept trying to get her to sell real estate with him.

"Could we just not talk about this now? I just got out of the hospital."

Daddy maneuvered the Hummer around the last of the curves and they came out on a long straightaway that led to a dead end.

"I'm sorry," Daddy said. "I'm just concerned about what you're going to do with yourself."

He wasn't going to come right out and say it, she knew that. He wasn't going to say, Don't be a pole dancer any more, do anything besides that, anything at all. He just assumed that her scar meant she'd have to find something else.

"I'm going to get a tattoo," she said, "from here to here." She ran her hand down her front like she was opening a zipper. Maybe a dragon, or a snake, with eyes that glowed in the black lights at The Kitty Palace.

It was worth it to see the look on his face. The way his lower lip bunched up. The way it made that muscle on the side of his face twitch.

"Oh," he said. "I hadn't thought of that."

The house was the last one on the road. She remembered all the times she'd driven down this road and seen her family sitting there in the living room, framed by the picture window. All of them safe and smug in their tidy home, like dolls in a dollhouse.

They pulled into the driveway and parked. The Hummer was too big to go in the garage.

Selling real estate, what a bore. All that stupid paperwork, and nobody bought a house from some cute young thing in her twenties. What was Daddy thinking?

"So don't worry about me," she said. "I'll be fine."

BROOKE HAD ALWAYS BEEN high maintenance, Marlene knew this. A colicky baby, a willful, manipulative child, and let's face it, by the time she was seventeen she'd tossed away her virginity as easily as if it were a dirty tissue. Thank God Justin was easy. If she'd had Brooke first she would have gone out of her mind. But this accident, this terrible thing that happened to Brooke, maybe this was an opening. Maybe she would change her ways now.

The stitches were appalling, a long line of black Xs like some enormous centipede squatting on the front of her body. The skin on either side of them was red and puffy. It made Marlene's whole body tighten up just to look.

She held Brooke's hand as she stepped into the shower stall, and then she stepped in behind her with the sponge. Marlene started on her neck, long and graceful like her own, the neck of a queen.

"How's the sponge?" she said. "Not too cold?"

"It's fine," Brooke said. "It feels good."

She had a lovely shape from the back, there was no denying

it. Marlene's bottom was flattening as she grew older. It had been a long time since Chuck told her she had a world-class ass. He used to say that to her all the time, and vulgar though it was, he had a way of saying it that made Marlene smile. She missed hearing it.

She washed the backs of Brooke's legs all the way to her feet and squeezed the sponge out. She dipped the sponge in the plastic tub of rinse water and washed her down again, faster this time. It was like having her baby girl back again, washing her this way.

"I used to bathe you in the kitchen sink when you were little," she said. "You probably don't remember."

"How could I?" Brooke said. "I was just a baby."

Marlene tugged on the bottom of her bathing suit before she asked Brooke to turn around. She'd worn the one-piece. She wasn't going to let Brooke see any more cellulite than was absolutely necessary.

"Please," Brooke said. "Don't stare at the stitches." The skin under her eyes was purple to black, but at least the colors were starting to fade. Her voice had a trembly edge to it, and her eyes were shiny and wet. She said, "I look awful, don't I?"

"You'll heal," Marlene said. "You'll use cocoa butter on the scar." Marlene had used cocoa butter on her cesarean scar after Brooke was born, and that scar was hardly noticeable.

She had Brooke lift up her arms. There was stubble in her armpits. She washed down one side of her body to her hip, and there was stubble on her legs too. She'd left a strip of pubic hair above her sex. Is that what young women were doing these days? It was vulgar, like an arrow pointing to her most private part. She hadn't noticed anybody at the gym who shaved themselves that way.

"Are you going to need help shaving?"

"No," Brooke said, "I'm not a cripple, Mom."

Marlene dipped the sponge in the wash water and dabbed

carefully at the skin near the stitches. Brooke's breasts were right there, still young and high. Thank God she hadn't had them puffed up like cantaloupes with silicon. The skin next to her stitches was inflamed, and she wasn't sure how close to get.

"You're lucky this missed your breasts," she said. She dabbed a little more, this was so awkward, not just the cut and the stitches, but was she really going to wash her daughter's breasts?

"Give me that," Brooke said. She grabbed the sponge right out of Marlene's hand. "I can do the rest," she said. "And I'm sick of hearing how lucky I am. There's not a fucking thing that's lucky about some old wheezer having a stroke and crashing his truck through the front of your house. If I was really lucky, he would've hit the house next door."

"I'm only trying to help." This was so like Brooke, touchy about every little thing she said, ungrateful. Pushing her away, using that kind of language.

"You've helped enough," Brooke said. "Get out of that ridiculous bathing suit and you can help me put the bandage on."

And insulting her. Where had she gone wrong? How had she raised a daughter who could be so cruel? She shook her head.

"You ought to be ashamed," she said, "talking to me like that."

There was no apology in Brooke's face. She was shameless, the way she enjoyed baiting her mother.

Marlene went to her closet and changed into a pair of creamy linen pants, loose enough so that her bottom still looked all right, and a silk blouse in a lovely teal. She wore the teal slingbacks with the two-inch heels. If she'd been home alone, she wouldn't have bothered with the heels, but they helped the shape of her bottom. She freshened her lipstick, ran a brush through her hair, and then turned to check herself in the full length mirror. Her tummy was still flat. All those hours in the gym. Brooke didn't possess that kind of discipline. She wouldn't look this good when she was forty-eight.

Brooke was lying on the bed in her old bedroom, putting the last strips of tape on her bandage. The bandage ran right up between her bare breasts. Shameless with her cruelty, and shameless with her body. She hadn't even bothered to cover up her lower half with a towel.

"Oh," Marlene said, "I thought you were going to have me do that."

"It's all right," Brooke said, "I can do it myself."

Don't stare at her naked mound. Marlene opened the glass door to one of her display cases, where she kept her collection of crystal figurines. They were all elegant women from different cultures. She picked one up, a geisha with a parasol, etched into the center of a block of glass. Exquisitely detailed, right down to the butterflies on her kimono.

Marlene held the figure out to her daughter. "Isn't this gorgeous," she said. "Such a lady."

Brooke blew a puff of air out from between her lips. So dismissive, she'd been doing that since she was a little girl. "She's like all of us," she said. "She's someone who gets dressed up to play a part."

"Or undressed," Marlene said. My God, she'd come right out and said it. She was so sick of pretending it wasn't true. Of lying to her friends about what Brooke did. "I'm sorry," she said. "It must be awful, having all those men stare at you."

Her cheeks were heating up. It was indecent talking to her own daughter about this. Brooke should just stop it, before the whole world knew.

"You're not sorry," Brooke said, "you're embarrassed."

Brooke was sideways to her, and sitting up now. Her shoulders back and her chest pushed out. This must be the kind of pose she struck in that awful place she worked. Her hands stroked up her sides in one long motion. So casual, as if she were just making conversation.

"You ought to try it some time," Brooke said. "You ought to

see what it feels like to have so many men want you." She rolled over on her side, facing away, and brought herself up on all fours. There was her world-class ass pointed right at Marlene's face. Marlene held the geisha close to her chest. The figure was heavy, there was so much lead in that glass. Maybe it would shield her from her daughter's cruelty.

"Except you couldn't pull it off," Brooke said. She was talking to the wall in front of her. "It's not as easy as it looks."

She twitched the muscles in her bottom, one side and then the other, back and forth. My God, where did someone learn to do that? It was so obscene. She looked over her shoulder and her lips made a pouty kiss. Her eyes were wide with desire, and she slowly closed them and let out a throaty moan. The flush in Marlene's cheeks spread down her neck. The curtains were open. If someone came into the back yard, they could see her.

The geisha, it was heavy enough to smash Brooke's face in. To put an end to all this.

She turned away, and set the figure back in the display case. Exactly where it had been. Her hands shook. She closed the door. When she turned back around, Brooke was sitting up on the bed again, studying the chipped polish on her toenails. "If you could learn to do that," she said, "I bet Daddy would pay for that kitchen remodel you want."

Marlene held very still. Not even her eyes blinked. If she moved, her daughter would strike again. Did she really think this was how a marriage worked?

She should slap her for what she'd said. What a little drama queen her daughter was. But Marlene took a breath, and she stayed calm. Calm would be her revenge. As calm as if they were simply having tea together.

"We don't do things like that in this family," she said.

Brooke scraped a fingernail across the polish on her big toe. It had taken her years to learn, but the thing that pained her daughter the most was to ignore her. Brooke was waiting for her to show how hurt she was. She could tell from the way her daughter glanced up.

Let her wait.

HER PARENTS WENT OUT to some charity fundraiser, a dinner and an auction, all the way in the city. They apologized for leaving her there alone, but her mother had helped organize the event and they simply had to go. Her mother was always so polite that way, even after the snit they got into that afternoon. Such a phony. If she really wanted to make it up to her, she could have invited Brooke along, not that she wanted to go. Brooke wanted to punch her, but they didn't do things like that in this family.

Her stitches still hurt from the way she'd moved, but her mother was shaking by the time she was done with her. It had been worth it.

In high school she'd loved nights like this when she could invite a few friends over and have the run of the house. A little wine, a little weed, topped off with a sportfuck in the comfort of her own bed instead of the back seat of her car or on a blanket in the woods. But tonight, this was lonely and deadly boring. She turned on every TV in the house and wandered from room to room with a glass of wine in her hand. It was entirely her parents' house now, filled up with their things. She didn't belong here any more. That girl was gone.

Justin's old room was full of their mother's Barbie collection. Floor-to-ceiling shelves on three walls with dozens of Barbies. Some were displayed with all their accessories carefully arranged. Some were stacked in their original boxes, never opened. Harley Davidson Barbie, Scarlett O'Hara Barbie, Star Trek Barbie, Vanna White Barbie, Shopping Queen Barbie. Her mother had two of those. Her mother liked to say that anyone who thought money couldn't buy happiness didn't know where to shop. Bewitched Barbie, I Dream of Jeannie Barbie, Goddess of Beauty Barbie.

God she had to get out of there Barbie.

Not one Pole Dancer Barbie. Not one Barbie who knew the power of her own naked body and how to use it.

She got her cell phone and started making calls. Somebody had to answer, somebody had to come out and get her. She got voice mail after voice mail, she got Dallas who was working a double shift at The Honey Pot and didn't get off until two, she got Danielle keeping a client waiting while she did her makeup, she got Phoenix whose kids were both sick.

There wasn't squat to do in Renata. There were three or four bars, a couple of restaurants, and five, count them, five places to rent videos. That said more about this town than anything else. The Bwana Lounge with its bizarre collection of wild game the owner shot all over the world. God, what a dive that place was, the taxidermied animals were moth-eaten. There was nobody she had the slightest interest in talking to, she'd kept up no friendships from high school. Nothing to smoke. The paramedics probably stole her buds.

But there was video poker at The Bwana Lounge. Better than nothing, and as close to the edge as she was likely to get in Renata. She put on some jeans and a sweater. Her eyes were a disaster, but at least the swelling had gone down. Although what difference did it make, out here, in this hick town, a woman with black eyes was just part of the scenery. She popped three of her pain pills. She would tough it out. Let them stare if they wanted to. The Bwana Lounge had cocktails, and she could get a decent buzz on.

She put on her coat and felt in the pocket for her car keys. Christ, what was she thinking, her car was at home. She finished off her glass of wine and wandered through the house, all dressed up and no way to get there.

Fuck it, her parents' cars were in the garage. They wouldn't be home for hours, she could go play a few hands and be back before they ever knew. The keys were on a rack next to the garage door. Her mother's Buick was right there, the space next to it empty. They'd gone in her father's Lexus, and that meant Daddy's Hummer was in the driveway. She pressed the button on the garage door opener. The garage door lifted up and there it was, on the far side of the driveway, wide and mean looking, an assault weapon of a vehicle.

Buick or Hummer? This was a no-brainer. Daddy would want her to travel in style.

A BLAST OF STALE cigarette smoke hit her as soon as she opened the door of The Bwana Lounge. At least at The Kitty Palace they had ceiling fans. What a freak show this place was. There were glassed-in dioramas everywhere. Two tigers fought over a dead antelope. An eagle swooped down to steal a rabbit from a puma, and a lion and a leopard leapt from the ceiling over the stage. Fake blood dripped from bared teeth, and the tigers' stripes had been touched up with magic marker.

The place was huge and nearly empty. A guy dressed head to toe in camo sat at the bar playing Keno. A buffalo head stared at her from behind the bar. She ordered a Heart Attack and the bartender looked at her like she was from Mars. God this place, so unsophisticated.

"It's Red Bull and a double shot of vodka."

"Why didn't you say so?"

Bitch. There goes your tip.

Brooke took her drink to the alcove at the end of the bar where the video poker was. A country song blared from the sound system and then abruptly changed to some hop metal hit from the nineties. The sad eyes of a dead elk watched her sit down.

She fed money into the machine. She had three hundred dollars in her pocket. The pills were starting to kick in. She was on the edge of the zone, she could feel it. She loved winning money, it made her feel like Wonder Woman, beautiful and sexy and strong and righteous.

She was up fifty in no time, but then things changed. Twice, after losing several hands in a row, she doubled her bet and won. But then she'd lost those little victories and more on the next few hands. She changed machines, she changed games. About an hour into it some guy with a big buckle and a handlebar mustache came up behind her and asked if he could buy her a drink.

She turned in her chair and let him get a good look at her black eyes. He had huge ears sticking out from under his cowboy hat, and she wasn't in the mood to tease. She set her lips in a hard line and looked up at him like he was the one who hit her. His mouth dropped open.

"I didn't think so," she said. The cowboy rocked back on his heels and left. So easy, it made her laugh.

Shutting the cowboy down was the most fun she had at The Bwana Lounge. Two hours later she was buzzed and broke. She'd had three Heart Attacks, one for each of the pills she took. When the last of her money disappeared into the chrome-edged slot she got up and staggered carefully out to the Hummer. She hated losing. Her mouth was incredibly dry, and she kept working her tongue around, trying to find some hint of moisture.

There was no traffic. She drove the Hummer down the middle of the road all the way to her parents' house. There were no lights on, they hadn't made it home yet. She pulled up in front of the house, and there it was, a bigger, nicer version of her ranch-style crackerbox back in Felony Flats. Her home, which now had a truck-sized hole in it. God what a rush before that truck ended up in her lap. All that flying glass, her house exploding right in front of her eyes, that truck bigger than life itself slamming into her chair and pushing her to the back wall.

There was nothing between her and that huge picture window but a decorative wood fence and some lawn. The Hummer was a tank, and it would go wherever she pointed it.

She backed the Hummer up and turned it to face the house. Her high beams were aimed straight at the picture window. She put the Hummer in drive. The Hummer wouldn't fit in the garage, but she could park it in the living room.

She was alive, so fucking alive.

She punched it.

On Formal Occasions, Hummingbirds

YOUR YOUNGER BROTHER, THE one your older brother chose to be best man instead of you, sends you to Hong Kong Tailors for a suit. Hong Kong Tailors turns out to be Mr. Wu, a small man with a feathery comb-over who sometimes holds the measuring tape in his lips. The quick way he moves around you, measuring your back and neck, stretching the tape down your inseam and sleeve and around your wrist, scribbling numbers on a pad, reminds you of the flock of goldfinches you saw that morning in the hawthorn tree.

There is a black and white photograph on the wall of an older Chinese man standing stiff and stone-faced next to a younger Mr. Wu. His father, you think, and the tape in Mr. Wu's lips hangs as it has a thousand times before, and always with his father's voice in his head. You can hear that voice telling him in fat chopped Chinese syllables: Work fast, no mistakes, your customer is your bowl of rice. The voice comes to Mr. Wu from an oblique angle, from above and behind, where the walls meet the ceiling.

Mr. Wu holds up three fingers. "Suit ready," he says, "three days."

You take a handful of peppermint candies from a bowl on the counter. You are buying this suit, in a creamy linen that you are sure you will spill mint ice cream or marinara sauce on, because the clothes you once wore to formal occasions like weddings and funerals hang off your body like an awning. You are buying this suit because, best man or not, there is no way your wife or your mother will let you stay home. You are tired of thinking of yourself in the second person but you can't stop, it's the only way you can keep yourself separate. Your wife, if you spoke to her about this, which you don't, would tell you that you are avoiding taking responsibility for your own life.

"Don't sleep in," she says. You are between employments. The gap in your resume is growing wider. They don't seem to be hiring second-person folk nearly as much these days. You manage to get out of bed and get dressed before your wife leaves for work.

"Tie your shoes," she says. You're wearing your Air Jordan XIIIs, $335 from a website that specializes in vintage Air Jordans. You told your wife they were $99, and you are stealing money from the grocery account to cover the credit card bill. You wear them unlaced, humiliating your fourteen-year-old son, who informs you that wearing your Air Jordans unlaced is beyond old school, it's before school, and he won't walk within twenty feet of you at the mall. Your sixteen-year-old daughter cannot be bothered to tell you how beneath her contempt you are, except by the way she takes her twenty dollars of allowance money from your hand with only the tips of her glued-on-at-the-beauty-salon nails.

You are planning to wear the unlaced Air Jordans with the creamy linen suit to your brother's wedding.

You put a peppermint candy to your lips and then you realize it still has the cellophane on. The cellophane crinkles so loudly as you unwrap it that it drowns out all other sounds. You fold the wrapper into a square, and then a smaller square, and a smaller one, and when you drop it on the floor of Hong Kong Tailors it sits there, unmoving, which today is a relief. You still have to buy a tie. The cellophane square is not quite origami, but it is an ordered shape nonetheless.

Tomorrow you will try the shoes on with the laces tied.

THE THOUGHT COMES TO you in your own voice: How to disappear completely. Wool blankets are a start. A fat duvet is better, but there is still the problem of the lump of your body. No duvet is fat enough to hide that lump completely. Practice pulling your limbs in. Yes, closer to the body is good, but to disappear completely you work on pulling the flesh along each bone in tighter. Shrinkage, you think, and your muscles begin to shake.

There are closets to hide in all over the house. Wear white and stand skinny in the broom closet. Practice practice practice, and one day your wife reaches in for a broom and grabs your arm instead. You haven't touched each other in months. A squeak escapes her lips and you squeak back, but these are not the squeaks of love. Your feet could be dustpans. Your hair could clean cobwebs from the corners where the walls meet the ceiling. You imagine clothing made of sticky tape, a coverall like mechanics or painters wear, only this is for rolling across the carpet picking up lint. Your wife will be pleased, one less room to vacuum, and you remember a piece of advice your mother once gave you.

"Be careful who you marry," she said, "because this is the person you are going to end up discussing laundry detergent with."

You ignored this advice of course. How a woman looked in lingerie seemed so much more important at the time.

You wanted children, but not these children. They think you're an idiot because you don't know who 50 Cent is. "That's a 'what,' not a 'who,'" you say, thinking they will laugh, but instead they walleye you and lean back, as if your aura of ignorance, of unhipness, of complete absence of the "phat" or the "tight" or the "kickin'," might be contagious.

The car sits in the driveway. It's time to go to your brother's wedding. Your shoelaces are all the way down there where your feet are, too far away to bend over and tie them. Your wife is wearing the Boucheron perfume that once made you slide your hand up the slit in that long black silk skirt.

She says she'll drive. She says she'll tie your shoes for you, if that's what it takes. She says it doesn't matter about the shoelaces, what about seeing a doctor? Your brother is a doctor, she says, he could write you a scrip after he cuts the wedding cake.

"I don't know," you say, "I feel pretty normal."

"You're not," she says. There's a hummingbird out the kitchen window, darting around the tall phlox.

You want to point out the hummingbird to your wife, but your hand moves too slow.

THE WEDDING IS AT an expensive hotel with valet parking. It's the kind of hotel that puts a large crystal bowl of perfect green apples on a table in the lobby. There are no flies anywhere and the women all have nylons on. Your brother, not the one getting married but the other one, the best-man-instead-of-you one, he's sitting in a chair in the lobby. He once played Falstaff in one of those Henry plays, and this is how you see him, always. Even though he's wearing an acre and a half of summer-weight black wool cut into a tuxedo jacket and pants with a shiny stripe of black satin down the outside seam, you see him with an enormous wide belt and a square brass buckle, you see him in boots with soft leather tops that fold down, you see him laughing with his mouth wide open and a tankard of ale in his hand.

"Apple juice," he told you after the play, backstage, his snowy white beard hanging off half his face and streaks of sweat running through his makeup. Here, in the hotel lobby, he sees you and he stands. You take an apple from the bowl and put it in the side pocket of the creamy linen suit, where it makes a round bulge that will never disappear completely. You walk over to him, drawn by the white carnation boutonniere on his lapel.

"You look terrible," he says, shaking your hand. "Can't you tie your shoes?"

The shoelaces, you want to explain to him, are carefully arranged. Untied shoes are part of a look that includes the three day's growth on your face. You are old school, you want to tell him, not before school. Creamy white linen, you want to say, Hong Kong Tailor you want to say, but when you open your mouth a hummingbird flies out and hovers in front of your brother's white carnation boutonniere.

A thought flies in at you: It's always hummingbirds at this kind of hotel. Not one of your own thoughts, you think, these are the thoughts that come from an oblique angle, from the corners where the walls meet the ceiling. The voice is familiar, but it's not your voice, any more than it's the voice that speaks in fat chopped Chinese syllables to Mr. Wu. It is a voice with a lot of authority. It's the voice that says, "Meds? Just say no."

Good advice, you think, it worked for Nancy and Betty and lots of other people including many family members but not, unfortunately, for Ron, poor president Ron, he was never the bright one, now was he. This thought comes to you in your own separate voice. The woman who wears your wife's clothing looks across the lobby at you, not for the first time, and she waves her fingers and points at the doors to the room where the wedding will be. She's talking to your mother, laundry detergent you think, they're talking about laundry detergent. "Shout," they are saying, "Dash" they are saying, "Tide." Your brother takes you by the elbow and together you move toward the door. Everyone has something black on, a belt, shoes, black buttons down the back of a red floral print dress, and you realize you have no black on anywhere. Your Air Jordans are Carolina blue, and they have a hologram of a basketball that morphs into the number 23 which morphs into what you always thought was his Air-ness leaping, but which you are now pretty sure is actually a hummingbird.

"Is this a funeral?" you say. But your brother doesn't hear you, he's talking to another guest, and you can't break the code. It's something about hummers, the man had just bought a yellow hummer, and now it was parked in the living room. High above you hummingbirds buzz the lights on the chandeliers. If you close one eye you can slow them down and see their tiny tongues reach out and drink the electric light. Their red throats shine brighter with each sip.

Your wife leans her head against your shoulder, she loves weddings, she loves you in your new suit. The disagreement over footwear is the only fly buzzing in your marriage, but you worry that her hair will stick to the creamy linen, so that when you stand up her head will be stuck to you at an oblique angle and she will have to follow you everywhere. You reach into the pocket of your creamy white linen coat for the apple but find instead a white dove folded from a small piece of paper. You set it free thinking it will fly up to join the hummingbirds, but it just lays there in your hand. Your wife smiles at the dove, happy that her hair does not stick to your creamy white linen suit, and she blows gently, and the wings shift from side to side, but then she is not your wife. It's maybe your wife's sister, you've always had a hard time telling them apart at formal occasions, or it could be your niece, the one who joined the Peace Corps and went to a country you never heard of, Bettystan or Nancystan or Medistan. The folded paper dove pecks at you once before it settles down.

The only way the bride could hide is if she found a bridal shop and stepped into the window. Her dress, which stretches out behind her where it is harnessed to two little girls wearing floral tiaras, is a creamy white that matches your new Hong Kong suit. What a couple we would make, you think, creany white and creamy white, satin and linen, and she is marrying entirely the wrong man, your older brother the doctor, a man annoyed by any mention of laundry detergent. You want to follow the bride up the aisle and whisper in her ear. "Ivory," you would say, "Cheer," you would say, "White King." She would lean back, the stiff netting of her veil scratchy against your warm cheek, and you would say this to win her heart: I can produce a beautiful hummingbird from my mouth at any moment.

The girls harnessed to the trailing end of the bride's gown are walking some six and one quarter inches above the floor. The minister is a woman in a charcoal gray pinstriped suit. The black Air Jordan XIs, the hightop ones with the three tuck and roll padded bulges under the ankles and the red flame trim on the outer edge of the soles, they would look terrific with that suit.

Your children are sitting in the back, on the bride's side, and they are whispering to each other, but not about laundry detergent. You're seated halfway up on the groom's side, and your mother's bald spot is directly in front of you. The bald spot is not an actual bald spot, but an extreme thinning of her bluish white hair, and you wonder how many of those missing hairs were lost to birds who needed them for their nests. What doesn't disappear down the shower drain ends up in bird nests, you've heard this, scientists are studying the use of your mother's hair in bird nests at this very moment. The bride passes by your row and you want to follow her but the bird in your hand needs a nest.

The wedding service is spoken in a bastardized version of English that allows "commit" to be both a verb and a form of punctuation. It's all code, and the minister herself is festooned with loose syllables that hover around her face, poking out their long slender tongues, drinking in the light reflected off her too-white teeth. At thirty paces you can see what only raptors see, every eyelash, the glint of a tear not yet fallen, the looped strings of tiny pearls in her iris.

From deep below, in a sub-sub-sub-basement, you hear the machinery start up. This whole room, this entire hotel on its one city block, is about to tilt up thirty degrees from front to back. Your brother, the groom, will grab the minister, who will grab the altar, and they will stay where they are while the bride slides down the length of the aisle, drawn to the dove in your hand, whose wings are fluffed and ready to fly. You will wait in the aisle to receive her in your arms. Your unlaced Air Jordans will hold you fast to the floor no matter what the angle of the tilt.

"Bold," she will say to you, "Surf," she will say, "Gain."

The white dove eyes your mother's bald spot. It plucks a stray hair and flies up to the chandelier.

You will say to her, "All."

A Gentleman, Under These Circumstances, Has No Idea

THE WAY IT HAPPENED, Ned's pickup truck was in a long line of cars working their way through the construction on a two-lane highway a few miles outside of Renata. The road was curvy, running alongside the river, so the big hang-up was a blind turn where they were only letting the traffic through one direction at a time. Ned's truck was the next car when the flagger put up her hand and stopped him.

So he looks over at her, and he's thinking why me, but what he sees is she's past fifty for sure, and she's got the standard-issue orange vest and the standard-issue orange hardhat, and she's got road grit on her jeans. There's something familiar about her, but it isn't something he can name right off. She's got these cheekbones like his ex-wife had, Robyn, the cheekbones he fell in love with when they were still in high school, rounded and full, not those chiseled anorexic cheekbones that models and starlets have.

And then it hits him, a face from his high school yearbook, damn near forty years ago, but it really could be her. Annie.

Annie Carr. The new girl in town. Her family had moved there from Lake Placid, New York. He had a crush on her after he started going with Robyn, who reamed him a new one when she caught him with Annie at The Hum Dinger on a Saturday afternoon when he was supposed to be helping his dad put up sheetrock in the new addition.

Yup, could be her all right. The day is unseasonably hot, hot enough to make even reasonable people want to kick the crap out of their own dog, and this flagger gal is looking off into the middle distance like she might actually be able to see what the flaming hell we're in this life to figure out. Her lower lip was caught up between her teeth and her eyes blinked a couple of times.

A look of actual cogitation, rather than the blank stare of someone who's for sure been standing in one place way too long. Her hands are long-fingered, he sees that from the way they wrap around her flagger's pole, and long fingers are something else he's got a weakness for, and Annie Carr, she had long fingers like that. Played the piano, Annie did, but couldn't sing to save her life.

"Annie?" he said. She looked over at him, squinted hard, then pulled a pair of glasses out of her pocket and took a step toward him. She put the glasses on her face and leaned forward.

"Who wants to know?" she said.

So that's how it went on, this thing they'd started way back in high school and never finished. Not really much of a thing, Annie thought, a burger and fries and a malted milk shake that she never got to finish because Robyn Sigafoos barged in on them. Lab partners in biology their senior year, that's how it started, Ned wisecracking under his breath about the chalk dust fingerprints all over the front of Mr. Regner's pants. She'd gotten all giggly, but it was perfectly harmless flirting, nothing more, until he called her up one Saturday and asked her to meet him. Out of bounds and they both knew it, but not by much.

Eons ago, and she'd never given Ned a second thought. She'd gone off to college, met David and married him, and a few years later they'd moved back to Renata. She'd owned the only bookstore in town. No kids, her husband didn't care much for kids, or so he always said, and she went along with that. They had dogs instead.

But then twenty-six years in, her husband sat her down and told her the marriage was over. He didn't love her any more, and he was moving out. "Where to?" she asked. There was nothing inside her right then but the sound of a great wind blowing across an empty field. He'd met someone new, he told her, but that had nothing to do with their marriage. Yes she was younger, and oh by the way, she was pregnant. Yes with his child. No there wasn't anything she could do to change his mind. A done deal, he said. She could keep the house. She could keep the dogs.

She lived on vitamins, vodka, and rage for a couple of weeks. She lost twenty pounds in the first twenty days. She watched the skin peel off her cheeks, only God knew why. She closed the bookstore for a month and stayed in bed with the dogs. With David gone she could do that now, let the dogs sleep right there with her.

A stripe of her hair turned gray starting at her temple. She re-opened the bookstore, and she slogged her way through the divorce. David wanted nothing from their life together, not the furniture, not the bookstore, not the dishes. She was relieved and insulted by this at the same time. He took his truck, he took his clothes, he took his tools. When he had turned into a man who wanted a child was something she never figured out. She never even met the woman he left her for.

Things slowly got better the next couple of years. The murder-suicide fantasies abated. She learned how to run a chainsaw, and she bought herself a little pickup truck. She cut her own firewood, and split it, and stacked it on the side of the garage where David used to park. Then times got tough. The dot-com bubble wiped out her savings. The bookstore failed. The dogs died. She still had the house, and it was paid off, but she was working this flagger job for nine-fifty an hour. Her truck needed tires. The house needed a roof. She was all right, most of the time, but there were nights when she woke into the dark fuzzy absence of light, the empty sound of the house filling her ears with nothing. She was brittle, her life broken apart like a raw egg dropped on the floor.

Six years a divorcee. She'd had a couple of boyfriends, but the boyfriends hadn't worked out. And now, Ned Scheible shows up and grins that five-hundred-watt grin at her, and flash, her belly goes popsicle cold and her cheeks go heat rash hot. Just like that she's back in high school again.

Except she's not. She's looking at herself in the full length mirror on the inside of her closet door at six o'clock on a Saturday night. The silk blouse or the plain cotton one? She's in her bra and panties, and when she turns sideways she pulls in her pooch of a belly, and that helps, but it doesn't fix all that cottage cheese skin where her bum meets her thighs, and why the hell should she care anyway, it's not like she was going to do anything but have dinner with the man. If that, even. She could seriously just not show up, because what would they do besides talk about high school, and how boring was that, and this was going nowhere because it had nowhere to go. His job, counting geese of all things, brought him here once a week, and she'd be damned if she was going to be his little Renata fling.

In the end she settled on her best jeans and the plain cotton blouse. She took out the diamond earrings her husband had given her on their tenth, and put in some dangly concentric loops. She pulled her hair behind her ears. She wiped the Rose

Maiden off her lips and put on Natural Sinner, which made it look like she was hardly wearing lipstick at all. She wore her blue flats, she was walking to The Cazadero after all, and she expected to walk back. Alone.

She checked herself in the mirror. She wasn't bad for fifty-four, no loose skin hanging off her arms, no wattle hanging underneath her chin. Her face was holding up reasonably well, the wrinkles not set too deep yet. But the Natural Sinner wasn't really doing much for her lips. Maybe she should risk a color that had a little more drama to it.

She rummaged through her makeup drawer, rejecting Coral Goddess, Hangup, Riveting, and Saint Nude. She settled on an old favorite, Viva Las Vegas.

God help us, she thought, who thinks up the names for these lipsticks?

ALL WEEK LONG HE carried the look of her walking into the bar at the restaurant in the back pocket of his thoughts, where it was within easy reach at all times. He was on a stool at the end, where he could watch the doorway, a Friday evening beer in front of him. When she walked in, she passed through some colored lights rigged into the ceiling, yellow and red, and then she stood in blue light. The blue light fell across the tops of her cheeks and got caught up in the folds of a white shawl she was wearing. That light on her a thing you could hold in your thoughts until the day you died.

His steak was a little better than passable, and she said her chicken breast was not too dry, soaked as it was in an herb-flecked sauce in an indifferent shade of red. They laughed together about that day at The Hum Dinger. They got the vital statistics out of the way, both of them divorced, no kids for her, his two all grown up. Something was moving inside him all evening long, something that started moving when she stood under that blue light. Something that said take your time. Don't blow this. He walked her home, and when they got to her door, he didn't ask if he could come in, didn't ask for a kiss goodnight. Instead he asked her if she wanted to ogle geese with him sometime.

"Ogle geese?" she said. "Ogle?" There was a giggle in her voice, she got the little joke he was making, and she said yes.

HE TOOK HER TO Hidden Lake, which was in a deep crease in the land below The Hogback. All these years she'd lived in Renata, and she never knew about Hidden Lake. Ned kept talking about geese while he drove, what smart birds they were, and fierce, and how they were adapting to urban life.

"Why fly thousands of miles to summer way north in Canada when you have everything you need right here?" he said. He drove with one hand on the wheel and a cup of coffee in the other hand. She could see him driving that way for hundreds of miles and never spilling a drop. He had a thermos of coffee in its own special bracket mounted on the dash.

"So," she said, "they don't migrate any more?"

"Oh, most of them still do," he said. "The cacklers, they still do, but they used to winter in California, and now they winter in Oregon. It's mostly the Westerns that have moved into the parks and golf courses year round. They're the big guys."

She told him about growing up in Lake Placid, and how her father took her outside one day when she was maybe five or six, and the sky was black with geese. "Great skeins of them crossing the sky in long ragged waves," she said. "I loved how my father used that word, skeins. But it scared me that first time. I knew the sky wasn't supposed to be black." She liked how Ned listened to her, waiting for her to finish instead of cutting her off with some thought of his own. David was forever interrupting her, it used to make her so mad.

"You lived in one of the main flyways," Ned said. "They'll wait for days for the right tailwind, and then they all go at once.

They fly thirty miles an hour on their own, but with a twenty-mile tailwind, they're doing fifty."

The right tailwind. Maybe that's what was missing from her life.

It was a scramble getting down to the lake. Ned parked his truck in a wide spot next to the road, grabbed his backpack, which he said had their picnic and a blanket in it, and he took her by the hand and led her to the trail.

Holding hands, such a simple pleasure. The trail was steep, straight up and down in spots. He went first, working his way holding onto bare rocks and tree roots that stuck out of the ground, then turning and facing her to help her down. She was plenty strong enough that she could have made it on her own, but she liked the way he helped her, and when he put his arms around her to lift her down at the bottom, her face came right up next to him, and the thought of kissing him flashed through her mind. She didn't, but she was pretty sure he was thinking the same thing.

God only knew if she was ready for this. The boyfriend thing had not been kind to her. She'd sworn off men a couple of years ago, after Frank, the second one, broke up with her. She'd gone out with him for more than a year, and they had a nice routine going, spending rainy weekends at his house in the city, and using her place as a base to do outdoorsy stuff if the weather was nice. Frank was a carpenter, but he had a degree in English. He read the books she gave him, and talked to her about them, and he had books of his own that he loaned her. He was two years into a separation from his wife when they met, headed for a divorce.

She had a lot of hope invested in Frank. He was so different from David, who couldn't sit still long enough to read a book. And David had a temper, he'd turn red in the face and throw his tools if he was working on his truck and things didn't go right. Frank never got angry, and when he wrapped her in his arms after sex she felt safer than she'd ever felt in her life. But they never talked of love, though that's what she felt for him. She believed that's what he felt for her right up until he called her one day and said he was getting back together with his wife. And then she felt like the whole thing had been a lie.

The trail flattened out and rounded a bend, and there was the lake. Long and narrow, maybe three hundred yards end to end. Doug firs growing right down to the edge, postcard pretty. There was a muddy beach at the far end, with a stream flowing out through a marsh.

"Goose country," Ned said, pointing at the marsh. There were a couple of dozen geese down there, most likely Taverners, he said, a subspecies of the Cackling Goose.

She said, "They mate for life, don't they." It wasn't a question. It was the big mystery, wasn't it, how geese could get it right when human beings kept screwing things up.

"Pretty much," Ned said. "Only there's research the last few years that says it's not quite that simple."

She was ahead of him on the trail, but she stopped and turned to look back at him. "What do you mean?"

"Well, mostly they do," he said, "mate for life. But that doesn't mean that some of them don't sneak off once in a while and, you know, get a little something on the side."

"Oh," she said. She didn't like the sound of this. "The males, they cheat on their wives?"

"Males and females both." Ned said. He was rummaging in his backpack, and he pulled out a pair of binoculars. There must have been a worried look on her face, because when he looked up at her, he quit fiddling with the binoculars and said, "It's not something moral with them. It's all instinct. They do pair off for life, and they're mostly loyal to each other. But it improves their chances of having strong babies if they mix up the gene pool once in a while."

Instinct. Good enough for geese, maybe, but it wasn't

enough for her. She took the binoculars when he handed them to her. The geese at the far end were all head down, grazing, except for one on the edge who had his long neck up, looking straight at her. On guard.

She handed the binoculars back. Maybe a guy who spent his time studying geese had a different perspective on human behavior. Humans were animals, after all. They'd traded divorce stories over dinner at The Cazadero. His mate had left him for someone else, same as hers. When she said she was sorry to hear that, he shrugged and said, "It happens," as if it didn't have much to do with him.

They walked on a ways. They had to jump over a tiny creek that waterfalled down the slope and then flowed across the trail. A few more steps, and then Annie turned and stood looking across the lake. She reached up and tucked a piece of flyaway hair back into her stocking cap. "You know what my ex-husband said when I asked him why he cheated on me?"

His lips twitched, like maybe there was something funny about adultery. "That you deserved it because you were such a terrible mate?" Ned's grin took its full width now. "That's what my wife told me—it was my fault. I made her do it."

Annie laughed. It was the kind of laugh you laugh when the joke's on you, a laugh without a smile behind it. "My husband said, 'Why does everybody have to be so damned married all the time?'"

The surface of the lake was still, with blue sky and clouds and trees reflected in it. The geese were talking to each other, a low conversation that seemed to be about the general satisfaction of finding food. Ned put his arm across her shoulders.

"Damned married," he said. "Nice thing to say to your wife."

Maybe he was the kind of guy who stuck to one woman. There wasn't really any way to know what she wanted to know. It was just the two of them out there, without a guarantee in sight. She leaned her head against him. "It's cold down here by the water," she said. She zipped her coat up. "Let's get over there where the sun is."

They spread a tarp on a patch of bare dirt littered with droppings, and then a blanket on top of that. "Goose dung," said Ned. "One of my occupational hazards." They were beneath a maple tree that hadn't quite leafed out yet. Ned got some sandwiches out, and a bottle of wine. She gave him a raised eyebrow, like what was he up to, but then she smiled big. "This your idea of romantic?" she said. "Ogling geese and drinking wine?"

She liked the way he tilted his head to the side while he thought up what to say. "You nailed me," he said. "I'm kind of goofy about geese." He opened the wine with a corkscrew, and he pulled two wine glasses out of a side pocket on the backpack. They were plastic, and they had stems that screwed on and off for easier packing. Nice, a guy who pays attention to the details. He poured the wine and handed her a glass.

"To geese," he said, "because they're doing the best they can."

She knew what he meant. That bit about being loyal, even if they weren't always completely faithful. She took a sip of her wine, and then, for courage, a big gulp. She leaned in, and put her hand on the side of his face, and she kissed him.

He was happy to oblige, she could tell. Not too fast, and not too slow, they let their lips feel each other. They weren't staking out claims, not just yet, but they were asking each other a question. She liked his answer.

She pulled back, and they looked into each other's eyes. He leaned in to kiss her again, but she put her hand on his lips and pushed him away. "Don't go getting any ideas," she said.

Again he tilted his head to the side. "Of course not," he said. "A gentleman, under these circumstances, has no ideas." The start of a smile was on his lips again, but this time she felt like maybe he was making fun of her. He said, "I leave that to the ladies."

Cold air seeped in underneath her jacket. The ladies, plural. She wasn't sure she liked the sound of that.

FIFTY-FOUR GOING ON SEVENTEEN, that was how he felt. Lovesick so bad he called her up on Monday and left her a voice mail about what he had for lunch, how the pickle that came with his sandwich was so crisp like the ones his Aunt Adelaide used to make. Had she ever made pickles? He'd helped his mother a couple of times, he kind of knew how, maybe they could do it together some time.

Christ, he hadn't even slept with her. The kiss at the lake, that was all her doing, so she had to be interested. Her eyes were cornsilk blue in that light. Her hair stuck out from the knit cap she wore, and she had that foxy gray streak in her hair. He liked that, it gave her the weight of a life lived. If she wasn't dyeing the gray away, she wouldn't be fussy about how she looked, or him either.

He felt foolish after he left her that voice mail. He was divorced, and damaged goods at best, a guy old enough to know better, and here he was, ready to start the whole thing over again. In Renata, of all places, the town he'd grown up in, and left behind, and now maybe his life was turning full circle on him. Renata, where he'd had a fling with Belinda Parry after he found out his wife was cheating on him. His older brother, Dale, had introduced them, and Belinda was pretty attractive, but he was just separated, and the timing was wrong. After his salmon assignment with Fish and Wildlife was done, he let it drop.

He'd called Dale a couple of nights after his dinner date with Annie. Dale had gone through the whole divorced-in-middle-age thing ahead of Ned, and he was a veteran cyber-dater. He'd sorted through maybe two hundred women to find the girlfriend he had now, gone on dozens of dates, probably broken a few hearts along the way. "You're a man," Dale told him. "So whatever your instincts tell you, it's wrong. You want to call her every day, let her know how much you want her. Don't. It makes you look desperate."

So he backed off. He hoped maybe she would call him, but when Thursday rolled around and she hadn't, he dialed her number. He'd be in Renata the next day, counting geese again, and he wanted to see her.

She sounded glad to hear from him when she picked up the phone. She was easy to talk to, and they chatted about this and that, the weather, a book she was reading, a movie he'd seen. She asked him who the goose count was for.

"The feds," he said, "Fish and Wildlife." He told her how he'd given up a desk job with US Fish and Wildlife, five years short of his twenty, to become a partner in a firm that went belly up two years later. Now he was back working for his old boss, but on contract now, decent pay but not steady work.

"Why?" she asked. "What difference does it make how many geese there are?"

"Lots of reasons," he said. "The goose population is a resource, so it has to be managed. Down here, in the lower forty-eight, hunters want to shoot them. Up in Alaska, the Inuits harvest the eggs for food."

"I'll bet that gets political," she said.

"You know it. There's a water quality issue, too," he said. He told her how there were a million geese in North America in 1950, and now there were eight million. A flock of fifty produced five thousand pounds of droppings a year. There were e coli bacteria in those droppings, the bad kind that made humans sick. You didn't want all that fouling your water supply. They ate farmers' crops, wheat, grass seed. They could do a lot of damage. And don't forget that airliner that had to land on the Hudson.

"So what's the solution?" she said. "Don't tell me your bosses want to poison them all."

"No," he said. "Not that it hasn't been tried. But you put poison out, it doesn't kill just the geese. And there's too many to shoot." He was sitting in his studio apartment, all he could afford on what he made now. It wasn't bad, it had hardwood floors and he'd fixed it up with fresh paint and a reproduction antique light fixture. He had curtains, for Christ's sake, he was a good catch.

"So what are they going to do?" she said.

He let out a long slow breath, too loud for it not to be called a sigh. Some people didn't like this part of his job. "Sterilants," he said. "There's an antibiotic they use on poultry farms. Turns out it makes the Canada goose sterile."

"Oh," she said. He didn't like how she let that word just hang on the line between them.

God he wanted her. He didn't have much to offer a woman except his smile and the fact that he got up every morning and did something, broke or not. His divorce had taken his house and split the equity between him and his ex-wife, and that money was gone now. His truck needed a brake job. He wanted to wine and dine her, but he couldn't afford to the way he would've liked. More than anything, he wanted to not be a part of the faceless "they" she was imagining.

"So," she said, "the geese get to live, but they don't get to have babies?"

"Well, the way it goes," he said, "is they put this bait out where the geese congregate. They have to eat it for about six weeks for it to work. In the field, it reduces reproduction by half. So half of them get to have babies." No need to tell her that his next job was going to be spreading the bait.

"What a waste," she said.

"It's a lot better than killing them," Ned said. "Even PETA thinks this bait is okay."

"Uh huh," she said.

This was getting sticky. Everything he'd ever heard about what women wanted was wrong at least half the time. The best advice he ever got was from Dale, who told him, "There are three rules for wooing a woman." While Ned got his pencil out to write them down, Dale waited for him, a look of infinite bemusement on his face. "Unfortunately," Dale said, "nobody knows what they are. Not even women know."

"I need to get off the phone," Annie said. "I've got stuff to do."

SHE HAD THE TV on, some cop show, the sound was off. Her silk blouse on a hanger on the doorknob, already ironed, and her pillowcases the next thing. She'd hoped to wear that silk blouse to dinner with Ned. But then she got all caught up in what he was telling her about sterilizing geese, and she'd got herself off the phone before he could ask her out.

She ironed because wrinkles were no match for heat and steam. Because when she lay her head down on an ironed pillowcase she knew she had gotten at least one thing right in her life. On the TV a man was sneaking around behind a building with a gun in his hand. She laid a wrinkled pillowcase on the ironing board, smoothing it out with both hands. She refilled the iron with water. She changed channels to a cooking show.

The chef was making a frittata. He had a bowl of eggs all whipped up, and he'd taken a big shiny knife and scraped the broken eggshells off his counter and into the trash. Her tears started about the time the chef finished chopping the vegetables with that big shiny knife. She slid the iron back and forth across the pillowcase, the wrinkles flattening out, disappearing, and what a beautiful shade of lavender this pillowcase was. She'd brought the new sheets home from the mall, maybe a week after her husband left. The day she bought them she ran them through the washing machine and dryer, and then ironed them, so that when she made up the bed it looked like something in a movie, something perfect.

A tear fell from her cheek to the pillowcase, making a darker spot of color in the lavender. She ran the iron over it, and the dark spot lightened. She ran the iron over it a second time, and the spot almost disappeared, but then another tear fell, and another. Each tear a dark spot on the smooth pillowcase. She ironed those spots too, once, twice. Crying now was ridiculous, she was years past crying about her divorce. What was the matter with her. She told herself to stop, but she let the tears come, and one by one, with the iron, she made them all disappear.

The chef brought his beautiful fritatta out of the oven. All those geese courting each other, pairing off, building nests, laying eggs that would never hatch. God help us, what a mess we've made of things.

She should join that ukelele group that was getting started in town. She'd been musical back in high school. And maybe she should get a cat. An orange cat, she'd heard orange cats were more affectionate. A cat could be home all day alone. Cats were independent, and uncomplicated. Not like a dog. Or a Ned.

She could handle a cat.

HE SAW HER THE next day on the road up the river. She stood next to her sign pole, looking down the road at the line of cars winding its way by. It was drizzling out, that kind of misty rain that fell so lightly it didn't even make a dark spot on your clothes. He rolled his window down when he got to her, and stopped long enough to say, "How about dinner tonight?"

She shook her head no. "It's ukelele night," she said. "I'm taking a class."

"Glass of wine after?" he said. "What time do you get out?" He checked his rear view mirror, he had three cars behind him, and he was blocking the road. Annie had a look on her face like she was all worn out. Like she was feeling every one of her fifty-four years. He wanted to put a smile on her face, that was all. The car behind him beeped its horn.

"I'll call you," he said. She gave him the barest of nods, and then she waved him on his way like he was just another car in the middle of a long day full of nothing but cars.

Anybody could play the ukelele. Even him.

A FLOCK OF GEESE flew overhead as Annie walked back to her car at the end of the day, maybe two dozen of them, in an orderly V. They were headed north and moving fast. The one at the sharp tip of the V slicing a wedge through the air for the others to follow, and all of them honking, onward, onward.

They must have a tailwind behind them, she thought. They flew with such purpose, as if they knew exactly where they were going.

Acknowledgments

TO THE MANY WRITERS with whom I have sat around The Pinewood Table, having the most remarkable ongoing conversation about this thing we do called writing, who are too numerous to mention here save to say for years you have made Tuesday the best night of the week for me, and for whom I hope this book's publication provides hope and inspiration

To Laura Stanfill, my editor, my publisher, my friend and fellow writer, and perhaps the only person who loves this book more than I do

To Gigi Little, a woman of wit and style, and the hardest working and best book designer ever, who has left the fingerprints of her skilled hands all over this beautiful book

To Laurie Paus, whose drawings capture so fluently the changing moods of my stories, who taught me the value of staring into the middle distance, and the magic of ironing away tears, and who told me years ago to "Dream Big"

To Joanna Rose, my longtime writing buddy and teaching partner, a poet, novelist, and essayist of great subtlety and even greater heart, who is wise in the ways of literature, and wiser in the ways of the world, and whose calm gaze from the other end of The Pinewood Table every Tuesday night anchors me

To Nikki Schulak, who asked me to read my stories to her so she could learn from them, who kept saying, "Promise me you'll get these stories published," who gave the manuscript a careful reading before I submitted it to the publisher, and who made several brilliant suggestions on how to link the stories more closely together

To Harvey Horne, who taught me it was okay to be a little bit ticky

To Mrs. Baumgartner, my fifth grade teacher, who laughed out loud at my first ever piece of creative writing

To Linda Mae Holmes Kibbler, who knew my writing all the way back in high school, and who magically reappeared after a forty-year absence, read the manuscript, and pronounced it ready for the world

To Natalie Goldberg, Kim Stafford, Craig Lesley, and Tom Spanbauer, extraordinary writing teachers all of them, who taught me, respectively, to spend it all, every time, to always ask 'what if?', to write about the work lives of my characters, and how to alligator wrestle at the level of the sentence

To Keith Jafrate, editor of *The Text*, who published my work early and often, and gave me an audience in the UK

To the people of Estacada, who welcomed me into their remarkable town, a place big enough to hold everything I need, and small enough to keep track of everything that matters

To Lori Ryland, Nancy Ritz, and Ruth Tuff, founders of The Artists Edge Salon in Sandy, for inviting me to join, for giving me such an amazing audience month after month, and for encouraging me to get this collection published

To Scott Sparling, who knows how to take the noir out of the night and put it into the broad daylight

To Bruce Barrow, who found a flying saucer buried in a mountain in Oklahoma, and a river of crickets at a party in LA, astounding me in the process, and shaking me out of my lethargy, and whose unflappable Okie countenance assures us that no matter how strange things get, he will edit the chaos until it appears coherent

To Yuvi Zalkow, who dared imagine that he could take a mess of half-finished essays and short stories and turn them into *A Brilliant Novel in the Works*, all the while declaring "I am a failed writer" when he is anything but, and who thereby punctured the basket under which I have hidden my light for too many years

To Cris Colburn, my longtime Poet Soul Brother, who has been reading these stories as long as I have been writing them, and whose lifelong friendship and support has been constant and true and always a joy

To Dale Woods, for sage advice on dating after divorce, delivered with the driest of wits, and a smile more understated than the Mona Lisa's

To Steve High, best friend for fifty years, who told me the story of his neighbor Whitey, the spar tree rigger who fell from the sky

To Jesse, my beloved orange cat, killer of rodents, rabbits, and snakes, and cuddler extraordinaire

To John Fahey, Mary Flower, Joe Morawski, The Shook Twins, and Jesse Sykes & the Sweet Hereafter, whose music keeps the darkness at bay in the pre-dawn hours when I write

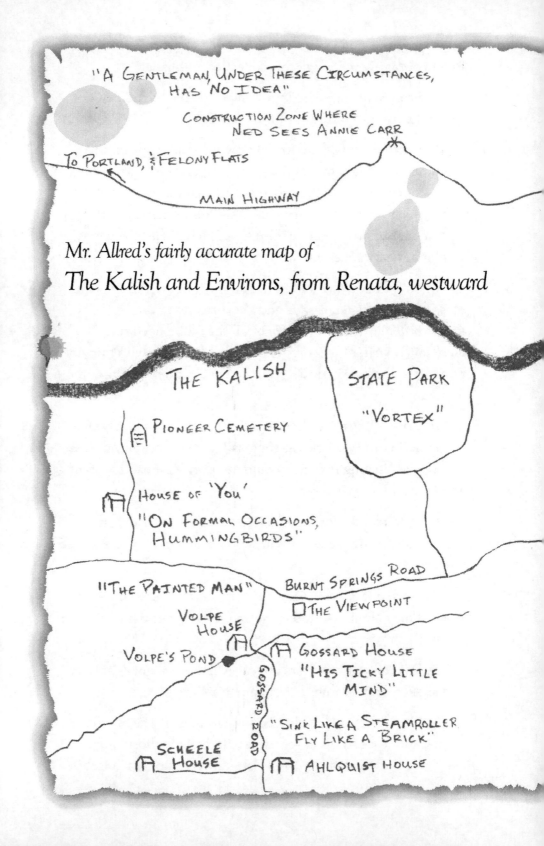

"A GENTLEMAN, UNDER THESE CIRCUMSTANCES, HAS 'NO IDEA'"

CONSTRUCTION ZONE WHERE NED SEES ANNIE CARR

To PORTLAND, & FELONY FLATS

MAIN HIGHWAY

Mr. Allred's *fairly accurate* map of
The Kalish and Environs, from Renata, westward

THE KALISH

STATE PARK

"VORTEX"

PIONEER CEMETERY

HOUSE OF 'YOU'
"ON FORMAL OCCASIONS, HUMMINGBIRDS"

"THE PAINTED MAN"

BURNT SPRINGS ROAD

☐ THE VIEWPOINT

VOLPE HOUSE

VOLPE'S POND

GOSSARD ROAD

GOSSARD HOUSE
"HIS TICKY LITTLE MIND"

"SINK LIKE A STEAMROLLER FLY LIKE A BRICK"

SCHEELE HOUSE

AHLQUIST HOUSE

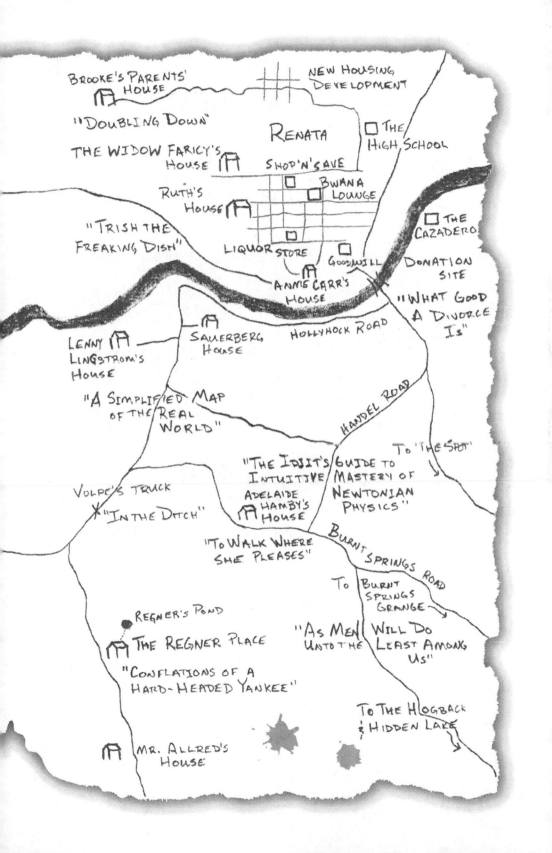

Story Trees

Pretty Legible Hand Lettering by the Author*

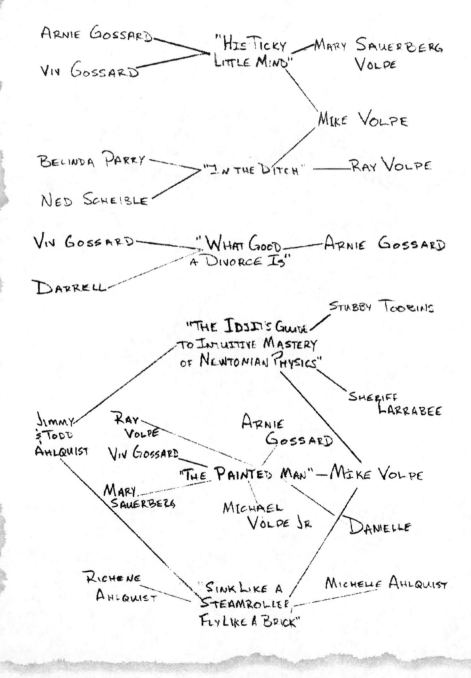

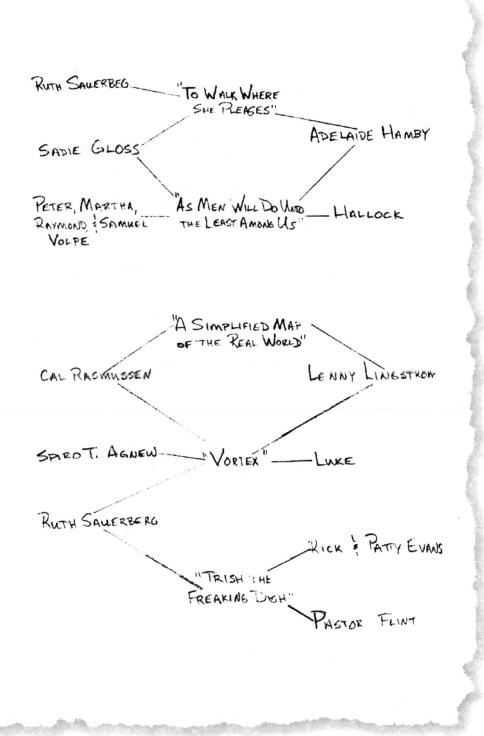

RUTH SAUERBEG —— "TO WALK WHERE
SHE PLEASES"

ADELAIDE HAMBY

SADIE GLOSS

PETER, MARTHA,
RAYMOND & SAMUEL
VOLPE

"AS MEN WILL DO UNTO
THE LEAST AMONG US" —— HALLOCK

"A SIMPLIFIED MAP
OF THE REAL WORLD"

CAL RASMUSSEN

LENNY LINGSTROM

SPIRO T. AGNEW —— "VORTEX" —— LUKE

RUTH SAUERBERG

RICK & PATTY EVANS

"TRISH THE
FREAKING DISH"

PASTOR FLINT

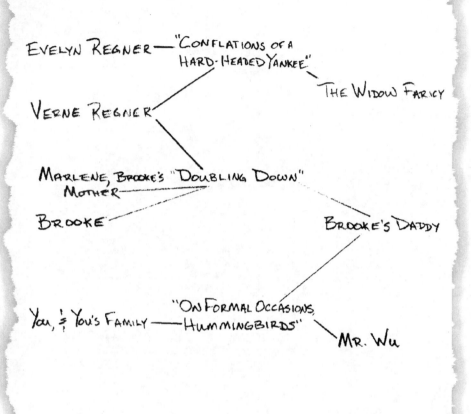

EVELYN REGNER —— "CONFLATIONS OF A
                   HARD-HEADED YANKEE"

                                  THE WIDOW FARICY

VERNE REGNER

MARLENE, BROOKE'S "DOUBLING DOWN"
   MOTHER

BROOKE   BROOKE'S DADDY

YOU, & YOU'S FAMILY —— "ON FORMAL OCCASIONS,
                  HUMMINGBIRDS"

                              MR. WU

NED SCHEIBLE —— "A GENTLEMAN, UNDER —— ANNIE CARR
                    THESE CIRCUMSTANCES,
                  HAS NO IDEA"

* Entirely free of grease spots and coffee stains

About the Author

STEVAN ALLRED HAS SURVIVED circumcision, a tonsillectomy, a religious upbringing, the '60s, the War on Poverty, the break-up of The Beatles, any number of bad haircuts, years of psycho-therapy, the Reagan Revolution, the War on Drugs, the Roaring '90s, plantar fasciitis, the Lewinsky Affair, the Internet bubble, the Florida recount of 2000, the Bush Oughts, the War on Terror, teenage children, a divorce, hay fever, the real estate bubble, male pattern baldness, and heartburn. His work has appeared in numerous literary journals, and he teaches creative writing with Joanna Rose at The Pinewood Table.

About the Illustrator

LAURIE PAUS HAS A bachelor's degree in English from the University of Washington. Over the years she has taken drawing and painting classes from the Pacific Northwest College of Art and Oregon College of Arts and Crafts, and recently, she has been studying sculpture at The Gage Academy of Art. She lives on the shores of Lake Union and works as a bookseller at The Elliott Bay Book Company in Seattle.

Reading Group Questions

Use these prompts to stimulate book club discussions or to enrich your own understanding of the text. To invite author Stevan Allred to attend your book club meeting, in person, by speakerphone, or online, email books@laurastanfill.com.

1. How do you interpret the title of the collection, *A Simplified Map of the Real World*? What is the simplified map? How do relationships change the inner landscape, the border between mine and yours? How does the map on pages 272-273 add to your knowledge of Renata?

2. How does the linked story format enrich our understanding of life in this particular rural town? Why do you think the author chose this format instead of writing a novel?

3. In the first two stories, a classic neighbor-to-neighbor rivalry unfolds. Who is more sympathetic, Arnie Gossard or Mike Volpe? How does your perception of Volpe change when you see him from his son's perspective in "The Painted Man"? And how do you view Arnie after hearing from his ex-wife Viv in "What Good a Divorce Is"?

4. The different points of view explored in *A Simplified Map of the Real World* suggest it's impossible to ever truly know somebody. What are some of the stories that might prove or disprove that statement? Is it possible to fully know another person?

5. The author plants a number of unanswered questions, such as whether Ray is Mike Volpe's son, whether Viv has slept with Mike, whether Viv will pay for the nail polish, and whether Richene spots her son in the waiting room. How do you interpret those ambiguities?

6. The word "church" is capitalized in the title story, "A Simplified Map of the Real World." Why?

7. When Cal and Uncle Lenny reunite in "Vortex," what has changed in their relationship? What remains the same? Is "church" still capitalized? How does the romance between Lenny and Luke parallel the one between Ruth and Cal? What are the differences?

8. Why is this collection illustrated? Did the images affect your understanding of the stories? Why or why not?

9. In "Trish the Freaking Dish," why does Ruth call Trish by her old nickname? What names does Trish use for herself, and how do those choices affect how we read her character?

10. In "On Formal Occasions, Hummingbirds," why did the author use second person? What's the effect of stumbling on that emphatic "you" near the end of the collection? How is this blast of second person different from Mike Volpe in "In the Ditch"?

11. Several stories play with magical realism. Where do ghosts appear, and what do they mean to the characters who see them? How do you interpret the endings of "Sink Like a Steamroller, Fly Like a Brick," when Jimmy visits the river, and "In the Ditch," when Volpe hears a goat's bell?

12. In the last story, "A Gentleman, Under These Circumstances, Has No Idea," will Annie and Ned get together? Why or why not? Does your answer affect your overall impression about the book's hopefulness or hopelessness about relationships?

13. Throughout the collection, the author exposes some of the rationalizations people make to justify their own behavior. Which character makes the biggest leaps of logic in defending his or her actions? Which character's justifications make the most sense to you?

CPSIA information can be obtained at www.ICGtesting.com
Printed in the USA
LVOW06s1517201113

362096LV00003B/473/P